I0572815

not me!

SPELUNCAPHOBIA, SECRETS, & HIDDEN TREASURE

CHARLOTTE STUART

Praise for *Not Me! Speluncaphobia, Secrets and Hidden Treasure*

"A wonderful heroine, interesting supporting characters, and a lot of adventure and fun make this a great book that is well worth reading, and I would recommend it to anyone who enjoys a good mystery with a lot of humor."
—Kathy Sickles for Reader Views

"Charlotte Stuart has a way of really bringing her characters to life and now they feel like old friends. They're characters that I'd be friends with in real life, but I'd need lots of Dramamine to go on a sailing trip with them . . . This is a five star cozy mystery that I recommend to all!"
— Christy Maurer, Christy's Cozy Corners

"The atmosphere and descriptive quality of the writing were a real high point, and Stuart's words make you feel as though you're experiencing every vivid detail of this wilderness adventure for yourself."
—K.C. Finn for Readers' Favorite

"Readers who like a good pulpy mystery that has plenty of danger and excitement but an underlying cozy and friendly atmosphere at its heart will treasure this story for its full length."
—Michael Radon for U.S. Review of Books

Copyright @ 2021 by Charlotte Stuart

Second Edition, 2025

All Rights Reserved

Published by Quartermaster Publishing, Vashon Island, WA

This is a work of fiction. Names, characters, places, brands, media, and incidents are either the product of the author's imagination or are used fictionally. Any similarity with real persons, places, or events is unintended and coincidental.

No part of this book may be reproduced, stored in a retrieval system, or transmitted in any form or by any means electronic, mechanical, photocopying, recording or otherwise, without the prior consent of the publisher.

Originally Published by Taylor & Seale in 2021

Cover design by Chris Holmes

Interior design by Interbridge

ISBN (paperback): 979-8-9924802-1-4

ISBN (ebook): 979-8-9924802-2-1

*To my adventurous husband Don
and to our Alaskan fishing partners
Tina Dinzl-Pederson & Gordy Pederson*

Phobia: an intense fear that is out of proportion to a specific object or situation. (As in "speluncaphobia.")

- *Approximately 5% of children and 16% of adolescents will have a specific phobia in their lifetime.*

- *On average, specific phobias begin between ages seven to eleven.*

- *Girls are more likely to experience a phobia than boys at a rate of 2:1.*

- *Phobias do not decrease with appropriate reassurance and provision of information. For example, a dog phobia persists despite telling your child that Grandma's dog is kind, has no teeth to bite because it is old, and will not scratch.*

Anxiety Canada - www.anxietycanada.com

"The cave you fear to enter holds the treasure you seek."
—Joseph Campbell

"It is when pirates count their booty that they become mere thieves."
—William Bolitho

a mysterious key

Every family has at least one—a crazy uncle, an eccentric aunt, an outlandish grandparent, a weird shirttail relative, or an odd hanger-on who has attached themselves to the family like a barnacle to a piling. In my family, we are blessed with several. Mostly unsympathetic characters I wished belonged to someone else's clan. Except for my unconventional Uncle Wade. I've always idolized him as a romantic figure in his own adventure story.

Even after his move to Canada, stories of his treasure seeking escapades traveled south to Seattle on the family grapevine. Trips to faraway places. The occasional discovery of a valuable antiquity. Unsuccessful treasure hunts. Sunken ships. Rumors of smuggled goods and near arrests. Unlike the mundane lives most of us lead, his was filled with fanciful dreams, risk taking and intrigue.

When I unexpectedly received a package from Uncle Wade, I was both surprised and a bit excited. He'd never sent me anything before. The possibilities seemed endless—something recovered from a shipwreck or unearthed in an ancient ruin. Something he'd picked up on an excursion to an exotic location. Or maybe a family keepsake. But surely something unique. He was, after all, my adventurous, part folk hero, Uncle Wade.

It was a small, light package. After shaking it once to see if it rattled—it didn't, I wasted no time in ripping it open. The only thing inside was a sealed envelope nestled in bubble wrap. The handwritten message on the front said, "*To be Opened Upon the Occasion of my Death.*" Straight out of an Agatha Christie novel.

I confess to a fleeting moment of disappointment not to find some ancient treasure in the box, a necklace worn by a Mayan warrior queen or a tattered leather bag filled with gems or gold nuggets. That was followed by an overpowering desire to know what was in the envelope. It was like leaving a child alone in the kitchen with a tray of cookies straight from the oven and warning her not to eat any. No one in the family had mentioned that Uncle Wade was in ill health or near death's door. So why had he sent me what looked like a message about his dying wishes? And why to *me*, someone he hadn't seen in ages? I fought with my conscience about whether to obey the instruction not to open the envelope until I got word of his death, but my dark side won.

Inside was a key wrapped in pink tissue paper and a handwritten letter in purple ink. I thought the letter would explain the long thin key with the number 356 engraved on its head, but it didn't. And reading the message made me sad and riddled with guilt for not making more of an effort to stay in touch.

Dear Bryn,

You are reading this for two reasons:

I died from terminal cancer. No, don't feel sad, I've made peace with it and am not cursing the gods or railing against fate. I've accepted the cliché "It is what it is." What I am doing is getting my affairs in order. That's one of the advantages of knowing you only have about six months to live.

You were always good at solving puzzles. Even as a child you enjoyed figuring things out. I think you are like me in that way. I've always liked a good mystery.

I guess there are three reasons, not two. The third is Ellie. She is a lovely and intelligent woman, but she is still vulnerable in so many ways. You looked out for her when you were children; I'm hoping you will continue to do that after I'm gone.

Finally, I know that you, like me, often succumb to curiosity and don't always play by the rules. So if you have opened this letter prior to my death, please respect my wishes not to share my impending departure with any other members of the family. Especially your mother. She's the only sibling with whom I share filial affection. She can cry for me after I'm gone.

You may be tempted to call and ask me to explain. Don't bother; even if confronted in person with this letter, I will pretend I don't know what you're talking about. This really is intended to give you a head's up, nothing more. I do not want advice, sympathy, or any assistance at this time. Your role will begin AFTER my death. All will be revealed then.

You and Ellie were always my favorites. I'm counting on you to be there for her, and I wish you both long and prosperous lives.

Your loving Uncle

I sat there staring at the letter, massaging the key between my fingers, imagining Uncle Wade no longer in my life. I'd been meaning to visit for some time, but this made it awkward. It would seem as though I was doing it *because* of the letter. And how do you act normal when you know someone is going to die in the near future? When did mourning begin? I could already feel his loss creeping up on me.

Rereading the letter for the third time, I smiled when I got to the part about him knowing I would read it. I'm glad I did, but it still felt like a betrayal of trust. And it made things complicated in other ways. He very clearly didn't want the rest of the family to know he was facing an early death. I could understand why—my mother was very fond of him, and this news would spin her out of control with heartache. But she would be angry if she found out that I knew and didn't tell her. On the other hand, if his two other siblings learned of his approaching death, they would undoubtedly start pressuring him to do this or that with his estate, greed more dominant than grief. That's who they were. And he knew it. For these reasons, his decision to stay mum was a request I needed to honor.

CHAPTER 2

Family Ties and Tribulations

My name is Bryn Geneva Baczek. It's a mouthful, more chewy caramel than smooth dark chocolate. My grandmother was named Geneva, and my paternal lineage is Polish. My mother has a Welsh first name, Gwen, so I'm indirectly named after her. I'm okay with "Bryn"—it's at least short. I complain a lot about my surname though because it's hard to pronounce. But I complain even more about my mother's side of the family in general. They are mostly misfits and wannabes, with only a tiny handful who can pass for normal. Fortunately, we don't have a lot of interaction with any of them because at one point there was a mass exodus of Paynes from Seattle to Vancouver, B.C. My side of the family owes both a thank you and an apology to Canada.

In addition to my Uncle Wade, my favorite relative on my mother's side is Elspeth Agatha Payne, the only female cousin my same age. When I was in grade school, Elspeth lived two doors down from us. She was a kind, soft-spoken girl, socially awkward and skinny. Her knobby knees were always on prominent display between her hand-knit knee socks and the hem of her hand-made dresses. The other girls whispered about her clothes behind her back. Even her unruly curls set her apart. Straight hair was "in." And although I hated my red hair, it was at least straight.

Another thing that made Elspeth vulnerable to teasing and bullying was her slight lisp. Some of the kids would follow her around chanting her name, replacing the "s" with "th," until I finally intervened and insisted she be called Ellie. *That* was a name they couldn't make fun of. Or so I thought. It turned out there were a lot of words that rhymed with Ellie. *"Ellie has a 'pain' in her belly from eating too much jelly." "Ellie is smelly." "Ellie from New Delhi."* The phrases didn't have to make sense to the kids taunting her; it was all about the tone of the rhyme.

Poor Ellie. There was something about her looks and demeanor when she was young that attracted the mean kids. One time two boys locked her in the supply closet just as the class was heading out for a field trip. She wasn't discovered until we returned at the end of the day. By then she was a nervous wreck. The boys had removed the light bulb, so she'd spent the entire time in the dark. The experience traumatized her for life. At least that's what the therapists told her parents when she was diagnosed with speluncaphobia and gephyrophobia, fear of caves and fear of bridges and tunnels. Actually, she was fine with bridges . . . unless they went through a tunnel.

I remember when my mother sat me down for the "phobia talk." She wanted me to understand so I would know what to do if Ellie had an attack when we were together. Not too long after that, we were playing with a group of kids in the woods when we came across a tiny cave scooped out of a steep embankment. One of the boys dared another boy to crawl into it to see if there was an animal inside. Out of the corner of my eye I saw Ellie backing away, her face pale under the umbrella of overhanging fir branches. Then one of the boys decided Ellie should be the one to crawl into the hole. She turned and ran, and they chased after her. I followed as fast as I could, yelling for them to stop.

When they caught up with Ellie and started dragging her back toward the cave, I attacked. Fired by adrenaline and anger, I pulled one of the boys off and punched him in the stomach as hard as I could. Then I swirled about and kicked another in the balls, like my brother had taught me to do if attacked. I bit a third boy on the arm when he tried to shove me away. Then I grabbed Ellie and raced off with her. It wasn't what my mother had in mind when she gave me the "phobia talk," but it definitely worked.

Later, two of the boys' mothers complained to my mother about me. My mother, one of the handful of normals from the Payne clan, assured them that she would deal with me appropriately. And she did. She took me aside and heaped on praise for standing up for Ellie. That evening she fixed my favorite macaroni and cheese dinner and let me watch TV for a full hour after my bedtime.

As for the boys themselves, they weren't about to admit to classmates that they had been beaten up by a girl, so they let it drop.

A year later, Ellie and her family moved to Vancouver. After that, we only saw each other at big family events like weddings, graduations, and funerals. She grew up to be a very attractive and accomplished woman who conquered her lisp and her tendency toward gephyrophobia, but still avoided caves. Then she married a grown-up version of the bullies who'd plagued her as a youngster and was soon a divorcee. She shed his name along with him and returned to being Ellie Payne. When her mother died, all the Seattle and Vancouver families attended the funeral. I didn't hear from her again for several years.

Not until our Uncle Wade died.

loveable ne'er-do-well

A week after I received the letter from Uncle Wade, Mom phoned me at 7:00 a.m. Both Macavity and I were luxuriating in the thin early sunshine that was sending a beam of warmth through the open porthole above the bunk where he sleeps. It landed on the triangular mahogany inset between the conjoined bunks in the forward berth on my 40-foot sailboat, the *Aspara*.

Macavity emitted a yowl of protest at the partying frogs ringtone that announced I had a call and rolled over on his back, exposing his white belly rimmed in dark orange fur. Maybe he thought the frogs were rapping; he doesn't like rap first thing in the morning.

"What's wrong, Mom?" I asked in a voice thick with sleep.

"It's your Uncle Wade." Mom faltered, her hesitancy ominous. Dread jolted my brain cells into full wakefulness.

"What's wrong?" I repeated.

"I'm afraid he's . . . he's dead."

I had known this call was coming, but not so soon. My plan to visit Ellie and Uncle Wade was still in the infancy stage. I had been juggling commitments and trying to find a good time to drive up to Vancouver for a few days but hadn't quite mapped it out. I'd desperately wanted to see him before he was gone forever. And now that wasn't going to happen.

"Bryn, do I hear crying?" my mother asked.

"I always liked Uncle Wade." I couldn't control the tears or the crackle in my voice.

"I liked him too. He was a good brother and a good person." She paused to blow her nose. "If a bit complicated. I wish we'd been able to see more of him after he moved, but . . ." Her voice faded into memories. Abruptly, she added, "We can talk about this on Sunday. We need to make arrangements about going to the funeral. You *are* coming to dinner, aren't you?"

I don't know why she asks; our first-Sunday of the month family dinners are a command performance. No one except my brother's daughter by his first marriage, Catrin, has permission not to attend if she has other plans. I've never understood how she negotiated that, but I adore her anyway.

"Yes, Mom, I'll be there."

"Good. Now I need to call your brother." She said a quick goodbye and hung up.

When we were in grade school, Ellie and I had adored our Uncle Wade. From our youthful perspective, he was our familial Indiana Jones, a bright star among the other lackluster adults in our family. Well known by locals for his treasure hunting expeditions, he'd been in the paper on numerous occasions. Once for finding some buried jewelry of uncertain origins in a remote area of Finland. Another time for announcing he had a lead on one of the missing Faberge Eggs made by Peter Carl Faberge. If he'd found it, it would have been worth millions, but the lead didn't pan out. At one point he was convinced he knew the location of Jesse James' gold stash near Mulmur, Ontario. Although he persisted tracking the elusive treasure for almost a year, the stash —if it exists—remains where Jesse buried it.

Uncle Wade's small finds over the years kept him in the news, but it was his most famous expedition that got him into trouble. It involved a sunken Spanish ship from the late 1700s off the coast of Florida. He retrieved several hundred coins and a massive gold ingot from the decaying wreckage and got caught trying to smuggle them out of the country. There were also rumors that he had sold some fake gold coins to unsuspecting dealers, but as far as I know, no charges were ever filed. Perhaps the dealers knew they were receiving stolen goods and therefore couldn't rat on my uncle without confessing their own illegal intent. That was probably why my mother referred to him as "complicated"—his dreams sometimes devolved into dubious activities.

My father once said that Uncle Wade was a "loveable ne'er-do-well." I was in middle school at the time and remember asking what that meant, and he had explained that a ne'er-do-well was a nice person with "big dreams and little to show for them." I always felt like he secretly admired Uncle Wade for daring to dream. But my father never strayed far from home and wouldn't have done anything with even a whiff of illegality.

Lying there, thinking about Uncle Wade, I felt a sense of loss out of proportion to the amount of time I'd spent with him over the years. People you admire when you are young tend to occupy a special place in your memory bank. And Uncle Wade had consistently fueled my childhood fantasies for adventure and derring-do.

Suddenly my cantankerous and handsome orange cat was next to me, kneading my arm with his claws, gently, as if he'd come over to comfort me for my loss. I rubbed his ears, still shedding a few tears that glistened on his fur as they fell. The idyllic moment didn't last long. Macavity dismissed me with an abrupt "murf," leapt off the bed and headed for the galley and his breakfast.

"Okay," I said. "I'm coming." I pulled on some clothes, a pair of jeans and a wrinkled tie-dyed T-shirt, and went directly to my Keurig. I usually make my coffee before feeding Macavity, and he knows the routine, but he never fails to protest at the injustice of having to wait the thirty or so seconds it takes me to put water and a K-cup pod in the machine.

I'd barely had time to pour my coffee and sit down at my settee when the partying frogs on my phone started in again. I didn't recognize the number. I doubted it was a prospective client this early. Still, most of my management consultant business comes word of mouth, so I tapped "answer" and said, "This is Bryn Baczek." I pronounced it 'bay-check.' Sometimes I say 'bay-sick' or 'back-sek' just to keep things interesting.

"Bryn, hi. Sorry for calling so early, but I need to talk with you."

I thought I recognized the voice, but I wasn't 100 percent sure. "Ellie?" I said tentatively.

"Have you heard?"

"About Uncle Wade?"

"Yes." Her voice broke, and I felt the urge to cry again.

"I'm so sorry," I managed.

"Me too."

"Mom called me," I said. "We'll be up for the funeral. It will be good to see you—it's been too long."

"There's something I need to tell you . . ." It didn't sound like she was about to share good news.

"Yes . . .?"

"I haven't said anything to the others . . ."

"But . . .?" It's hard for me to prompt someone over the phone. I need visual cues to read feelings. In this instance, it wasn't surprising that she was upset, and she seemed to be leading up to something she wasn't sure she really wanted to talk about. Perhaps she knew about the key Uncle Wade had sent me or was privy to the other stuff he'd hinted at in his letter.

"Don't tell anyone, okay?"

"It depends on what it is," I said truthfully. I'm always hesitant to make blanket promises without knowing the details.

"When we were kids, you were always there for me."

"Ellie, whatever it is, I'll do what I can to help."

"Did your mother tell you how Uncle Wade died?"

"No." And I hadn't asked; I assumed cancer had taken him

earlier than he'd expected, even though I knew that predictions like that can be off.

"He fell down the stairs."

"What? That's awful." With only six months to live, he has a fatal accident. It *was* awful. Or perhaps a blessing. Maybe it saved him from months of pain.

"The police say it was an accident. He'd taken a sleeping pill, and they think he was groggy and slipped on the throw rug at the top of the stairs."

"But . . ." My thoughts leapt ahead as I visualized a throw rug at the top of the stairs. "Are you suggesting that you don't think it was an accident?"

"That's why I've called. I *don't* think it was an accident. For one thing, his bedroom is on the ground floor. For another, there was never a rug at the top of the stairs. He hasn't felt well recently, so I've been checking in on him every few days. I'm almost positive that rug was from one of the bedrooms on the second floor." Ellie hesitated, and I heard her take a deep breath as if bracing herself for her next comment. "Everyone knows throw rugs can be dangerous, so why would there suddenly be one there at the top of the stairs?!" Her voice ended on a strong, accusative note.

"Did you tell the police about your suspicions?"

"I talked to an officer about my concerns, but I don't think he took me seriously. He said that maybe Uncle Wade moved the rug for some reason. Or maybe the cleaning woman had."

"But you don't think either is likely?"

"The second-floor bedrooms were never used as far as I can remember. And Bianca never goes out of her way to clean *anything*. Last time I peeked in one of the upstairs bedrooms, there were dust bunnies on the floor and cobwebs hanging from the ceiling."

My mind took a side trip to the spider web hanging from the ceiling in my office before asking, "Okay, anything else?"

"Yes, he was always pretty secretive about what he was up to, and I never pressed. But the medication the doctor had him on made him drowsy and, well, sometimes he talked a lot. About random things. Then, a couple of days ago he insisted 'they' weren't going to get his secret out of him. He had a plan. Then he seemed to realize I was there and told me what a clever girl I was and that he was counting on me to figure things out. And he mentioned you, said you would help me."

"Did you ask him about it when he was more lucid?"

"I never got a chance. But I assume it was something to do with his latest treasure seeking project. He never quit looking, you know."

That made me smile. Indiana Jones to the end. "But he didn't talk to you about what the treasure was or where he was going to look for it?"

"No, and if he didn't tell *me*, I doubt he told anyone else in the family. They always treated him like the 'crazy old uncle.' The cousins never visited him, and Aunt Regina and Uncle Max made fun of his treasure hunting behind his back."

"So, is there something you want me to do?" My mind was racing. Since she hadn't mentioned it, I didn't think it made sense to bring up the key just yet. It might best be done in person.

"I just wanted to tell someone I could trust. And . . ." She paused. ". . . I would like you to assess the situation, see what you think might have happened. Maybe together we can come up with something to convince the police to investigate his death."

I was willing, but I didn't want to get her hopes up. "What about your father, is he around?" He was actually Ellie's step-father. Her biological father died in a car accident when she was five. Her mother remarried after they moved to Canada, and then she died of a heart attack shortly after Ellie's graduation from high school. I didn't think Ellie and her step-father were close, and now wasn't the time to ask. Still, I was fairly certain that he'd never become entangled in family politics, so he might be able to offer a neutral perspective on the current situation.

"No, he's on a world cruise with his new wife. I haven't called him yet. He was never close to Wade, so I don't think he would want to interrupt their trip to return for the funeral. I'll wait a few days before getting in touch, make it easy for him to say he can't make it back in time."

"Okay, I'm not sure we will be able to discover anything the police can't, but we can poke around a bit."

"How soon can you come up?"

"You mean *before* the funeral?"

"I would really appreciate it; I . . . I feel so alone."

It was a plea I couldn't ignore. I liked Ellie, and Uncle Wade had made her well-being after his death partly my responsibility. "Give me a day to sort things out, and I'll give you a shout, okay?"

After the call I sat there drinking a second cup of coffee and mulling over what Ellie had said. It wasn't much to go on, but his fall did sound suspicious. Then there was the key he'd sent me along with the enigmatic letter. I would have to check my calendar, but I didn't think I had anything on my plate that couldn't wait. I could either go up on the train or take a bus and come back with my parents after the funeral. Even if we didn't find anything to substantiate her concerns, it would be good to catch up with Ellie. And to perhaps figure out what the key unlocked.

CHAPTER 4

where there's a will

My office is in an old three-story building with sloped wood floors and vintage fixtures located at the foot of the marina dock where I moor the *Aspara*. Upon entering, I always check to make sure my goldfish aren't floating belly up. I'm on the fifth generation of fish named Bubbles and a spare that I call Friend. As soon as I feel my niece is old enough to cope with the death of a pet *she* named, I will end the charade. Fortunately, Bubbles V and Friend were busy chasing each other around their fishbowl home with its miniature treasure chest nestled in a floor of colored pebbles. Standing at a slight angle next to the chest is a pirate skeleton holding onto a sunken ship's wheel. It's my attempt to give the goldfish something to think about other than their next meal and possible premature deaths.

I'd already exceeded my one cup limit of coffee for the day, but that didn't stop me from making another. I have a Keurig on a wobbly table in the corner next to rows of bookshelves. I don't have running water in my office, so I have to keep water in a jug that I fill from a faucet across the covered walkway. It isn't much of an inconvenience, but it does require some effort, so it helps reduce my coffee consumption when I'm working.

As I waited for the coffee to brew, I considered giving the

place a thorough cleaning. It certainly needed it. Maybe tomorrow. No, that's right, I was leaving for Canada as soon as possible. The cleaning would have to wait. "Considered" and "checked off."

My work calendar was suffering from a mid-summer lull, so it didn't take long to shift a few things around and postpone the two appointments I had scheduled for late the following week. Having to attend a funeral in Canada was a pretty good excuse; they didn't need to know the details.

Then I called my landlord, Hudson Hiller, to see if he was in. He's a kind man, in his early 60's, with wavy grey hair and an easygoing manner. "If you're going to be there for a few minutes, I'd like to drop by," I said without preamble.

"Not the goldfish again!" Apparently, I needed to drop by more often when I wasn't requesting a favor.

"Remember, I have 7-day block feeders now, so you won't need to feed them more than once or twice."

"But what if they die?" He's been fish sitting upon more than one occasion when one of my goldfish died. Although I've assured him that it wasn't his fault, he still takes it personally.

"Don't worry, if they die, I'll replace them. Besides, Emma's getting almost old enough to handle the death of a pet. Either way it's a win-win." From my point of view, of course. Not from Hudson's and definitely not from the goldfishes'.

Then I called my good friend Logan. He and his partner Judd live on a 53-foot Ferro Cement sailboat on the next dock over. He has red hair like mine and people often assume that we are brother and sister. But he has freckles, the one curse of redheads that I've escaped, although I find them appealing on Logan. A grown-up Tom Sawyer. "Do you have plans for tomorrow morning?" I asked.

"What's the offer?" Logan said.

"The chance to take me to the train station and feed Macavity for a week or two."

"How can I resist?" He laughed. "I'm assuming there's a story here somewhere."

"I'll explain over your choice of breakfast, lunch or dinner today."

"Sounds like you don't have a Friday night date."

"When was the last one?"

"You need to work on that. But, sure, I choose dinner. I have some grading to catch up on and have scheduled office hours for this afternoon. But just so you know, I don't think a single dinner covers the cost of cab fare and two weeks with Macavity. It will require more than one meal—unless we go someplace really fancy."

"Put it on my tab. And did I hear you correctly? Office hours on a Friday afternoon in July? Sounds suspicious to me."

"You caught me." I envisioned him holding up his hands in mock surrender. "Seriously, I have some things I need to get done. And if a student really wants to see me—"

"Got it. Give me a shout when you're ready for dinner."

The rest of the day went quickly. I dropped off the goldfish, bought cat food and some of Macavity's favorite snack treats to make up for leaving him for a week, made train reservations, retrieved a duffle from my cluttered land locker, and packed for the trip. I would have to steam or iron my funeral clothes after having them rolled up like that, but between my duffle, my backpack, and my preference for casual dress, I would manage. I could always buy something if I needed to. The last thing I did was call my mother to inform her that Ellie had asked me to come up early and stay with her until the funeral.

"You'll miss Sunday dinner," she complained.

"Sorry, Mom, but under the circumstances, I couldn't say no to Ellie."

After a short hesitation, Mom agreed, "It's nice that the two of you are still close. It's sad when families grow apart." In addition to a smattering of relatives who were distant by blood ties as well as by actual distance, my mother didn't have a lot of contact with family members outside of our tight little group. The two siblings she'd been closest to—Ellie's mother and Wade—were both gone now. That left her older brother Max, her older sister Regina, and their children. Although there hadn't been a specific rift with them that I knew of, she didn't talk about them much and never encouraged visits. Maybe that was why our Sunday dinners were so important to her; she wanted to keep her immediate family close.

I have my differences with my mother, but my growing up years were good, and I loved my family in that "family love" sort of way. Maybe I needed to be more amenable, focus on the positive and let go of little irritations. Like my brother's wife Angelina giving me a red sweater as a present when she knows I look terrible in red. On second thought, I might want to wade in slowly on this amenability thing.

On the bright side, I was off the hook for Sunday, ready to travel, and was having dinner with a close friend. Life was good. Except for the sad void I felt at the loss of Uncle Wade.

Logan and I met at one of our favorite Italian restaurants, a short drive from the university and not far for me either. Even though it has white tablecloths and good wine, it's a casual place that has been there as long as the old brick houses in the surrounding neighborhood. We go there often enough to be treated like old friends rather than customers. Although I attribute the friendliness partly to Logan's generous tips. He's from a wealthy family and sometimes forgets he lives on a professor's salary. On the other hand, we both live on boats and don't spend much on "stuff." Every inch of space on a boat has to be devoted to essential items. Why buy something non-essential if you are going to store it in a locker?

We placed our orders for an antipasto platter and risotto Milanese, Logan making a show of getting the right wine pairing and insisting we save room for Tiramisu or he was going to order it to go. All to squeeze more out of his advance payment for services to be rendered.

Once we were settled, I explained that Uncle Wade had died and that was the reason for my trip to Canada.

"I'm sorry," Logan said. "I didn't realize this was that kind of dinner. I know you were fond of him."

"I wish I had made an effort to visit more often."

"We tend to assume people will be there when we have the time for them. And that isn't always the case."

"It makes me feel guilty for complaining about family dinners."

"Does that mean you aren't going to complain about them anymore?" Logan sounded skeptical.

"At least for a month." I picked up a garlic-stuffed green olive, but before eating it I added, "Especially since Mom excused me from this Sunday's dinner."

Logan gave me that sidelong look he reserves for questioning someone's motives or when quoting Oscar Wilde. Which he often does. Then his eyes wandered over the antipasto offerings and he chose a slice of Havarti. "So, when's the funeral?"

"I'm not sure yet. But since Ellie asked me to come, I think I'll stay with her until then, depending on the timing."

I helped myself to some tomato-basil bruschetta while Logan dove into a bowl of marinated veggies. We chewed and savored for a few minutes before I got around to the other unpleasant topic I wanted to discuss. I quit eating and took a deep breath. My shift in demeanor caused him to put down his wine glass just as he was about to take a sip. "There is something I want to run past you," I began.

"I'm not sure I like the sound of this."

"It's the reason Ellie wants me to come early." I hesitated. Her suspicion was an ominous supposition that I hated to give voice to. "She thinks Uncle Wade's accident wasn't an accident."

Logan blinked morse code for surprise. "She thinks he was murdered?"

"Pushed down the stairs and set up to look like an accident."

"That's quite an allegation. Any proof?

"It's mainly conjecture on her part. For instance, his bedroom was on the first floor. And he allegedly slipped on a throw rug at the top of the second-floor stairs in the middle of the night."

"Strange, but not impossible. Maybe he heard a noise and went to investigate.

"Even so, Ellie doesn't remember there ever being a rug there."

"Hmmm. I see. That *is* suspicious."

"He may have taken a sleeping pill. Which would have left him groggy and even less likely to have gone upstairs."

"Did he have pets?"

"I don't know." There was so much I didn't know.

"Could it have been a burglary interrupted? Was anything missing?"

"I'm not sure she's been to the house since his death. But the police didn't apparently think the situation suggested a burglary."

"He wasn't prone to falling, was he?"

"Not that I know of."

"Will there be an autopsy?"

"My guess is that the family will oppose an autopsy, even if foul play is suspected."

"Why?"

"That would postpone the distribution of his estate. Sorry, that was snarky, wasn't it? Anyway, I'm just guessing."

"But if the police decide it's a suspicious death?"

"Then I think there would be an autopsy. And if he was shoved hard enough, there could be bruises on his back or shoulders. Although, I'm not sure they would be distinguishable from other bruises caused during a fall. Besides, in my opinion, a clever killer would simply have lured him to the top of the steps and pulled the rug out from under him."

"Remind me never to cross you."

"Ellie doesn't feel like she has enough to convince the police to investigate further. That's one of the things we're going to strategize."

"So, what do *you* think based on what you know at this point —accident or . . .?"

"I don't know what to think. There's not much to go on, but I trust Ellie's instincts."

Our meal came and we ended the conversation about death and murder and got lost in the flavors and textures of a truly fine meal. It wasn't until we were drinking dark rich coffee after splitting a Tiramisu that we returned to the topic of Uncle Wade's death.

"There's something I haven't told you," I said.

Logan raised his eyebrows. "A *secret*?"

"I was going to tell you, but I only got the package a few days ago." I pulled the letter out of my purse and handed it to him. "Read this."

His eyes raced down the page. Then he reread it more slowly. "And two days later he's dead?"

"Well, the package was in the mail for several days, and I didn't pick it up at the PO Box right away. But in addition to not wanting the family to know he had cancer, it seems like he had some other secret he wanted kept from them."

"That makes it sound a bit like Ellie may be right about the so-called *accident.*"

"I'm hoping she isn't, because if she is, the most likely suspects are family, the Canadian contingent. Not my favorite relatives, but family nonetheless."

"So where do you start when you get there? Interrogate the relatives? Remind me how many we're talking about."

"The immediate family consists of my mother's remaining siblings, her older brother Max, and her older sister Regina. Max has three boys: Kent, Dennis, and Tuna."

"Tuna?" Logan interrupted.

"It's a name his brothers pinned on him when they were young. He was always eating tuna sandwiches and they claimed he smelled like a tuna."

"That's kind of stupid."

"But it stuck. Anyway, Regina has two kids, Candy and Vinny." I held up my hand. "Don't ask. No, her name is *not* Candace, but Candy. And Vinny is not short for Vincent or Vincenzo. It's just plain Vinny."

Logan chuckled. "So *you* have a cousin Vinny."

"You didn't have to say that."

"Oh, but I did."

"Anyway, Ellie is going to see if there's a will. She doesn't know if he had much to leave, other than the house. But he could have money in the bank or maybe some illegal gold coins hidden in the wall of his house."

"You're joking, right?"

"I doubt he has anything hidden in the walls, but Ellie thinks that recently he had a good lead on a big treasure of some sort."

"Maybe someone killed him for a treasure map. Now that's romantic."

"Don't forget, this is my favorite uncle we're talking about."

"A favorite uncle who was a treasure hunter, who with only six months to live is concerned about what could happen *after* his death, and who sends you a mysterious key with no explanation. You've certainly got *my* attention."

family secrets

"It's so good to see you," Ellie said when she met me at the train station in Vancouver. Then she threw her arms around me and gave me a big hug. I'm *almost* six feet tall and Ellie is only 5'8," so I had to bend down a bit for the hug, an uncomfortable and awkward position. Being *almost* this and *almost* that has plagued me all my life. My red hair is *almost* strawberry blond, but too coppery to be a warm reddish hue. My eyes are *almost* the same color, yet people know immediately that they aren't. I'm *almost* ambidextrous, although mostly left-handed. I was *almost* good enough to make the swim team in college. And, as my mother keeps reminding me, I'm *almost* forty.

"I shouldn't have waited for Uncle Wade's death to visit," I said.

"I know, but time passes so quickly, doesn't it?"

"It feels like it was just yesterday when you moved away."

"Yet so much has happened." We stood there a moment, each lost in our own thoughts about the past. Then Ellie grabbed my bag, "Come on, let's get you settled in so we can have a good talk . . . and maybe a good cry over a glass of wine."

"Make that several glasses of wine and you have a deal."

Ellie lives on the outskirts of downtown Vancouver not too

far from Grenville Island in a two-bedroom condo on the third floor. "I got the condo as part of the divorce settlement," she explained as I drooled over the view of the Bay and the waterside trail that she told me ran all the way to Stanley Park. "To be honest, I would rather live in a hovel than have gone through a nasty divorce." Then added, "To say nothing of the nasty marriage."

"I'm sorry. You didn't deserve to marry a miserable sod." I'd heard all about it from my mother who heard it through the family rumor mill. My Aunt Regina in particular was always eager to pass along bad news that was happening to *other* family members, but never shared any problems her own brood might be facing. Unlike the rest of us, *they* were a perfect family unit, each member supposedly exemplary in their own way. In retrospect I could kick myself for not getting in touch with Ellie during that difficult period in her life.

"That's one of the reasons I'm going to miss Uncle Wade so much. He was there for me when my mother died and again when I was going through my divorce. He even helped me deal with one of my phobias—but that's a story for another time. Meanwhile, my step-father didn't cope well with Mom's death and was already off on a series of world jaunts by the time of my divorce. I was only married for two years, but it seemed like forever. Purgatory without the prospect of moving on."

Ellie fixed us a plate of cheese and crackers with apple and pear slices. We took that along with two glasses of wine out on the covered balcony to enjoy the late afternoon sun and conversation.

"Did you find out if there is a will?" I asked.

"Uncle Max and Aunt Regina are convinced he didn't leave a will, but Uncle Wade's housekeeper is just as certain there is one."

"How's Bianca doing, anyway?" I remembered her as a slow-moving but pleasant older woman who wore colorful aprons.

"Well, she's in her 70s, not very nimble, and as you know, she was never much of a housekeeper even when she was younger. But she was with him for almost twenty years. He could never bring himself to demand more work from her. And firing her wasn't an option he would entertain either. He was a softie that way. She doesn't show her emotions much, but I think they were fond of each other, each in their own way. I'm sad for her."

"It sounds like his death will leave a big hole in her life."

"I caught him making tea for her one day." Ellie smiled. "Whatever works, right?"

"I like the image of him serving her tea," I said. "But back to the will, Bianca thinks there is one, but it sounds like she didn't find it."

"No, but what she *did* find was a card with a lawyer's name on it. When I called him late yesterday, he confirmed that he had Uncle Wade's will, and hadn't heard about his death. He also told me that in addition to the will, Uncle Wade left a letter for me. But by then it was almost 5:00, too late for me to come by and pick it up."

"A letter? That sounds intriguing." I hoped it was more specific than the one I'd received.

"It's apparently completely separate from the will. Something he asked the lawyer to hold for me until his death. I'm to pick it up on Monday."

"What about the will?"

"The lawyer wants to wait until your mother gets here so he can share it with all of us at the same time."

I was about to tell her about the key Uncle Wade had sent, when she took a deep breath and said, "There's one more thing I need to tell you. You won't believe this. Our vulture cousins already raided Uncle Wade's house looking for something, maybe the will. Who knows what they would have done if they'd found it and didn't like what was in it."

"How did you find out about the house being searched?"

"Bianca told me. She was pretty upset. She said that she went back to pick up a few of her things and found everything in disarray."

"Glad Bianca found the lawyer's card before that happened.

But what makes you so sure it was the cousins who are responsible?"

"Who else knew about his death? I'm assuming they were looking for the will, although maybe they thought there was something else of value to be found. Like a strongbox filled with money, or gold coins pilfered from some ancient site, or a treasure map leading to untold riches. They are a greedy bunch. Bianca said they made a huge mess of things. She called to ask what she should do."

"What did you tell her?"

"I told her to leave things as they were and that I would check it out. I'm torn about reporting a break-in to the police."

"You mean because you're convinced it was the cousins?"

"Yes. And I need to take a look around first anyway. The police will ask what was taken."

"Poor Bianca."

"I told her not to worry about the house for a while and assured her she would get paid for the month. And, hopefully, Uncle Wade left her something in his will."

"You think he did?"

"I would be surprised if he didn't."

"Have you told the rest of the family about the will?"

"Not yet. I don't want the lawyer pressured by Uncle Max and Aunt Regina to let them see it before your mother arrives. And I keep thinking about some of the conversations I had with Uncle Wade this last month."

"What haven't you told me?" Maybe we both had a few secrets to share.

"I'm not trying to be evasive; I'm embarrassed by what's crossed my mind. Lately he kept hinting about having a line on something big, something really big. But then, he was always boasting about a potential find, wasn't he?"

"He could have believed *this* time was the big score. That's what kept him looking for lost treasures, right?"

"Yes, he never gave up on the dream. But that doesn't make it real. Still—"

"Do you think your cousins heard the rumor and thought it might be true? Maybe they hoped to find a treasure map in his house. Maybe they *did* find one." I shook my head. "Sounds like a bad movie plot."

"I can't imagine Uncle Wade leaving anything important lying about where just anyone could find it."

"So, if he did have a map, or other valuables, you assume he would have hidden them somewhere he considered safe. Maybe the letter he left with his lawyer will tell you where."

"That's what I'm hoping, but I don't want to wait until Monday to have a look around. Do you?"

"No. I say that tomorrow we go on our own treasure hunt of sorts to see if we can uncover whatever secrets our uncle was hiding from the rest of the world." That almost sounded like fun. Uncle Wade had been right—I loved solving puzzles.

"On the one hand, I don't care about any valuables he may have kept hidden away. But I resent the other cousins not telling me they were going to search his house, and I don't want to see them benefit from his death."

I put the key on the table next to the cheese plate. "Uncle Wade sent me this a few days ago, but he didn't tell me what it's for. He seemed to assume we'd collaborate on something after his death. Any ideas?"

Ellie picked up the key and studied it. "No idea."

"Well, tomorrow, in addition to looking for things the cousins might have overlooked, we should see if we can find a lock that fits this key."

creative cartography

Saturday evening our conversation meandered from speculation about what we might find in Uncle Wade's house to a lot of reminiscing. A verbal scrapbook of the past. Sophie, my current best friend, was also my closest friend in grade school, but Ellie and I had spent considerable time together because of proximity and family connections. There were gatherings at the lake, camping trips, backyard bar-b-ques, and various types of celebrations as well as shared classroom experiences. We relived some of the good times as we sipped our pinot noir, always starting with "Remember when . . .?" and ending with a smile or a sigh of satisfaction. It was a long time ago, but some experiences are indelibly imprinted in childhood memories. Although I sometimes worry that not all such remembrances are reality based. The family retelling of stories or even a picture in an album can reinforce a particular aspect of an event, obliterating other features, sometimes transforming the event entirely. It's like seeing what happened through a kaleidoscope—a couple of twists to the right or left and a new image invades your recollections.

We also touched briefly on what the grade school bullies had done to puff themselves up by badgering us. We laughed about the time I'd defended her at the river by attacking the three boys who were trying to force her into a cave. And she reminded me of an incident that I've tried to suppress. In the fourth grade, some kids started poking fun at me because my eyes are two different colors, a condition called heterochromia. They mocked me for having "fake-eyes" or "rainbow eyes." Then, one day a boy I'd never liked came up with "snake-eyes," even though few snakes have different colored eyes. I'd had enough and punched him in one eye and said, "There, now *you'll* have two different colored eyes." That ended the teasing. Although when I think back, "rainbow eyes" wasn't all that bad.

We also caught up on more recent life experiences. How my family was doing. My Dad's adjustment to retirement. My mother's insistence that we all have dinner together once a month and her persistent aspiration to see me married. Dylan's second marriage and his three kids. My lousy luck keeping goldfish alive. What it was like to creep up on the big 40. The death of Ellie's mother. Her disastrous marriage and ugly divorce. And the strained relationships between Uncle Wade and other members of the family living in Vancouver.

"I know you can't choose family," Ellie concluded. "But if I could, I'm afraid most of my cousins would be voted off my island." I understood exactly what she meant. From what she told me, they hadn't changed much since we were young. They were still aggressive and self-centered, with a handful of underachievers' meanness thrown into the mix. Aristotle said, *Give me a child until he is seven and I will show you the man.* I assume he would have said something similar about women if he'd considered them worth thinking about. As for me, I always want to believe that people can change, but there has to be a catalyst.

Sunday, we stopped at a local diner for coffee and muffins before heading to Uncle Wade's house. Vancouver is almost as obsessed with coffee as Seattle, and they love their pastries. I had a lemonpoppyseed muffin topped with a tart, lemony glaze. It was promoted as "slightly crisp on the outside and moist on the inside," and it lived up to the promise. As a bonus, their French roast coffee was smooth and full-bodied.

Uncle Wade's house was on a block with other older houses, a slice of the fading elegance of another era. It was a three-story structure with a veranda across the front and a projecting upper bay facing north. Painted a gloomy dark green with white trim, it had a Mansard roof with two gables on each side. The lot wasn't large, and the houses were cheek by jowl, but rows of bushes lined both sides of the lot, providing an illusion of privacy. A weed-filled flower garden separated the sidewalk from the house.

I'd only visited once that I could remember, after the reception for Candy and Vic's wedding. My impression then was the same as now—the house was much too big for one person and obviously required far too much upkeep to maintain curb appeal. But Uncle Wade had apparently not only liked its proximity to downtown Vancouver, he loved the house itself, in spite of its rundown appearance. I could understand his attachment. The house's looming presence conjured up charming images of past occupants. In my mind's eye I could picture a large family with well-mannered children playing in the yard. The parents straight-backed and well-groomed. Prim girls wearing dresses with matching bows in their hair and pink-cheeked boys in short pants and caps. Vancouver had been a thriving city when the house was built, and only the well-to-do lived in this part of town then. Today, the truly wealthy had moved on, families were smaller, and historic homes were being replaced by giant condos and modern structures. It was amazing that this older neighborhood had survived.

We parked out front and made our way along the cracked cement walkway to the front steps. The handrail's peeling green paint felt gritty, and tiny flakes came off on my hand when I steadied myself against the uneven steps. "It needs some work," I unnecessarily pointed out.

"The family will probably sell it 'as is.'" Ellie said. "Money in hand and all that."

"But you don't know who inherits it yet. What if it's you?"

"Oh, I can't imagine Uncle Wade would have left his house to me; he knew that I wouldn't want to live here. Even though it's rather nice inside. There's some lovely woodwork and vintage stained-glass."

"You think it goes to the three remaining siblings?"

"That would be my guess. In spite of their differences, they were still his closest next of kin."

Ellie unlocked the front door and we went inside. There was a short hallway that opened into a large living room on the left and continued on toward the back of the house. The main thing I remembered clearly was the built-in, cushioned seat in the bay window off the living room; a lovely place to sit and read. To the right was a beautiful stairway with curved handrails made of dark wood and polished by many hands over the years.

"Why don't we start in his study?" Ellie said. "It's on the third floor, an attic room with a view of the surrounding area, but only through a couple of small windows. The kitchen and his bedroom are at the back of the house down here. The second floor has three bedrooms and a single bath. I don't remember him ever using the second floor. But all the rooms are furnished."

We trudged up the stairs to the third floor, both of us glancing uncomfortably at the two critical spots marking Uncle Wade's fateful fall. The rug was no longer at the top of the stairs; someone had moved it, probably the police. His attic study was an open space that was divided by function: office, lounge area, and storage. The desk in the office area was littered with papers, as was the floor around it. There were also files and papers scattered in front of the filing cabinet next to his desk, its drawers open and empty. The couch was upturned and its cushions removed. A lounge chair lay on its side next to an upside-down end table. The storage area was a tumble of boxes with their contents strewn across the floor. All of the books on the shelves along one wall had been removed and tossed aside.

"When Bianca described it as a mess, that was an understatement," I said.

"The cousins and I were supposed to come here together to *go through his things*," Ellie grumbled. "Not toss the place."

"And yet, if we are correct, they came without telling you, and now we are here without informing them. Not exactly teamwork."

"I can understand why they wanted to be here on their own, but why did they tear everything apart? Did they think I wouldn't notice?"

"Maybe it wasn't the cousins. Whoever searched the place, they were obviously determined to find whatever it was they were looking for." My eyes roamed over the results of their search. "And it was something they thought could be under a cushion or on a bookshelf."

"Maybe they *were* looking for a treasure map. As if he would have put something like that under a cushion on the sofa."

"Or hidden it in a book? I have my doubts."

"At least they didn't slit the couch cushions. I guess we have that to be thankful for."

"The question is whether whoever pushed Uncle Wade down the stairs got what they wanted the night of his death or came back and went through everything later."

"It's possible they deliberately came when they knew Uncle Wade was here so they could force him to tell them where to find the map or gold or whatever valuables they thought he possessed."

"That doesn't seem like the M.O. for the cousins, does it?" In spite of my dislike for them, I didn't want them to be responsible for Uncle Wade's death. It would destroy what little remained of our family connection.

"No, I think they were more likely to come by when they knew he wasn't here."

"Did they know he sometimes took sleeping pills? Maybe they thought they could do a quick search without waking him up."

"I'm not sure," Ellie said. "I suppose it's not impossible that he mentioned it to Aunt Regina or Uncle Max."

"Well, I can picture Uncle Wade surprising someone in the act and confronting them at the top of the stairs. They try to get past him, they struggle, and Uncle Wade falls. Or he surprises them and they deliberately push him down the stairs. In either instance, they left him there after he fell. For all we know, he was still alive. Accident or not, it was a despicable act."

"And," Ellie said, picking up on my scenario, "in either case, the rug would have been placed there *after* he fell. Whether the person deliberately pushed him and wanted to make it look like an accident, or because it *was* an accident and the person panicked."

"That makes sense. And in either instance they could have left in a hurry, possibly intending to come back later to finish the job. Unless we're dealing with two separate invasions."

"Well, we may not be able to find evidence to support one theory over the other, but we can look around to see if whoever searched the house missed anything. And I'm afraid I need to report this. In case Uncle Wade's death really wasn't an accident and the break-in is connected."

We found some rubber gloves in the kitchen so we wouldn't be destroying any fingerprints left behind. Then we spent several hours going through the contents of Uncle Wade's office. We started with the papers on his desk and the surrounding floor. Next, we looked at book titles and flyleaves before putting books back on shelves. We perused the stuff spilled out of the storage boxes. Replaced cushions. And kept our eyes open for a lock to fit the key he had sent me. There was a lot of memorabilia that needed sorting, but based on our cursory search, we found nothing to explain what someone might have been looking for or what the key he'd sent me unlocked.

"I suppose whoever was here could have found a locked box

or trunk or piece of luggage and taken it with them," I said. "Although I can't imagine Uncle Wade sending me a key and then leaving the thing it opened where it was easy to find."

"Me neither," Ellie said. "I need a break. Let's go have a cuppa. There should be something to drink in the kitchen." She pushed her dark brown curly hair away from her face, revealing a smooth tanned forehead. An older but recognizable version of the girl I'd known in grade school.

"I could use something to drink. Unless they dumped out all the coffee and cut up the teabags." I said it as a joke, not a premonition.

On the way down we stopped to peek in the second-floor rooms. There was very little furniture and few personal items in them, so the clutter left behind was less egregious. But the rooms had definitely been searched. Bedding was on the floor, mattresses askew. Drawers open, contents tossed aside. Pictures taken down and removed from their frames. There hadn't been much in the medicine cabinet in the bathroom, but its contents had obviously been examined and the cabinet itself pulled away from the wall about a quarter inch.

"More to clean up," Ellie said. "But not too bad."

Then we went downstairs and saw the kitchen. It looked like a small tornado had swept through. Appliances were still upright and drawers intact, but there was debris everywhere. Dishes and food items pulled out of cupboards, cannisters opened and contents dumped, food and packages strewn across the counter. The refrigerator door stood open, very little remaining inside. Food from the freezer had melted on the floor, bags and miscellaneous containers of food tossed hither and thither. The room smelled faintly of sour milk and rotting fruit. There was, however, a kettle on the stove, and the jar of tea bags on the counter appeared to be intact.

Ellie was stalled in the doorway, staring as if she couldn't believe what she was seeing.

"Let's have a cup of tea, okay?" I suggested to divert her attention from the catastrophe by prodding her into action.

"How could they have done this . . .!"

"We don't know for sure that it was the cousins." I was holding onto a thin thread of hope that it wasn't. "Maybe you should have Bianca clean it up."

"I don't think Uncle Wade would have wished this much clean-up on Bianca."

"You're probably right. If the three siblings inherit the house, they can hire an entire team of cleaners." I motioned toward the kettle on the stove. "I'll get the water going. See if you can find two cups." I filled the kettle and turned on the stove while Ellie searched the mostly empty cupboards and found two mugs that were still in one piece.

"He would have been so upset," she said.

"All the more reason to see if we can figure out what, if anything, he was hiding. In case it's still here."

While I was standing there waiting for the kettle to boil, I found myself studying a handcrafted switch plate cover on the light switch by the kitchen door. "This is interesting," I said.

Ellie came over and stood beside me. "Uncle Wade made it out of clay," she said. "He told me the picture he painted on it is based on a dock from an abandoned cannery on the Inside Passage. He rented a boat last year and made part of the trip through the islands to Alaska. He described it as the trip of a lifetime."

"Really?" I stared harder at the switch plate. It wasn't all that attractive. A thought was trying to move from a vague tickle at the back of my mind to a full-formed idea that I could articulate. "Did *you* ask *him* about the switch plate design, or did he make a point of telling you about it?"

Ellie blinked. "I'm not sure I remember. But he did emphasize that it was a place he hoped to return someday."

"Do you remember his exact words?"

She thought about it and shook her head. "Not really. But he mentioned it more than once. I thought he was proud of making it himself. A craft phase he was going through." Then she looked at the mug in her hand. "He painted the design on this mug, too. He told me it was 'my' mug. At the time I didn't say much because I thought it was ugly." She held it up. The picture depicted a wooded trail leading to a cave entrance and someone going inside. "He always treated my speluncaphobia with respect. Not like the rest of the family. That's why I was surprised he put a cave on a mug that he painted especially for me."

"But he definitely said it was *your* mug."

"Yes, he said that someday I would appreciate the picture."

"Anything else?" I asked, experiencing a tingle of excitement. "Anything else he mentioned that *you* personally might find interesting or that you should pay attention to?"

She thought about it for a minute. "He asked me recently what I thought of his placemats."

We walked over to the table and looked at the laminated map placemats. If we hadn't already been thinking about the Inside Passage, we might have simply thought they were maps of the western half of British Columbia. "The Inside Passage," we both said simultaneously.

I laughed. "Either our uncle was toying with you and went out of his way to lay breadcrumbs leading nowhere or . . ."

"He was leaving me a message."

"Maybe it will all be explained in the letter he left for you with the lawyer. In the letter he sent to me he said that my role would become clear after his death. I assume we are meant to put our heads together and figure this out." I still hadn't broached the subject of his cancer; the timing hadn't felt right. Nor had I told her everything he'd said in his letter to me. If he hadn't referred to Ellie's vulnerability and asked me to look out for her, I would have simply shown her the letter.

"If he was going to lay it all out in a letter, why leave strange clues like these?" Ellie asked.

"Well, we don't know yet what's in the letter. It could be

about something else. But I can think of two possibilities for leaving these clues. The first is that he wanted to engage us in 'the hunt.' My second thought is that he anticipated that someone, maybe our cousins, would ransack the place looking for his latest treasure map, and he didn't want to leave anything obvious lying about."

"What if he intended to tell me more but didn't live long enough?"

"Then we work with what we have. I say we collect all of the possible clues we can find and see if they take us anywhere. We need to look room by room with this in mind."

We quickly drank down our tea and started searching for anything remotely suggestive of a clue to be found in the living room. Someone had removed the giant globe from its stand in front of the window and cracked it open. "The globe," Ellie said. "He loved to twirl the globe and point to places he'd been. The scale makes it difficult to pinpoint specific locations though."

We picked up the two halves and put them on the coffee table. "It doesn't look broken," Ellie said. "I think these two halves can be put back together." She ran her fingers over Vancouver Island. "The globe may not be a clue, but it definitely reminds me of Uncle Wade and his adventures."

While I was listening to Ellie talk about the globe, another part of my brain was actively seeking connections. "So, we are looking for a place in BC, probably an abandoned cannery on the Inside Passage, and a trail to a cave," I summarized out loud as I googled abandoned canneries in British Columbia on my cell. "Wow," I exclaimed as the results popped up. "BC was cannery heaven at one point. Mostly for processing salmon. And it looks like there are about a dozen abandoned canneries in the Inside Passage."

"Even if we find a location that fits, how do we know it's for real?"

"We don't. Not unless we find something more concrete."

We continued our search. In the bathroom someone had

taken the back off a framed watercolor of a trail going up to a small lake. Pretty amateurish. The initials W.P. were in the corner. Ellie said, "He told me this picture was his vision of a trail leading to someplace special, like the yellow brick road."

"He actually referenced the yellow brick road? Well, we can follow a trail, but we need to know where it starts from." I picked up the painting and added it to our pile on the kitchen table.

"Maybe the trailhead would be obvious if we knew which cannery."

"I can't imagine it's a well-traveled trail. Or maybe it is, and the trick is to find the cave and then know where to look once inside."

Ellie shivered. "I won't be able to go in a cave with you."

"Hey, no one said anything about actually searching for buried treasure."

"But if we figure this out, you will try, won't you? *We* will. For Uncle Wade."

I'd been caught up in solving the puzzle from the random and elusive clues Uncle Wade had left behind and hadn't considered the practicality of next steps. But with Ellie's plea for action, I felt myself catching the fever. Uncle Wade had gone to a lot of trouble to leave a trail for us. One he couldn't be certain we would find and interpret correctly, no matter how much faith he had in my puzzle-solving skills. Still, it seemed like he'd been hinting rather blatantly to Ellie about the possibility of a hidden treasure near an abandoned cannery in BC, and he'd sent me a letter to encourage me to provide backup. And if the end goal was to get us to dig for treasure in a remote cave in the Canadian wilderness, no wonder he wanted me to assist Ellie.

"We might be able to narrow the location down a bit, even with what little we know," I said. "Unless the cave is a tourist attraction, it won't be on any maps. But lakes will show up. And with satellite pictures and topography maps, we should be able to make a pretty good guess about whether there are any caves in a particular area."

"Let's say we're able to identify some possibilities. Could we check them out on our own? Just the two of us?"

As soon as I'd started seriously thinking about searching for the treasure, I thought of asking Logan to go with us. Not only is he an experienced sailor, but he'd be handy to have along if we actually found the cave. I'm not phobic, but I've seen enough horror films to have a healthy respect for what one might encounter. Falling rocks. Bats. Spiders and snakes. Bears. Human remains. But with Logan along, I was confident we could handle it. Nothing is ever as scary with a loyal friend at your side. However, that's where my optimism petered out.

"I have a friend who I'm sure would love to take a cruise up the Inside Passage with us," I assured her. "But even if we find the right cave, we need an X-marks-the-spot to succeed."

CHAPTER 7

upon my death

"I'm not sure I know what this means," Ellie said. We were in the lawyer's office. The sealed envelope with Ellie's name on it had said "To Be Opened Upon the Occasion of My Death." Just like my letter. She had quickly slit the end of the envelope and pulled out a single sheet of paper. After reading it several times, she handed it to me.

Ellie, if you are reading this, then I'm no longer of this world. I hope I went peacefully in my sleep. Although I know there are those who would have gladly murdered me to possess the map I have found to an ancient treasure. It was believed that this treasure had vanished forever. Stolen by Spanish invaders from the Aztecs only to disappear, along with some of the Spaniards, before reaching Spain. It has probably gone through many hands over the years, eventually to be hidden away and abandoned. The last person in possession of the treasure died before he could retrieve it. But he left behind a map. And I managed to acquire it.

Unfortunately, there is no safe place to hide something you want to keep secret. Someone clever may find it or someone could come across it by chance. Therefore, I have the map in my head, and if I'm dead, that map is gone too.

You are a smart woman, Ellie. (As is your cousin Bryn.) We've shared many moments about places I've been and places I'd like to go. I would have left you the map if I hadn't felt it would put you in danger. I'm confident you will value some keepsakes of our friendship. And if you ever have the opportunity to take a boat trip, please think of me. It was one of the true pleasures in my life.

Your loving Uncle Wade.

"What do you think?" Ellie said when I looked up after reading the letter, twice.

"I think he cared for you." I stood up. "When do you anticipate reading the will?" I asked the lawyer.

"I would like the three siblings and Ellie to be present. Bryn, your mother said she will be here by Wednesday. How about Thursday morning?"

"What about our other cousins?" Ellie asked.

"That's up to the family, but they don't need to be present."

"Does that mean . . .?" Ellie paused.

"Why don't we wait until Thursday to discuss this further."

We went to a corner coffee shop to talk about the letter and what the lawyer had said about the reading of the will.

"I'm not surprised that you may be named in the will," I said.

"You think that's what the lawyer was suggesting?"

"I have no doubt about it. You're in, and the rest of us cousins are out."

"I'm sorry."

"Don't be sorry for me," I said. "I didn't keep in touch. But I'm glad I have fond memories, and I'm glad you did stay connected. Now about that letter—"

"If he wants us to look for the treasure, why didn't he give me more to go on?"

"Two things cross my mind," I said. "The first is that the letter isn't just for your eyes; I think he wants you to share it with other family members. To emphasize that he did have a map but it no longer exists. That provides you with cover.

"Second, I think it's partly because what he always enjoyed most was the hunt. It was less about getting rich than looking for hidden treasure. He left you clues so you, too, can experience the joy of being a treasure seeker. And he obviously wants me to help you."

"What you say makes sense to me," she said, "particularly the part about the thrill of the hunt—I can see it. Maybe even the smuggling he was accused of was the romance of the chase to him."

"We could be reading too much between the lines, but I don't think so. He made it clear that he didn't want to take the chance of writing anything down. Although I'm surprised that he would destroy a historic map. If that's what he did."

"Okay, so even though I don't really want to, I'll let it drop that I got a letter from Uncle Wade. That should do it. Aunt Regina will insist on seeing it."

"And it will also let the family know why we're thinking of a sailing trip—because we're two overly sentimental women, right? We just want to take a boat trip to honor his memory, like he suggested. All we need is to find a few more pieces of the puzzle, and we're set."

"Yeah, that's *all*."

We drank coffee in silence for a few minutes. Uncle Wade had certainly gone to a lot of trouble to create a script for us to follow. A more complex character than the folk hero image in my head.

"Now that he's gone, I realize there's a lot I never knew about him. For example, after he quit as an electrical engineer, did he ever have a regular job again?" I asked.

"If he did, I don't remember it."

"So where did he get his money for treasure hunting?" I asked.

"I don't know. It will be interesting to see if he actually had any money to speak of."

"Yes, I think the reading of the will on Thursday will be interesting in more ways than one."

In spite of our earlier resolve to let someone else do the clean-up at Uncle Wade's, we decided to do more of it ourselves so we could continue searching for clues. On the way, Ellie called Aunt Regina to tell her about the letter, and as anticipated, Aunt Regina asked if she could see it. Ellie said she'd bring it with her for the reading of the will. Then, playing the role of the disappointed heiress, she added, "I was hoping that there was a treasure map and that the cousins could have gone on an expedition together. Now it looks like the most we can do is take a boat trip to honor his last wishes."

Ellie also mentioned that someone had searched Uncle Wade's house and left a mess behind, and that we were headed there to do some clean-up. "I've reported the break-in to the police, and they sent someone to take a look around. But until we know if anything was stolen, there isn't much they can do."

Aunt Regina muttered something about the increase in crime in the area, then offered Candy's services for the clean-up. We could hardly refuse. Although it seemed unlikely to me that she was trying to be helpful, maybe she wanted Candy to keep an eye on us, or maybe she hoped Candy would find something of value. Either way, it would make our own further search of Uncle Wade's house more difficult.

Candy arrived at Uncle Wade's not long after we did. She had her daughter Pastel in tow along with a miniature dachshund named Shorty. "Pastel named him," Candy announced proudly.

I managed a neutral "Really?" instead of a sarcastic, "Clever child." Ellie just smiled.

I hadn't seen Candy in a while. With her bleached blond hair and round face, she looked like a slightly older version of her daughter. Pastel had brown hair, the color of Candy's roots, and a round face. They both had pouty red lips, although Candy's were slathered with lipstick that I imagined was called something like "Retro Ruby" or "Scarlet Passion." They were both wearing pink shirts and tight jeans. Shorty boasted a gem studded hot pink collar.

We were just starting on the kitchen when they arrived. Pastel and Shorty disappeared into the living room. Candy looked around and asked, "What do you want me to do?" She sounded like she was hoping we'd ask her to serve the martinis or test the cushions on the couch in the living room. Instead, I said, "We have some bags for things that need to be tossed; otherwise, we're just putting things back for now."

"Okay." She peeked in the fridge and made a face. "Gross."

"Pretty bad," Ellie agreed as she started to pick formerly frozen packages off the floor. They were still soggy, like something you'd find at the bottom of a swamp.

Candy daintily removed a brown head of lettuce from the fridge and put it in a discard bag. "By the way, Bryn, you're looking good. Don't have a boyfriend, do you?"

"Thanks, and no. How's Vic doing?"

"My chubby hubby is doing good. The real estate market is hot right now." She glanced around. "We won't have any trouble unloading this house."

I felt Ellie bristle at the words *we* and *unloading*. Given its location, the house would most likely sell quickly. There might even be a bidding war. If Vic handled the sale, he would get a nice fat commission. "Not sure who the 'we' is until the will is read," I said. More to needle Candy than anything else.

"Mom and Uncle Max will most likely inherit it, don't you think?"

"He may have left it to his siblings," I said, not calling attention to the fact that she seemed to think my mother didn't figure into the equation.

"I'm hoping he left us cousins a little money too," Candy admitted. "It would be nice to have enough for a tropical vacation." She was examining each item she removed from the refrigerator, even though after a week of non-refrigeration, nothing was worth salvaging. I was reading the dates on spices as I put them back, smiling to myself. They were almost as old as some of mine that I had only recently parted with. Why was it so hard to find the motivation to replace aging spices?

"I'm not sure he had much money," Ellie said.

"Oh, I think he did," Candy countered. "He was a wily old man. Maybe it's hidden in some secret location in the house."

"You think that's what someone was looking for when they made this mess?" I asked innocently.

Candy's face suddenly turned the color of her shirt. "I wouldn't know," she said quickly.

Based on our childhood memories of the terrible trio—Kent, Dennis, and Tuna—Ellie and I assumed they were the ones who had searched the house. But given Candy's "tell," I wondered whether she, and maybe Vinny, had been involved too. Although they could have known about it but not participated. We had decided not to point fingers . . . yet. Even though we were dying to know what, if anything, they'd found. But until we had some leverage to encourage a confession, we were going to bide our time.

"Did your mother tell you about the letter he left for Ellie?"

"Yes, she mentioned something about it."

"He wrote that he had a treasure map in his head. Sad that he didn't leave the real map to someone in his will."

"I can see why he wouldn't want something like that to fall into the wrong hands," Candy said.

"I was referring to family," I said. Candy's face got pinker. It was almost the color of Shorty's collar. She turned away and started studying the contents of the stuff on the drain board. I couldn't help noticing that she didn't seem interested in cleaning up any of the ugly mess on the floor. My recollection of her when we were kids was that she didn't like to get dirty, and even back then she had a preference for the color pink.

Pastel came in with Shorty padding along behind her on his

stubby legs, pausing to sniff a package of thawed sausage. Apparently, it wasn't up to his usual standards because he didn't bother trying to claw it open.

"Look what I found," Pastel said, holding up a ceramic Gollum crouching on a rock. "It's like the movie," she explained.

"Nice," I said. I almost turned away . . . then I noticed something odd about the figure. "Can I see it?" I held out my hand. Pastel didn't respond, reluctant to surrender her precious find. I knelt down and said, "I'll give it back in a minute. I just want to take a look." I couldn't very well forcibly pry it out of her hands in front of her mother. Although it was tempting.

"Promise?" she said.

"I promise." She thrust it at me and I barely grabbed it before she let go. The rock base had some letters and numbers around the bottom that didn't look like part of the original design. I handed it back to her. "Let me take a picture of you with it, okay?"

She gave me a big smile and started to pose. "Here," I said, "turn it like this." I made sure the numbers were included in the snap. I took one to give to her and another close-up to make certain I could read the numbers easily. Then I turned the figure part way around to get the remaining numbers and had her pose for a second photo. If she tired of her Gollum and left it behind, I'd pop it in my purse. But if she hung onto it, I would at least have the information that I think Uncle Wade intended Ellie to find.

At one point Candy wandered off. Although it seemed highly unlikely that she would find something we'd overlooked, I had to admit Pastel had done just that. I whispered to Ellie that I was going to see what Candy was up to, and she whispered back that she had been thinking about doing the same thing.

I found her in Uncle Wade's bedroom, examining the paintings on the walls. "Oh, we were wondering where you were," I said.

"Just trying to decide if there's anything I would like to keep."

No one had said anything about distributing the contents of Uncle Wade's house, but if his siblings inherited everything, they would probably divvy up what they considered worth keeping or selling. So, she wasn't really out of line. Maybe I should be thinking about a keepsake, something to remember him by.

"Well, we're going to have lunch soon. Did you bring anything?" I asked.

"No, I think we'll take off then. I have some shopping to do." She'd barely been there an hour and done zip. Nor did she offer to come back later or return another day to help finish up. But I wasn't about to complain. Pastel had done us a favor, and not having them around made things easier.

After they left, I showed Ellie the picture of the Gollum figure with the numbers someone had added.

"He loved that movie," Ellie said. "He was so proud of having found that ugly thing in a thrift store. I should have remembered his comments about Gollum having secrets."

Ellie and I stayed late, filling garbage bags with spoiled food and putting things back in order, all the time hoping to find more clues. But we didn't.

As we were getting ready to leave," Ellie said, "Bianca can probably handle it from here." Glancing around, she added, "Poor Bianca; this will be more work than she's been asked to do in years."

"Maybe you should tell her she can hire some help. Hopefully the rest of the family will agree. Getting the house ready to sell involves washing windows and some outdoor work Bianca may not be able to do properly anyway."

"Good idea. Vic will know the value of having a house look its best when it goes up for sale. Besides, it doesn't seem fair to ask Bianca to do much housework now that he's gone. In spite of his gallivanting and womanizing in his younger days, I think Uncle Wade was lonely. I'm glad Bianca was here for him."

That evening after dinner we studied the numbers on the pictures I'd taken of Pastel holding Gollum. She'd made off with the actual figure, holding it close, watching to see if I would try to take it away. The kid had good instincts.

"I hope putting a message about a treasure map on a Gollum figurine isn't a warning against greed," Ellie said.

"Or a comment on obsession," I added.

"Is it possible these numbers are as obvious as they seem? So many steps or feet either straight, right or left? 'S' for straight, 'L' for left and 'R' for right?"

"At first glance I thought it might be latitude and longitude, but I think you're right—after all of the vague clues he left you, this one seems pretty straightforward. A simple formula . . . once we find the cave."

Ellie paled and her breathing became audible. "When 'we' find the cave?"

"You really do have it bad, don't you?"

"Just the thought of going into a cave makes me uneasy."

"Don't worry, you won't have to go inside. As I've said, I'm sure that's one of the reasons he included me in this. Assuming, of course, that we find the right cave in the first place."

Ellie shook her head. "I've spent years in therapy. First to get rid of my lisp, and off and on since then to control my fear of caves and tunnels. The cave thing has never been much of a problem; caves are easy to avoid. But I used to go through some convoluted planning to avoid tunnels when driving." She paused and looked directly at me. "You probably think I'm crazy."

"No, because of you I know more about phobias than I might otherwise have known. For example, I know they are fairly common. One in ten adults has some kind of phobia. I also know that phobias run in families and that there's all kinds of them. Including some strange ones like spectrophobia—fear of mirrors —and globophobia—fear of balloons. My understanding is that as long as the phobia isn't impacting your day-to-day life, you are okay."

"Did you know that Uncle Wade had a phobia? Acrophobia, fear of heights. It's one of the really common ones. More than six percent of the population suffers from it. When it interfered with a couple of his explorations, he tried exposure therapy and then combined it with cognitive behavioral therapy and was basically cured."

"Impressive."

"That's why he was sympathetic with my situation. I ended up going to his therapist, and it helped some. But I've never managed to get the cave thing under control. Sorry."

"Don't worry. When we find the cave . . . Hey, I'm starting to sound like searching for this treasure is a done deal. I do think we may have enough to go on to give it a good shot. Besides, it could be fun."

"Do you really think your friend will want to go with us?" Ellie sounded uncertain. "It's not that I don't have confidence in you, but if there were three of us, I'd feel better about it."

"I can't imagine Logan passing up a chance to come along on a bona fide treasure hunt. Once we find the cave, all you'll have to do is guard the entrance while we schlep around in bat feces, dodging spider webs and trying not to step on whatever creepy crawlers live there."

"You're right—that definitely sounds like fun."

an attic surprise

Monday evening I called Logan and filled him in on what was happening. As I knew he would, he became instantly captivated by the idea of hidden clues and wished he could have been there to help us look. "Are you thinking about doing what I think you're thinking about doing?" he asked.

"And if I am?"

"Then I want to go with you."

I laughed. "You are already part of the plan. We need a muscled male to do the digging and haul the loot."

"Have shovel, will travel."

"Seriously, keep in mind that it may not be a realistic venture. But Ellie and I are leaning toward giving it a shot. It depends on what else we learn."

"I'm available in mid-August," he said. "Although I might be able to fudge that a bit if you want to go earlier."

"I like a professor who knows his priorities."

"I could make it an assignment and a field trip for my students."

"I can see it all now—a new class offering: *'English students read Agatha Christie and follow clues.'*"

"That's not bad," he said, "but there are more *literary* options."

"*Treasure Island*?"

"A good adventure with moral lessons for young boys, but no."

"*Treasure of the Sierra Madre*?"

"Some good lessons about greed and betrayal, but it's not about buried treasure."

"How about Poe's short story, *The Gold Bug*. That's got it all —secret codes *and* buried treasure."

"Okay, you've made your point," he said. "My students don't need a field trip, but I would definitely enjoy a boating vacation with you and Ellie. Treasure or no treasure."

"Judd won't mind you taking a trip without him?"

"No, he can't take that much time off work, and we have a trip scheduled for the end of September already."

Next, I called my mother. She told me that she, my father, and my brother would probably arrive about 2:00 Wednesday afternoon. They were going to stay in a downtown hotel not too far from Ellie's condo. She would give me a call when they got settled and planned on meeting Ellie and me for dinner.

Tuesday morning Ellie and I decided to take the day off to unwind. We started with a long walk in Stanley Park followed by a Cuban sandwich at a tiny hole-in-the-wall café. After lunch we went shopping. I've never been much of a shopper since I dress casually most of the time and only have one tiny closet on my boat, but Ellie is a clothes hound. Shopping to her is an art, and it was a welcome distraction for both of us. I even bought a trendy jacket in autumn colors with a geometric pattern. A bit more stylish than I'm used to, but Ellie egged me on.

We barely managed to get in an hour at the Edith Heath and Emily Carr exhibit at the Vancouver Art Gallery before it closed.

At that point we were both tired, so we picked up some groceries and had a simple pasta and salad for dinner.

"It feels like we're in limbo," Ellie said. "Marking time. Treading water. Waiting—"

"More like the lull before the storm, I fear." I poured us each more wine and we sat back, feet up, more relaxed than I've been in a long time.

"You think the cousins are going to be upset if Uncle Wade named me in his will?"

"Yeah. Of course they will be upset," I said. "No matter how insignificant the bequest."

"You think he may have left me his library," she asked, "or the leather jacket he always wore on trips, that sort of thing?"

"What do *you* think?"

"I still think the house will be left to the three siblings. And I can't imagine him singling me out for a special bequest of some sort. He never cared for the Vancouver cousins, but he always liked you and Dylan."

"Personally, I think the fact that he wanted to pass along his obsession to you is touching," I said. "After all, if he simply wanted to make sure you knew where the treasure was, he could have given you two letters—one to show the relatives and one with a map. But he didn't."

"Maybe like Candy said, there's something hidden in the walls or in a secret compartment under a floorboard."

"Are there any other storage areas, inside or outside?"

Ellie hit her forehead with the palm of her hand. "Duh, I feel so stupid. I didn't even think about the storage space in the attic ceiling. He told me once he was too old to go up there anymore. I don't remember him ever mentioning it again."

"Well, first thing tomorrow, let's take a look. Just in case."

Wednesday morning, fortified with a bowl of cereal and three cups of coffee, we returned to Uncle Wade's house and hurried up to the third floor. There, over the area where his storage boxes had been stacked, was a door access panel with a recessed pull ring. It didn't take long to find the pole with the hook on the end that he used to open it. The door opened with a squeak, and we were able to easily access the pull-down stairs.

"Slick," Ellie said.

"Do you want me to look?" I asked.

"I'm not claustrophobic," she said. "Caves are different than other small spaces. Caves are, well, it's hard to explain. But . . . why don't you go ahead anyway. You're the one who thought of it."

I climbed up the ladder and found a light switch. The overhead light produced a dim glow that barely illuminated the one item in the tiny crawl space, an antique wood chest with metal straps on either side of the locking mechanism, its lid tilted up. It was on a piece of plywood about fifteen feet from the opening, too far away to see what was inside.

"Nothing up here but one small wood trunk," I called back to Ellie. "It looks a bit like the treasure chest I bought for my goldfish, only human size. I'm going to take a look."

I crouched down and made my way across a series of stringers under the low roof. When I reached the chest, I pushed the lid back and could see immediately that it was empty. I snapped a couple of pictures with my cell and returned to the ladder.

"Well?" Ellie said.

I leaned over and held out the shadowy picture of the empty chest before starting down. "I think the cousins beat us to it, whatever 'it' was. The cousins or the murderer. Or the murdering cousins. The jury is still out, right?"

"If there was something in the chest, why do you think they tore everything apart?"

"Maybe they started downstairs and worked their way up. Did the cousins know Uncle Wade's office was up here?"

"Probably not," Ellie said. "I don't think they ever visited. And even if they had, I doubt he would have brought them up here."

"What about Bianca? You don't think she would have known about the chest, do you?"

"I have no idea."

"Why would he be so mysterious with all of the clues he left for you if there was a map in the attic?" she asked. "That doesn't make any sense."

"Maybe he had some artifacts from past treasure hunts in the chest."

"Too obvious. It's almost like . . . he was setting a trap."

I turned my eyes toward the ceiling and held up a hand: "Uncle Wade, why couldn't you just tell us what you had in mind?"

CHAPTER 9

Executor Woes

My family made Wednesday dinner reservations at a nice downtown restaurant on the second floor of a high-rise where the waiters were formal and the food a visual and taste treat. Our table was in front of a large window that had a view of a busy street and other high-rise buildings. Although it wasn't the same as looking out over fields of flowers or a picturesque lake, it had the feel of an aerie, isolating us from the rest of the world.

"What are we celebrating?" I asked.

"Nothing," my mother said. "It's a restaurant Wade once recommended. We were going to come here with him, but our visit kept getting postponed for one reason or another." She suddenly looked as though she was going to cry. "You never know when life is going to be cut short. I just wish . . ."

My father put his arm around her shoulder and squeezed. "It's okay, Gwen. Wade knew you cared." His gentle voice conveyed love and comfort. Seeing them together at times like these made me wish I was in a relationship like theirs. But I was resigned to the idea that it might never happen for me. Resigned and not unhappy.

My brother Dylan reached across the table and put his hand

on her arm. "We all have regrets. And he must have felt good about your relationship. After all, he made you his executor."

Ellie and I both said "What?" at the same time.

"Mom, you're the executor for Uncle Wade's will?" I hadn't been thinking about who the executor would be. But his choice of Mom made sense.

"Yes, the lawyer called me yesterday. He wants me to come in early to discuss a few things before the others show up."

"Did he say what he wants to talk about?" I asked.

"No, so don't bother probing. I don't know."

Dylan was seated next to me and jabbed me in the ribs with his elbow. "She knows you better than you know yourself," he said.

"I don't *probe*."

Ellie grinned and, with comedic sarcasm, said, "Sure. Right."

"In my defense, it's what I've been trained to do as an OD professional."

"No, you have that backwards," Mom said. "You chose organizational development as a profession because you like to ask questions. Your first words weren't mama or dada but 'what am I doing here?'"

Everyone laughed. Even I smiled.

"Well, I'm in good company—Einstein claimed he had no special talent, only passionate curiosity."

"Now you're comparing yourself to Einstein?" Dylan jabbed me again.

"Hey, cut that out." I jabbed him back.

"Now, kids," Dad said, grinning. "I miss those days when you two were always going at each other." For a brief moment I saw my father as I remembered him from childhood, before his hair started to turn gray and move back from his forehead, before the chiseled lines around his mouth became prominent and the hint of jowls dragged at the lower part of his face. It was a face I loved and cherished, then and now.

"They weren't that bad," my mother defended. Then she faked an exaggerated eye roll and added, "Except occasionally."

"Unlike our other cousins," Ellie threw in with a serious edge to her voice.

Everyone stopped kidding around and turned toward her.

"Sorry, I shouldn't have said that."

"They've been misbehaving," I explained. "At least we think it was them."

Ellie and I filled my family in on the chaos left behind by whomever searched Uncle Wade's house. We also mentioned the letter Ellie received from her uncle and the empty chest in the cramped storage space above Uncle Wade's office. We did not, however, as agreed upon earlier, share anything about the map clues we'd discovered. We wanted to wait at least until after the will was read. Maybe even longer. Not that we didn't trust them to keep a secret, but we didn't want to put them in the position of having to lie to the rest of the family. Especially if they couldn't do it convincingly. And I had my doubts about whether they could.

"You don't suppose he had anything of value in the chest, do you?" Dylan asked. "I mean, a space with pull-down stairs and only one item in it isn't a very good hiding place."

"My brother always loved a good practical joke," Mom said.

"You don't think . . .?" It looked as though she might confirm one of my wildest speculations.

"Do I think he could have anticipated that someone would ransack his house looking for treasure and treasure maps? Yes, I do."

"Did he say something to you about that?" I *probed.*

"See what I mean about my daughter?" Mother looked at the others for confirmation.

"Okay, I admit to being a *prober.* Now, did he?"

"I hadn't seen Wade in person for a long time, but we kept in touch by phone. A couple months back, he told me he was about to make a big score. I didn't think too much about it because he was always on the verge of finding something huge. But he also said something about another treasure hunter sniffing around. And a trick he was going to play on him."

"What kind of trick?"

"He didn't give me any details, but I assumed from what he *did* say that it involved some kind of phony lead, possibly a map."

Ellie and I exchanged looks. Then we both started laughing. "We can only hope," I said.

"You think the cousins rather than another treasure hunter found the phony map?" Dylan asked.

"It would serve them right," Ellie said. She was no longer laughing.

We hadn't yet mentioned Ellie's suspicions about Uncle Wade's fall not being an accident, but Mom's revelation about the other treasure hunter added another twist.

Dylan said, "Maybe it was the treasure hunter who searched the house and turned everything upside down. You may be unfairly blaming the cousins."

"I hope whoever was involved found the map and it takes them on a long and expensive trip for nothing," I said. Everyone held up their wine glasses and toasted the sentiment.

"Maybe the will contains some information about his latest dream," Mom concluded. "We'll know tomorrow."

The dinner conversation turned to other topics and the evening ended pleasantly. I hoped my mother wasn't going to be angry when I later told her about the letter Uncle Wade had sent to me and what Ellie and I had pieced together about his last treasure hunt, his potential "big score." Nor had it seemed like the right time to ask if she had known about his cancer or to bring up the possibility that his death wasn't an accident. There was too much going on, too many unanswered questions. Maybe the will would clarify a few things. One way or the other, there would be time to talk after it was read.

My mother was already there with the lawyer when Ellie and I arrived. Dad and Dylan had decided to go for a walk instead of engaging in the family drama. Uncle Max, Aunt Regina, and the five cousins—Kent, Dennis, Tuna, Candy, and Vinny—showed up right on time. The cousins looked pleased with themselves, whether because of something they'd found in Uncle Wade's house or in anticipation of an inheritance, I could only guess.

The lawyer began by explaining that he had started processing the will. He had posted a notice to creditors and had informed the bank not to release the contents of Wade's safety deposit box to anyone but the executor.

"Safety deposit box?" was the echoed question around the crowded conference room. My mind immediately went to the key he had sent me. Could it be . . .? Ellie and I'd been thinking it opened a personal lock box or a storage locker, something private. If it was a key to a safety deposit box, why not simply leave it with his lawyer?

One lone voice said, "Executor?" I think it was Aunt Regina.

"Yes, Wade named his sister Gwen as his executor . . ." Before he could finish the sentence, there was a ripple of comments from the cousins that sounded suspiciously like they were not pleased to hear that he had bestowed the role of executor on my mother.

Candy turned to me and said, "You knew this, didn't you?"

I shook my head. "Not until last night."

Mom spoke up in her own defense. "I think he saw me as supportive. It was my impression when we talked that you two .. ." She looked pointedly at Max and Regina ". . . didn't want much to do with him."

"That isn't true," Regina protested. "It was, well, his lifestyle that we didn't approve of."

The lawyer jumped in. "Let me read the will before you carry this discussion further. I don't think there is much to complain about in terms of equity."

They fell silent, and he read the will out loud in a singsong voice, like someone who's read similar scripts many times before.

The money from the sale of the house was to be evenly split six ways and the money held in trust until the recipients turned 18. The six named were the grandchildren of his siblings: Flint, Finn, Pastel, Noah, Emma and Catrin. He had added that he was leaving shares to Flint, Finn and Pastel "in the hope that they were more deserving and successful than the previous generations." That brought some grumbling from Regina, Max and the other cousins and a smile from Ellie and me. My mother somehow managed to keep a straight face. It was also noted that since Catrin was already 18, she would receive her share immediately upon sale of the house.

The lawyer continued with specific bequests. The contents of the house and personal possessions went to Ellie to dispose of as she saw fit. "What?" Candy said before a look from her mother stopped her from commenting further. The money in his bank account was designated for settling any outstanding bills, with $50,000 to Bianca for her years of service. It was Aunt Regina's turn to interrupt, "Fifty thousand dollars to the maid?" she said. "Unbelievable." The final bequest produced another murmur of complaints from the cousins. Any remaining money was to be donated to the Museum of Anthropology at UBC.

Ignoring the complaints and comments, the lawyer continued. "Finally, the contents of the safety deposit box are to go to Ellie." The lawyer looked around. "That's it. Questions?"

"Ellie inherits all of his personal belongings?" Candy asked, obviously upset about Ellie receiving more than her."

"To distribute as she sees fit," the lawyer reiterated.

"How much does he have in his bank account?" Uncle Max wanted to know.

"The executor will check into that."

"And the safety deposit box? Do you know what's in it?" Aunt Regina asked.

"No idea."

Aunt Regina turned to my mother and said, "I want to be there when you open it."

"You don't trust me?

"I insist on being there."

"Fine. And since the contents go to Ellie, she should be there too."

Kent finally spoke. "I don't see why she should get so much and the rest of us get nothing."

"Neither Bryn nor Dylan got anything," my mother pointed out.

That shut Kent up, but the other Vancouver faction of the unnamed-in-the-will cousins still looked displeased, like they were going to demand a recount.

Candy was apparently doubly upset. "Well, I don't think it's fair that two shares of the house go to your kids, Dennis, and three to yours, Dylan. Pastel only gets one share. What if I have another child?"

Dennis frowned but didn't say anything. I thought it was a reasonable distribution and was pleased for Catrin in particular. Even "as is" the house was probably worth more than a million given its location, history, and potential. And if Vic ended up handling the sale, it was my opinion that Candy should be satisfied with that little windfall and shut up about the rest.

"If we're through here," Regina said, "why don't we go to the bank now?" I wondered what she was hoping we'd find in the safety deposit box. Although I admit that I was very curious myself.

The lawyer shifted in his chair. "There's one problem, I'm afraid. I don't have a key. We may have to wait until the bank can arrange for another way to access the box." Then he added, "I understand that some of you have been to his home, did anyone see a key that looked like it belonged to a safety deposit box?"

I assume he'd been referring to Ellie, Candy, and me, but the other cousins immediately looked down. Aha. I knew that was my cue, but I let the silence build to see if they would say anything. When no one did, I confessed, "I think I may have the key."

All eyes turned in my direction.

"I said I *think* I do." I pulled it out of my purse and handed it to the lawyer. "Does this look like a safety deposit key to you?"

"Yes." He held it up to the light. "This is the correct number."

"Where did you get that?" Kent demanded.

I could practically see his mind working: they had searched the house and hadn't come across a key. Sometimes a moment calls for the perfect comeback, and for once, I had one.

"In his desk. In the top drawer."

CHAPTER 10

eight pieces of gold

Regina, Ellie, and Mom left the rest of us in the lobby of the bank and disappeared into the inner sanctums with an employee wearing a dark blue suit and striped tie. Approved bank attire for the men, judging from what the other male employees were wearing. The women apparently were allowed more flexibility. Their dress ranged from pants suits to floral dresses with plunging necklines. I caught Vinny and Tuna ogling one particularly voluptuous clerk and had to bite my tongue not to make a caustic remark about their boorish behavior.

We seated ourselves in the sofas and chairs arranged for people waiting to see a bank specialist, avoiding small talk. Almost everyone immediately started looking at their cell phones as if they contained important messages. Whereas I found myself staring out the window at the busy street. Nothing too interesting going on there, unless you enjoyed seeing cars whiz by. No answers about why Uncle Wade sent the key to me, unless it was simply to needle the other cousins.

Vinny suddenly spoke, lobbing an accusation at me. "You didn't find that key in Uncle Wade's desk." Everyone looked up from their phones, waiting for my response.

"How would you know that?" I challenged.

"Because . . ." He hesitated, his eyes blinking rapidly, as if suddenly realizing his faux pas.

"He was our uncle, too," Dennis interceded. "We had a right to go through his things."

Apparently, the pretense was over, and we hadn't even needed to waterboard anyone. "No, you didn't actually. But Ellie did."

"We didn't know that at the time," Kent pointed out.

"And neither did Ellie or you," Tuna chimed in. "You two went there on your own, just like we did."

I could feel anger welling up and had to force myself to remain calm. "Ellie was under the impression that you were all going there together, but you jumped the gun. When Bianca told her that someone had been in the house, we went to take a look. She doesn't care what you took; she probably would have given you anything you wanted if you'd asked anyway. But the mess you left behind was . . . irresponsible and totally unnecessary." I couldn't think of a word strong enough to describe what they had done to Uncle Wade's belongings. Finally, I added, "And disrespectful."

"Well, I helped you clean the place up," Candy said, straightening her shoulders. I had to bite my tongue.

"And there was no key in the top drawer," Vinny said.

"Not my fault that you didn't see it," I retorted. A minor triumph, but a satisfying one nevertheless.

The cousins fell quiet, but it was clear they weren't buying my explanation about the key. However, they probably didn't want to make too much of a fuss about what Ellie and I might have found and removed. After all, they had been there first, and they weren't saying what they'd made off with. And Ellie was now the custodian over Uncle Wade's belongings.

At that point, Ellie, Regina, and my mother returned. Ellie was carrying a cardboard shoe box. She looked pleased. "The papers were all in order, so the bank said I could have this now. Want to see what was inside the safety deposit box?" she asked. She definitely had everyone's attention.

She set the shoe box down on a side table and glanced around to see if any other customers were paying attention. When she was satisfied that we had some privacy, she waved us closer. We gathered around, shoulder to shoulder, leaning forward expectantly as she made a show of removing the lid, like a magician revealing what's beneath a magic handkerchief.

There was a collective intake of breath when we saw the gold objects. A quick count told me there were eight. Eight gold artifacts.

Ellie removed them one at a time and placed them on the table for everyone to get a better look. There was a bell in the form of an eagle warrior. A god figure with an ornate headdress. A female statuette that was probably a fertility goddess. A jaguar brooch with jewel eyes. A serpent labret like I had seen in a museum display on Aztec artifacts. A gold ring with a protruding Aztec face. And two flat coins depicting skeletal faces surrounded by symbols.

"Holy shit," Vinny said. "He actually found something."

Kent looked around. "You should put them away," he said. We all agreed, and Ellie quickly returned them to the shoe box.

"You should share those," Candy said.

"I want to do some research first," Ellie explained. "Then I'll decide what to do with them."

"You need to sell them and divide up the proceeds," Regina said. Her comment was delivered like a royal command.

"It's possible they should be turned over to a museum," I said.

"That's easy for you to say," Candy snapped. "You don't have a family."

Ellie hesitated. "I thought that each of us might want something to remember Uncle Wade by. As I said, I'll do some research and let you know what I decide." The cousins started to argue, but Ellie ended the conversation by picking up the box and heading for the exit. I hurried to catch up, my mother not far behind.

We rushed to the car and got inside like we were being chased by predators and we were the prey. I held the box of relics while Ellie drove. "Was there a note with these?"

"No," Mom said. "Nothing. No explanation, no provenance, nothing."

"You think Uncle Wade came by them legally?"

"Who knows?" Ellie said. "But I'll find out. And when I do, I'll do the right thing. Uncle Wade left them to me; he must have known I would try to figure out where they came from."

"Another mystery. You gotta love Uncle Wade's flair for death."

Max and Regina insisted the funeral and reception should be held on the upcoming Sunday; they had already started making arrangements. Mom and Dad hadn't expected it to be so soon. None of us had. They were going to have dinner with Max and Regina to divvy up the errands and tasks that needed to get done ASAP to meet the Sunday deadline. If everything went as planned, Mom, Dad, and Dylan would probably go home on Monday. I still hoped to hitch a ride back with them.

Ellie and I stopped by and picked up a pizza for later before returning to her place to examine the artifacts from the safety deposit box. "I'll take them in to a man I know at the UBC museum tomorrow," Ellie said. "Maybe he can tell us what they're worth."

"You don't think Uncle Wade obtained these illegally, do you?"

"Even if he found them on his own, that doesn't necessarily mean it's okay to keep or sell them. It's possible they should be handed over to the authorities or to a museum." Ellie picked up the bell and held it next to one of the coins. "When the lawyer said that Uncle Wade had left me the contents of his safety deposit, I didn't expect to find much. Maybe something sentimental that he didn't want to leave in the house. Now I'm wondering—you don't suppose these are *part* of the treasure he boasted about? Maybe he already found what he'd been looking for and, for one reason or another, he only brought these eight pieces back with him and left the rest in that cave above the abandoned cannery."

"Or maybe these are all he found," I said. "And he would have told you that if he'd lived."

"No, he was giving me hints the week before he died. If he already had everything from the cave treasure in his possession, he wouldn't have been leaving me breadcrumbs or reaching out to you."

"That makes sense. But I can't wait until tomorrow. I say we go online and see what we can find before you take them in for an expert's opinion."

"Okay, and let's keep our fingers crossed that we don't discover they are from a stolen collection."

"I don't think he ever actually stole anything. Although he obviously didn't report all of his discoveries."

"That may be considered a form of stealing by whichever country thinks they have rights to them."

"I see your point, but I have mixed feelings. Probably because I want to see it from Uncle Wade's perspective. I sympathize with countries whose antiquities have been looted, but if someone *discovers* them after they've been missing for centuries—"

"Maybe you've nailed the issue—it comes down to word choice: *looted* versus *discovered.* Looting implies a premeditated illegal act; discovery is an in-the-moment finding."

"But either way, if they were once looted, aren't they still the product of an illegal act?"

"I suppose that's why there are finders' fees—to reward discovery and to discourage keeping findings secret."

"Okay, let's do some research. We might also check on Canadian guidelines for what you should do if you come into possession of what might be valuable artifacts."

It turned out to be surprisingly easy to find images of gold artifacts similar to those from the safety deposit box. The distinct Aztec flavor came in varying motifs and was instantly recognizable. There were also quite a few references to Spaniards making off with Aztec treasures, jettisoning or hiding them when the Aztecs followed in pursuit. Thus, the origins of myths about lost Aztec treasures.

We also learned that not all that glittered was gold in the Aztec empire. A lot of their art was apparently made from an alloy called tumbaga. Not only did many Spanish invaders lose their lives trying to make off with Aztec gold, much of what they stole wasn't actually gold.

"It looks like there's a possibility that there is still some Aztec treasure out there somewhere," Ellie said. "Lost treasure waiting to be found. And, although there may be finder fees, the black market is probably more lucrative."

"But in Canada? Doesn't it seem unlikely that South American treasures would end up in Canada?"

"I asked Uncle Wade about that once. As you know, he traveled all over the world looking for different kinds of treasure and antiquities. Jewels, jewelry, gold, artifacts, art. But some of his explorations were in Canada. He told me that there's always been a chain of thieves stealing from each other, each trying to keep their latest acquisition out of sight until it was either safe to bring it into the open or they desperately needed the money. Like pirates used to do. That's why treasures often end up in unlikely locations."

"If these are real, even if they aren't pure gold . . ." Something didn't feel right about this. "Why leave them hidden away? I feel like we're missing something."

"I agree," Ellie said.

"I have a thought, but it's so far-fetched, I hesitate to mention it."

"I promise not to laugh."

"Well, the picture we've been building of Uncle Wade is part ne'er do well, part rogue, and part prankster. He loved the hunt.

Didn't think much of his kin for the most part—you, me and Mom seem to be among the exceptions. And he knew he was dying." I stopped abruptly as soon as I realized what I'd said.

Ellie cocked her head to one side. "What do you mean 'he knew he was dying.'"

"I should have mentioned this earlier, but it never seemed like the right time. In the note that came with the key, he mentioned he had cancer and had been given about six months to live. He asked me not to say anything to any family members. Then he died. And somehow, because of the way he died, the fact that he had cancer didn't seem relevant."

Ellie looked sad but not surprised. "I wondered about his poor health and all of his references to death. I wish he had told me."

"He was probably waiting as long as possible so as not to stress you."

"I can kinda understand. Telling you was easier because you didn't see him on a regular basis. But why do you think he sent you the key instead of giving it to me or leaving it with the lawyer?"

"I think it's like we talked about earlier, to pique my interest. He knew we would eventually figure out it was to his safety deposit box."

Ellie started to cry, and my eyes teared. "He put a lot of thought into all this, didn't he?"

"He obviously wanted you to carry on his legacy. I think he would have been more specific if he had lived a little longer. But, at the same time, he didn't want to give you information that would make you a target."

"If he left a phony map in that chest to divert attention from the real location of the treasure, then why put artifacts in a safety deposit box that he had to know the whole family would insist on seeing?"

"Maybe these artifacts are part of his grand deception for the rest of the family. The number may not be coincidental but planned. One for each cousin. Then, when the map turns out to be useless, and if the eight artifacts aren't worth anything, everyone will lose interest in Uncle Wade's final project. And you are free to go after the real thing."

"Could he really have set up such an elaborate scheme?"

"It wouldn't have taken all that much—"

Ellie suddenly giggled. "I just had a delicious thought."

"A way to get back at our greedy cousins?"

"Yes, I'll have these checked out. And if they're real, we'll figure out Plan B. But if they're fake . . ."

"You'll gift them to the cousins!"

not an accident

"First they want to rush the funeral, now we have to delay it," Mom complained. Her face was beginning to show age lines, and the ones around her mouth deepened with anger, her face a rain cloud before the downpour, a hint of thunder in her voice. In the small café, heads turned in our direction.

Ellie and I were trying to enjoy breakfast with my parents and brother. The cafe was packed with a combination of people—those quickly scarfing down food to fuel their workday and those taking their time over the menu, their food, their tea or coffee. We weren't in a hurry to get somewhere, but my mother was all wrought up, so it was hard to be relaxed and leisurely.

"I thought it was a question of finding an opening at the funeral home," I said, addressing the first half of her complaint. My father flashed me a warning look: *don't encourage her.*

"First, Regina and Max reserved a space at the funeral home for this Sunday without consulting me, and I went along so as to not make waves. Knowing full well that it didn't leave much time to make arrangements and let people know about the service."

"Did they ever explain why so soon?" I asked, ignoring my father's not-so-subtle signals to change the subject.

"They told me it was either this Sunday or we would have to wait three weeks."

"That seems rather strange. Did the mortality rate suddenly soar? Was there a mob war or a mini pandemic?" As soon as the derisive words left my mouth, I wished I'd heeded my father's warning.

"Are you implying they were lying about the lack of availability?" my mother asked, matching my caustic tone.

I knew I'd stepped in something and was afraid to check the bottom of my shoe. Dad finally ended the uncomfortable silence that hung in the air. "Your mother doesn't want to admit it, but she called the funeral home and asked whether there were any openings for the following week. That's the real reason she's so upset."

"There was something so hasty about the whole thing," Mom said defensively.

"And?"

"And there were two openings for the following weekend."

"Did you ask Aunt Regina and Uncle Max about it?"

Mom sighed. "I decided not to make a fuss."

"Yet, here you are, obviously distraught."

"Why would they lie about something like that?" Dylan asked.

Ellie was looking more and more uncomfortable with the conversation. I turned to her and asked, "Are you okay?"

"Not really," she said. "It's about the delay . . ."

Mom turned to Ellie, and Ellie squirmed under her gaze, like a small child caught with their face smeared with chocolate minutes before dinner. "It was *you*!" Mom said suddenly. "Wasn't it?"

"Please don't tell them," Ellie pleaded. "Let them think it was the police who asked the coroner to investigate. But I admit it, I contacted the Coroners Service and suggested they might want to look into Uncle Wade's death. They said I could stay anonymous."

"But why? What's this all about?" Mom asked. The tiny wrinkles etched on her forehead intensified, highlighting her confusion.

Ellie looked to me for support, but I wasn't about to step in it a second time. "I called them because I'm not convinced it was an accident," Ellie said softly. "I think someone pushed him down the stairs and left him there to die."

Mom looked shocked, but it didn't leave her speechless. "When they notified me this morning about not being able to release his body right away, I asked for the reason, and all they would say is that they were looking at cause of death. I thought he might have taken too many sleeping pills. Something like that."

"With Aunt Regina and Uncle Max trying to rush the funeral like they are, it makes me wonder what *they* know that we don't," I said.

"Bryn," Mom scolded. "You are such a cynic at times." Then she paused and looked from me to Ellie and back. "You two really believe his death wasn't an accident?"

Ellie reluctantly shook her head, and I nodded in agreement.

"The findings could be inconclusive, even after an investigation," I offered. "But there are some anomalies that place the accidental ruling in question."

"Such as?"

Ellie explained about the rug and his bedroom being on the first floor.

"But couldn't he have gone up to his office for something and slipped on the way down?" Dylan asked. "Of course," he said, answering his own question, "that doesn't explain why the rug was there in the first place."

"You don't think any family members could have . . ." Mom couldn't bring herself to complete the sentence.

"Our cousins are obnoxious," Dylan said, as if it was a fact, ". . . but murderers?"

"I can think of a couple scenarios that puts what happened in perspective," I said. "For instance, say they had a little too much to drink and decided to search for a treasure map at Uncle Wade's in the middle of the night. He hears them, goes upstairs to investigate and there's a struggle. When they realize what they've done, they panic and try to make it look like an accident.

"Or maybe it was that other treasure hunter that he mentioned to you, Mom. Same scenario—Uncle Wade catches him in the act, they struggle, he falls. Or, he forces Uncle Wade to give him the map before deliberately pushing him down the stairs."

"Or," Dylan interrupts. "The housekeeper moved the rug. He goes upstairs for something, trips and falls. And now she doesn't want to admit it because she doesn't want to be blamed for his death."

"I wouldn't rule out that possibility except for one thing—it doesn't look like the second floor has been cleaned for eons, so why would she suddenly move a rug?"

"It sounds like you won't be satisfied with a 'death by accident' finding," Dad observed.

"Not one hundred percent. For the family's sake, that's still what I'm hoping for. But *if* someone, including one or more of the cousins, is involved in any way, I want them to pay for what they've done." I paused, then asked Mom, "What are you going to do about the funeral?"

"Well, the police said it could take several weeks before they release his . . . body." She obviously had a hard time referring to her brother as a "body." I understood. The word "body" is an intimate, personal term when someone is alive, but it sounds so clinical after their death. "That means we can't bury him. Or cremate him, which was his wish. Max and Regina are furious. I think they're calling every official they know to protest. And they absolutely refuse to postpone the ceremony."

"I keep telling her not to worry," Dad said. "Fighting with those two isn't worth it."

"You can still hold the service," I pointed out. "It's not ideal, but it can be done. You weren't going to have an open casket ceremony anyway, were you?"

"No, but it won't seem quite right to *pretend* he's there when he isn't."

I could tell that both Dylan and Dad were thinking the same thing I was, Uncle Wade wouldn't be there with or without a body.

Our food came, but I barely tasted it. We all tried to lighten the mood by talking in great detail about the weather, even though it was a typical summer day. Dylan brought up some sporting event that I knew absolutely nothing about, and no one else seemed to either. The topic fizzled. But I gave him credit for trying.

As the waiter removed our plates, my mother handed around copies of what she had written for Uncle Wade's obituary. She asked us to read it and let her know if there was something she should change or add. That was the point at which I finally brought up his cancer.

"He told me just a few days before he died," Mom said. "But I didn't know he'd told you."

"Are you going to mention his cancer in his obituary?" I asked.

"I don't see any reason to, do you? In fact, under the circumstances, I think we should avoid saying anything about cause of death."

It was a nice obituary, highlighting his life as an adventurer and explorer, listing some of his successes in general terms. But when Ellie got to the sentence starting with "He will be missed by . . .," she scoffed and shook her head. "Are you sure you want to list all of his surviving relatives there?"

"You could say "survived by" instead," I suggested.

"I know it's petty," Ellie admitted, "but I would prefer that."

"I guess obituaries are like resumes," I observed. "Mostly true but with enough BS thrown in to make them appealing to the reader."

"I really think you are being too hard on your cousins," Mom said. Dylan, Ellie, and I rolled our eyes in unison, like synchronized swimmers.

We would all remember that moment on the day of the funeral service without a body.

CHAPTER 12

fake funeral

After breakfast, Dylan came with Ellie and me for a long walk in Stanley Park. I was already thinking about how nice it would be to go home. I hated to admit it, but I missed Macavity. Logan had put him on the phone the last time we'd talked. I thought I'd heard a muffled meow of protest for being forced to say something when he didn't feel like talking, but I may have imagined it. I also missed my routine, and my privacy. After living alone as long as I have, it's hard to be around someone, even someone you like, all day every day. Still, I was determined to enjoy the last few days of time away from the office, even though it had turned into an intense and somewhat uncomfortable family experience.

"How's Catrin doing?" I asked Dylan as we were strolling along a sandy stretch at Third Beach, dodging people lying under umbrellas or sprawled on towels or mats. She hadn't been at the last Sunday dinner I'd attended.

"Same ol' same ol'. She's getting good grades but can't decide on a major. And she's let me know that she doesn't like it when I call her 'kitten' anymore." He shook his head. "They grow up so fast."

"And the twins?" Ellie asked "I haven't seen them in a while."

77

"As energetic as ever. And they, too, have their demands about what to be called. I'm not sure if they picked this idea up from Cat, but now they've decided they don't like being referred to as *the twins*. And they told Angel they no longer want to be dressed alike. Angel has always kind of color coordinated them, although she's never gone overboard with it. But now if one is wearing stripes, the other insists on plaid. That sort of thing."

"I can understand that," Ellie said. "How you dress makes a statement."

Dylan raised his eyebrows at me and grinned.

"I like to be comfortable," I said in my own defense.

"Being red-haired twins probably gets them a lot of attention, doesn't it?" Ellie said.

"Sometimes a little too much," Dylan replied.

"I remember someone trying to nickname me 'Red' in spite of me hating it," I said pointedly.

"And I remember someone trying to track where she got her red hair from when she discovered it was a recessive gene." Dylan turned toward Ellie. "That was after her fantasy about being adopted because at that time no one else in the immediate family had red hair."

"And I seem to remember someone saying I was a *mutant* because the trait is caused by a series of mutations."

"And Mom tried to convince you that you were *special* but you insisted you were cursed." We laughed at the old conflicts that were part of our shared memories as kids.

"You have a nice family," Ellie said wistfully.

"Hey, you're part of *our* family," I said. "It's just too bad your parents moved up here with the predatory side of the clan."

Dylan said, "When we were kids, I used to have fights with Kent. Fistfights. He was something else."

"What did you fight about?" Ellie asked.

"Anything and everything. He always wanted things done *his* way." Dylan grinned. "And I got bossed around enough by my younger sister." He turned to me, "You were a feisty one."

"Funny what you remember. What I occasionally come back to is the time you stepped in when Tuna and Vinny were holding me under water at the lake. I couldn't get away and was sure they were going to drown me."

"Oh yeah. They were really mad at you for some reason. I can't remember exactly why. You probably made some smartass remark or showed them up by doing something they couldn't."

"People don't change," Ellie commented. Dylan and I quickly agreed.

<hr>

Friday afternoon I spent some time on my laptop catching up on email and responding to a request from a potential client. I was careful not to commit to anything mid-August in case Ellie, Logan and I followed through on a trip to explore trails near abandoned canneries during Logan's break. Ellie had already put in for vacation then, just in case. Logan had been checking out topography maps, and there appeared to be at least three areas that were a good match for the puzzle breadcrumbs Uncle Wade had left for us.

I was just logging off when Ellie came into the room and said, "Ta da. Guess what? The eight pieces of gold are . . ." She posed with her hands in the air and her head cocked to one side.

"Come on . . . don't keep me in suspense."

"They are as fake as cousin Candy's diamond wedding ring."

"Zircon?" I asked, momentarily sidetracked by the thought that Candy's wedding ring wasn't as expensive as she made it out to be.

"My best guess."

Refocusing, I said, "And the eight artifacts are fake? For sure?"

"For sure."

My mind suddenly went into overdrive. "That means he really did put them in the safety deposit box as a not-so-subtle message.

Part of his larger, extended subterfuge. And maybe as a hint as to what we should be looking for."

"I think you're right on both counts."

"Sending the key to me makes more sense then. It could have been his way of saying that the contents of the box were a part of the puzzle as well as part of his con."

"What amazes me is how much effort he put into this, assuming we're right about everything. Although getting the replicas wasn't hard. I went online and found similar ones ranging in price from $17.50 to $200."

"To me the most significant fact is that there are eight of them. That had to be deliberate."

"I agree. Eight artifacts, eight cousins."

"You could hand them out at the reception after the service. Say he would have wanted them each to have something to remember him by."

"And do I gloss over the fact that I said originally that I was going to have them checked out?"

"Absolutely. All you have to say is that they are from a collection of Aztec artifacts. They won't care. All they will see are shiny gold objects."

Ellie did a victory tap dance, swinging her shoulders back and forth as she hummed a tune I didn't recognize. "I can hardly wait."

"Give them the fanciest ones. Dylan and I will be happy with the two coins."

"We should explain the joke to him, don't you think?"

"Yeah, but let's hold off telling him about the other clues we're looking into. Until we decide what we want to do. Meanwhile, Dylan will get a real hoot out of you pranking the other cousins."

On Saturday, Dad, Dylan, and I played tourist. I couldn't remember the last time the three of us spent time together. Mom was helping Regina and Max with last-minute plans for the funeral service and the reception to follow. She was also working on a eulogy. Ellie was running errands and planned on meeting a friend for lunch. For me, it was one of those rare days when I was able to simply enjoy things in the moment without dwelling on yesterday or tomorrow.

Dylan had dinner with Ellie and me at her place that evening, while Mom continued the funeral planning over a shared meal with Max and Regina. Dad begged off joining us; said he was looking forward to a relaxed evening on his own. Given all the stress and controversy of the last few days, my guess was that we would all be more than ready to head home on Monday morning.

The highlight of our evening was when Ellie told Dylan about the fakes and her plan for handing them out at the reception following the service.

"We could place bets on how long it will take them to find out they are replicas," Dylan said excitedly. "Which will only happen if they decide to try and sell theirs. Who do you think the first one will be?"

"I bet on Candy," I said. "Candy before five pm on Monday."

"How much? Ten dollars?" Dylan asked, removing a ten-dollar bill from his wallet. "Kent by end of day on Tuesday." He put the bill in a bowl on the coffee table. I grabbed my purse and found two fives.

"You are both wrong. I say Tuna *before* noon on Monday." Ellie whipped out her ten dollars and tossed it in the bowl. The game was on!

Sunday morning I put on my freshly pressed funeral outfit, a dark pants suit I also use for interviews with new clients. The lapels were probably outdated, or maybe back in style for all I knew. But the suit has classic lines, and it looks fine with shirts of any color. In this case, I'd chosen a sea green shell that matched one of my eyes.

Ellie and I arrived at the funeral home at the same time as Candy and her husband Vic. As we walked up the stairs together, Candy started crying. "He will be missed," she said, delicately dabbing at her tears with a pink handkerchief, careful not to smudge her mascara. I almost asked who she was referring to but forced myself to take the high road, although I couldn't resist a small dig.

"I'm sure you'll miss having tea and biscuits with him," I said as sweetly as I could manage. Ellie's lips quivered as she quickly turned her head away to hide the smile that was trying to break out.

But Candy was so caught up in her own drama that she simply sniffed and said, "Yes, I will." Vic at least had the decency to look embarrassed by the exchange, embarrassed and annoyed. He probably knew that we were aware Candy never visited Uncle Wade.

Kent and Tuna were standing just inside the door, laughing loudly about something. Feeling irritable because they were acting like they were at a party instead of a memorial service— or a funeral sans body, depending on how you looked at it. I peeled off from Candy and Ellie and joined them. "Hey, how's it going?" I asked, as if I was one of the gang. They immediately stopped laughing.

"Well, we should probably go in," Kent said. He took off with Tuna hurrying to catch up. For an instant I pictured them as kids, running off to play, Kent the leader and Tuna the follower. Ellie was right, some things don't change.

Ellie was talking to three older men next to the montage of pictures Mom and Regina had put together of Uncle Wade. I wandered over to the photo display, but before I got a chance to look at any of the pictures, Ellie pulled me aside and introduced me to the three men. "Bryn, these are the friends Uncle Wade had breakfast with at least once a week: Abe, Drake, and Doug." She gestured at each in turn. "And this is my cousin Bryn from Seattle."

"He often talked about you and your mother," Drake said. "He was very fond of your mom."

"Yeah," Abe said. "She always defended him from the jackal pack."

"The jackal pack?" I asked, even though I knew who he meant.

"Regina, Max, and their kids made fun of his treasure hunting behind his back. They apparently thought he didn't know, but he knew. From time to time they invited him over and made nice, in case he was lucky someday and struck it rich."

"The rumor is that just before he died, he did have a new lead, something he was pretty excited about." I threw that out there to see if they had taken his latest project seriously.

"Yeah," Abe said. "He seemed pretty upbeat about something he'd come across, but he didn't share any details. That's not what treasure hunters do."

"And we didn't press him."

"Did he mention finding a map?" I asked.

"Nothing that specific," Drake said. "But he must have found something to point the way because he dropped a number of hints about an upcoming jaunt he was planning."

"Too bad he had to trip and fall," Abe said. "Bummer of a way to die. I just hope he didn't suffer."

We all fell silent for a moment of collective mourning. Then the music started up in the other room, beckoning us to the beginning of the celebration of an ending. Without a word we all automatically obeyed.

It wasn't a large room, and there weren't that many people— mostly family with a sprinkling of friends. As I made my way to the front to sit with the other family members, I took in a number of sad faces and hoped that, unlike Candy's, their tears were genuine.

Bianca was seated near the middle, empty seats on either side of her. I tried to catch her eye, but she was staring straight ahead.. She looked so forlorn that I wanted to go over and give her a hug, but the ceremony was about to start.

One of the biggest arguments Mom had with Regina and Max after agreeing to the Sunday funeral sans body was how to represent Uncle Wade's presence. Regina wanted to rent a casket, but Mom insisted they instead display the container they would eventually use for his cremated remains. Regina and Max pushed for a family vote on the matter, obviously because Mom would be outnumbered. But Mom played the executor card. She informed them that they were free to personally pay to rent a casket, but as executor, she was paying for an urn and the funeral out of estate expenses. End of argument.

Instead of a traditional urn, however, Mom chose a lovely wood box with a treasure chest carved on the side for Uncle Wade's final resting place. It was still empty, of course, but it was in the place of honor on a table on the raised stage, surrounded by containers of white and multicolored flowers. The flowers had been another bone of contention. Mom thought her brother would have appreciated simplicity, but Regina preferred colorful and fussy. Regina had informed Mom that Wade wouldn't be there and that appearances were important. So instead of a solemn look, it was part circus atmosphere.

The piped in music continued, a medley of unidentifiable selections that had been chosen by Regina and Candy with the help of a funeral home employee. I had to tell myself that none of this mattered—the music, the flowers, the arguments about caskets and urns. Uncle Wade had lived a good life, and he was gone. The only thing to do was support those left behind. My mother in her loss. Bianca, the bereft housekeeper. And Ellie, the cousin Uncle Wade requested I look out for after his death.

My mother's eulogy was short and touching. She told a story about her brother creating a treasure hunt for the neighborhood kids when he was in junior high. The treasure was just a couple of candy bars in a cardboard box, but the clues leading from one place to another were quite elaborate for someone his age. She said that was the beginning of a life devoted to solving riddles and searching for treasure. She acknowledged that he hadn't always been successful, but he'd remained optimistic about "next time." And, she concluded, based on what we knew about his last few months on this earth, his passion and optimism had been with him to the end.

Max and Regina made a joint presentation, putting on a show of grief in an unusual back-and-forth performance. Their emphasis was on him being their baby brother, and the way they talked about how much he loved his nieces and nephews made me nauseous. So much drama. Between them I didn't detect one authentic note of sincere sadness.

The only cousin to speak was Ellie. She mentioned how fascinated she and I had been as children listening to Uncle Wade's treasure hunting tales. She explained that it was the hunt and not the treasures themselves that had been important to him. And then she said something that made me wish we'd talked about what she was going to say in advance. She said that even in the last days of his life he was planning his next adventure. My mother had said something similar, but Ellie made it sound as though he had shared that plan with her. With a possible murderer in the audience, I didn't think that was a very smart thing to mention. I was in the front row with my parents and brother, so I couldn't look around to see how people were reacting to her comment. And from the podium, I doubted Ellie would notice any unusual responses if she wasn't specifically looking for them. Hopefully, if someone approached her at the reception for more information, she would make it clear that he hadn't shared any details. None. Zero. Nada. I didn't want her to be the next victim.

After Ellie, Drake spoke on behalf of the "breakfast buddies." He told a story about Wade joining a team of divers to look for a sunken ship off the South Carolina coast. "According to Wade, the Spanish and the Portuguese lost a fair number of ships carrying looted treasures in the 16th and 17th centuries, and he had a hot tip about where one had gone down. He was pretty sure he was going to make a bundle off of what they found.

"Well, they didn't find a chest filled with gold or jewels, but they did come up with some odds and ends. A rusty cannon. Some broken pieces of pottery. And a piece of worm-eaten wood with part of the ship's name on it. He was so pleased that they'd actually found an old ship sunk in the mud with a few items still intact that we couldn't bring ourselves to say what we were thinking: *that's* all you found?" Everyone laughed. "He and the crew also brought up a few silver and gold ingots and a cast iron anchor with a curved head and a long shank, but after all their hard work, they ended up having to turn everything of value over to the state.

"That didn't discourage our good friend, Wade. It just made him more determined. We'll miss his tales of lost shipments of gold . . ." Drake had to stop because he was choking up. He ended with, "We'll miss you, Wade." He glanced briefly at the empty carved box and then quickly took his seat.

A few more people I didn't recognize spoke. One was a neighbor who said he bragged to his friends about living just a few houses down from a big explorer. Another was an aspiring treasure hunter who praised Wade for being generous with advice. The final speaker was a woman who described Wade as a "sweet man" who was always willing to help a friend. I had the sense she was really going to miss my uncle.

The reception that followed had been catered by my mother's third choice due to the short lead time, and it showed. The food platters looked suspiciously like they'd come from Costco. There were even those Belgian cream puffs that I knew from experience you could buy at Costco in huge containers in frozen desserts. I was tempted, but then, my goal wasn't to eat but to talk to as many people as possible about their knowledge of Uncle Wade's last treasure hunt plans.

I was looking around for the three breakfast buddies to follow up on a few questions I had when I spotted Abe with a full plate of food standing off to one side by himself. I caught up with him just as he popped a mini quiche cup in his mouth. He struggled to chew and swallow so he could respond to my very direct question: "Earlier Drake mentioned that you all thought Uncle Wade had made plans to check out a big lead. We've gone through his belongings and didn't find a map or any indication of where he might have been headed. Any idea who he might have talked to about this?"

Abe gulped and choked. I grabbed a glass of water off a nearby table and handed it to him. He took a couple of sips and his color returned to normal. "No, but he mentioned a safety deposit box one time. Have you been to the bank yet?"

"No map there." I said. But it was interesting that Uncle Wade had mentioned the box to his breakfast buddies.

"Do you remember what he said about the safety deposit box?"

"Just that he'd opened one. I kinda thought he would put things like maps and leads in it. Or maybe gold coins from past hunts. But he never said." Then Abe grinned. "Have you checked the floorboards and tapped the walls in his house for hidden compartments?"

"*Someone* did a thorough search," I said, watching for his reaction.

His mouth opened but nothing came out. Finally, he said, "Really? Are you serious?"

"Yes. Any idea who might have done that?"

"No," he said. Unless all of my instincts were as dead as last year's tennis shoes, he was telling the truth. Then his eyes flashed. "Those cousins of yours—I wouldn't put it past them." Then he looked contrite. "Sorry, I probably shouldn't have said that."

"That's okay. I think you already referred to them as jackals."

"One thing Wade *did* mention . . . just a couple of weeks ago, I think it was. Some reporter came around asking him questions. Said he'd heard Wade knew about a treasure that had found its way from Europe to Canada. Wade was pretty upset. Told us not to talk to him if he approached us."

"Do you remember the reporter's name?"

"Yeah, something Walker. Tom or Tim. First name began with a T."

"Did he say how the reporter got wind of whatever he was up to?"

"He thought a rival sicced the reporter on him. Someone who was ticked cuz Wade wouldn't share information."

"Wade didn't mention the rival's name, did he?" The suspect list was growing rapidly.

"No, not that I remember. And there may have been more than one. From what Wade said, it's a pretty small circle."

Drake suddenly appeared with a couple of drinks, one for him and one for Abe. "Nice service," he said to me.

"I enjoyed your story about Uncle Wade," I told Drake.

"He's a big loss to our breakfast group." Drake raised a glass in a salute to Wade's memory and Abe joined him.

"I understand there was a reporter trying to get a story out of him."

"Yeah, a local guy, Todd Walker. He did a piece last year for the Vancouver Sun on missing treasures that are supposedly still to be found somewhere in Canada. A surprising number. Did a couple of interviews with treasure hunters for a podcast. He wanted to interview Wade, but Wade told him to bugger off."

Doug joined us. With all three breakfast buddies present, it was a good opportunity to ask a few questions. "Any chance you remember the name of the rival that was hounding him?" I looked from Doug to Drake.

Doug shook his head "no," but Drake shifted his weight from one foot to the other and said, "You seem awfully interested in who your uncle might have talked to about his next project."

"I am," I admitted.

"You going treasure hunting?" Drake asked with a chuckle.

"Just wondering who wanted the map enough to push him

down a flight of stairs." Sometimes the best way to get an honest reaction is to be abrupt. In this instance, my pronouncement was a showstopper—all three men gaped at me, literally with mouths open.

Drake recovered first. "No one has said anything about his death being anything but an accident."

"It's being investigated. That's all I know." If any of the three were involved, I wanted them to sweat. But they seemed sincerely shocked at the idea.

"I find it hard to believe someone would do that for a map that probably isn't worth a dime. You know your uncle was a great guy, but most of his attempts to find treasure failed."

"I know. But he had a few successes over the years," I said. "And someone may have thought he was onto something." I thanked the three men for coming and took my leave.

It was almost time for Ellie's meeting with the cousins. That was one gathering I was definitely looking forward to. And not just to receive my share of the booty.

CHAPTER 13

mementos

Ellie had commandeered a small side room for the presentation of keepsakes. There was an extra person standing next to Kent when I joined the group. He was tall and attractive with thick blond hair that begged to have someone's fingers running through the lengthy strands. But when Kent referred to him as a friend of his, I tried to turn off my attraction button.

"River Robinson," the friend said, extending his hand. "You must be Bryn."

River? Really? I shook his hand and moved closer to Dylan as Ellie started to speak.

"I'm now able to tell you that these artifacts are all part of a larger find from a missing Aztec collection from the 1500s. These pieces were originally stolen by Spaniards, many of whom were killed while fleeing from Mexica warriors. Some of the collection ended up in Lake Texcoco. But it's alleged that a small band of the Spanish invaders escaped . . ."

"We don't need a history lesson," Kent interrupted.

"Let her finish," Dylan said.

Ignoring Kent, Ellie continued. ". . . that's where the story fades into rumor. No one is sure how much of the treasure made it back to Spain. There's some indication that at least part of it ended up in the Southwest. And since Uncle Wade traveled all over in his search for treasure, we can't be sure where he found these pieces. But since he put *eight* of them in the safety deposit box, I'm confident he wanted each of us to have one to remember him by."

"Where's the rest?" Kent asked.

"This is it, as far as I know," Ellie said.

She started walking around, handing each cousin one piece from the box she was carrying. The cousins barely glanced at their own gifts before eyeing what she was giving the others. Kent immediately ran his fingers over the gold fertility goddess as if it were an erotic miniature. Candy seemed pleased to get the jaguar brooch with jewel eyes, not realizing they were worth less than her zircon ring. Vinny looked unhappy with his gold ring; it wasn't as big as the goddess or as flashy as the brooch. She gave the bell in the form of an eagle warrior to Dennis. It was probably the most valuable of the lot—if it had been real. Tuna got the serpent labret. I wanted to suggest that he try it on but stayed in character awaiting my turn.

When she handed Dylan his coin, he said, "This is all I get?"

"You weren't around that much," Ellie said, firmly but politely. "Sorry."

She handed me my coin. "Thanks," I said with flat enthusiasm.

River came over and whispered in my ear: "Some rare coins can be worth a lot of money."

I accepted his consolation with a nod. Dylan was going from one cousin to the next asking to see what they got and was doing a pretty good job of grumbling. I hoped he didn't overdo it.

As the group started breaking up, River was still beside me. I tried to tell myself I wasn't attracted to him, but part of me was ignoring that advice. To dampen any romantic thoughts that might be creeping into my psyche, I asked, "How long have you known Kent?"

"Since high school. We were on the football team together. I've been living in Europe since college," he said. "I came back two weeks ago for an extended visit."

"And immediately hooked up with your old buddy, Kent?" That definitely earned a left swipe on the dating app.

"We ran into each other yesterday at a coffee shop. When he mentioned Wade's funeral, I decided to come. Your Uncle Wade was an inspiration to me. I almost became an archeologist because of him."

"Almost?"

"I ended up with degrees in finance and art and currently work for an import-export company, the Cruzzan Group." He smiled. "Better money and you keep your hands clean. What about you? I understand you live in Seattle. On a sailboat."

"Did Kent tell you that?" I was surprised Kent knew even that much about me. Although maybe Aunt Regina considered my single, liveaboard status as indicative of failure, and as such something to be shared with other family members.

"Actually, Ellie did. Kent told me you're staying with her."

"Yes. I'm headed back to Seattle tomorrow." I thought I detected a flicker of disappointment. Was that possible?

"Maybe we could go for coffee as soon as you feel comfortable leaving here."

My suspicious mind wouldn't let me consider that he was simply as attracted to me as I was to him. Instead, I was pretty sure he was using me to get information about Uncle Wade's treasure seeking aspirations. But at the same time, I told myself that it would be interesting to see how he went about it, so I said, "Sure. Another hour should do it. Does that work for you?"

"I'll look for you at the entrance in an hour." He gave me a toothpaste smile and went over to talk to the Vancouver cousins.

Dylan waved me over. "Let's go," he said. "I can't keep this up much longer."

"You've talked with all of them—how do they feel about their gifts?"

"They are all busy checking out what the others got, probably worrying that someone else's is worth more than theirs. Can you believe it?"

I caught Ellie's eye, and she headed in our direction. Once in the other room, we hurried outside so we could talk in private.

"Could it have gone any better?" Ellie asked. "If Uncle Wade's watching, I know he is having a good laugh."

"If they see us out here, they will probably think Bryn and I are complaining to you, so don't smile," Dylan cautioned Ellie.

"I do have a question though," I said. "What's with Kent's friend, River?"

"Oh, I was surprised to see him here," Ellie said. "Once he moved to Europe, and his parents left the area, I thought he was gone for good."

"Did you know him in high school?"

"He was the football team captain. All the girls had a crush on him."

I have never been a football fan, not even in high school when it was the hub of the universe for most of my classmates. "All muscles and no brains?"

"Actually, my recollection is that he was Valedictorian the year he graduated. It was a big deal at the time because he also got a football scholarship." She glanced around before flashing me a smile. "He asked about you."

"I know; he told me. I'm wondering if Kent suggested he ask me out for coffee."

"He asked you out for coffee?" Ellie said. "You're going, aren't you?"

"Yes, but only to find out what he wants."

"Hey, I know you're my sister, but it strikes me that there's a possibility he finds you attractive," Dylan said. "After all, he doesn't know you like we do."

"I appreciate the compliment. But doesn't it also strike you as odd that he's turned up now after all this time?"

"Sometimes a coincidence is just a coincidence," Dylan said.

"But most of the time it isn't. Just don't tell Mom about me having coffee with him, okay? It could be a long ride back to Seattle if you do."

We returned to the reception, and Ellie and I walked around together for a while so she could introduce me to a few people and explain who others were. She finally wandered off to talk to some of the neighbors, and I approached the woman who had referred to Uncle Wade as sweet. "I'm one of Wade's nieces," I explained. "I really appreciated what you said about him."

"I'm sorry for your loss," she said.

"How did you know him?"

"Ah, I didn't know him well." I noticed that she was holding a full plate of food. Some people eat when stressed. But for some reason, I suddenly had a hunch about her.

"You aren't a neighbor, are you?"

"Not really." She took a bite of a chicken wrap. A little drool of sauce came out and she dabbed at it with a napkin.

"Friend of a friend?" I tried. She swallowed hard and her eyes darted around, as if she was looking for a means of escape.

Making a wild guess, I said, "It's okay with me if you crashed his funeral."

She took a sip of juice before replying. "I read his obituary. He sounded like a nice man."

"He was. Thank you for coming." I left her with her plate of food. Who would have expected an uninvited guest to get up and speak about the deceased? Then again, why not? As I walked away, I thought about how Aunt Regina would have asked her to leave if she'd known the woman had never met Uncle Wade when he was alive. Whereas my mother's instinct would have been to find out if she needed help. It was hard to believe that the two sisters came from the same family background.

When I was ready to escape the small talk and sadness, I made my way to the entrance. River was waiting for me, studying the pictures of Uncle Wade through the years. I hadn't had a chance to look at them yet, so I stopped alongside him to take them in.

"Hi there," he said, his greeting soft as a caress.

"Hey," I said, concentrating on the pictures. "That's Ellie and me with Uncle Wade." I put a finger on a very old photo taken at a family picnic when Ellie and I were about eight or nine.

"You were a real cutie," River said.

Me? A cutie? More like an awkward kid who didn't care about appearances and always had her nose in a book. I pointed to another photo. "There's the entire group of siblings. They look so happy in that picture."

"No one chooses pictures for a funeral that make people look bad or sad," he said.

"Not a very realistic view though."

"Are you implying that there have been bad times?"

"There always are, aren't there?"

"You mean 'what family doesn't have its ups and downs'?"

I liked the fact that he could quote Eleanor of Aquitaine, even if it was only from a movie. "Well, I certainly hope everyone in our family isn't scheming to one-up everyone else."

"It's tougher for the royals than for us peasants." He nodded toward the exit. "Coffee?"

He'd slipped past that bait with the skill of a star athlete. I'd have to be on my toes not to give away more than I managed to learn.

Our conversation over coffee turned out to be more pleasant than I anticipated. We chatted about movies and books and food. Then he mentioned the housing market in Vancouver.

"Are you looking for a house?" I asked.

"I am. A smallish one. Or a condo. I haven't decided yet."

"Real estate in Vancouver is expensive."

"I know," he said. "I've already started checking online real estate sites. Kent's hoping Wade's house is worth a fair amount. Given its location, my guess is that it is."

"Did he mention that the money from the sale is to be held in trust for the grandkids?"

"No. That's interesting."

"I think he was disappointed in the will."

"But I understand Ellie was bequeathed the contents of the safety deposit box. It was certainly nice of her to share with everyone." He paused. "Could I take a look at that coin you got again?"

"Of course." Here it comes, I thought. I wasn't sure what was coming, but my gut said this was the reason he had asked me for coffee. I handed him the coin.

"It looks like it's about the 16th or 17th century."

"You know a lot about coins?"

"I've picked up a little on the job," he said. "And I like watching documentaries on archeological digs."

"You're not a treasure hunter then?"

He handed the coin back. "No, too busy with my job for that. But I can sympathize with the dream."

When it was time to leave, he asked for my cell number. "I get to Seattle from time to time. Maybe we could have dinner."

"I would like that," I replied. And in that moment, I meant it.

home sweet boat

It's no fun shouting "I'm home" when there's no one there to hear you, not even your cat. But I was happy to be back. Macavity always has to punish me for leaving him on his own for longer than a day, so I would need to make a trip to the grocery to pick up some special treats for him to ease the transition. And I needed to make a run to Fran's Chocolates to buy some salted caramels for Hudson for taking care of my goldfish. He always insists I don't need to get him anything for fish sitting, but he never turns down Fran's salted caramels.

The trip home had been both pleasant and painful. Pleasant because I was with family. Painful because I was with family. For the most part my mother was on good behavior. Then Dylan made the mistake—on purpose?—of asking about my coffee date with River.

"Not that good-looking blond man I saw you talking to?" Mom immediately put two and two together while Dad muttered something about "What kind of a name is River?"

I told them he just wanted to examine the gold coin from Uncle Wade's safety deposit box. Then I'd dropped the bomb about all of the artifacts being replicas. Things definitely took a downward dip at that announcement. Mom couldn't decide who she was the maddest at—Uncle Wade for storing fake artifacts in a bank rather than at home, thereby encouraging family members to assume they were worth a lot of money. Ellie for letting the cousins believe she was giving them something valuable. Or me for not telling her they were phony. She even gave Dylan a bad time for not being up front about it.

I didn't explain that Ellie and I thought Uncle Wade had used the safety deposit box ploy to divert attention away from the real treasure he had his eye on. Because then I'd have to admit how we had discovered some clues as to its whereabouts and planned on following up. But I did confess that we let the cousins think the artifacts were authentic in part because we were angry about them searching Uncle Wade's house and leaving a huge mess. Dylan and Dad were on my side, agreeing that the cousins got what they deserved. But Mom thought I should tell them the truth. In spite of their bad behavior, they were still family. I pointed out that if they kept them as mementos, it wouldn't matter. It was only if they tried to sell them that they would discover the truth. And that would mean they cared more about money than about memories of Uncle Wade.

Dylan further defended me by saying that he was pleased to have the coin and to be in on Uncle Wade's joke. It made the keepsake doubly precious. Mom made a few more feeble protests about it seeming unkind to keep the other cousins in the dark, but when I reminded her that it was Uncle Wade and not us who was responsible for the deception, she suddenly smiled.

"He was always a tease," Mom said, before adding: "I hope they don't try to sell them." Dylan and I avoided looking at each other, and neither of us suggested she contribute ten dollars to our pool on who would sell first.

Macavity came home just as I was getting ready to run my errands. He paused briefly when he saw me in the galley, then turned tail and went back out his porthole door to let me know he would socialize when he was good and ready. He probably guessed I hadn't had time to buy him any treats yet.

After restocking my pantry and exchanging salted caramels for my two goldfish, I found myself at my office computer feeling like I'd never been gone. The clutter was right where I'd left it. The table with my Keurig still wobbled. Bubbles V and Friend were still swimming in circles, Bubbles V in the lead—at least that's what it looked like to me. The only thing that had changed was the overwhelming number of emails in my promo and spam files. I'd let deleting them slide while I was in Vancouver. There were a zillion promos and even more spam emails with colorful emojis— my unclaimed winnings, payment verification requests, final notices, warnings that someone was running a background check on me, and a slew of comments on how to enhance my sex life.

I should probably move *strengthening spam filters* from "do soon" to "urgent" on my priority matrix. Or maybe I should get rid of my "to do" matrix altogether; it seemed to spur more guilt than action.

There was also an email from River. It had slipped past the spam filter and made it to my inbox. He said he was coming to Seattle next Friday, and if I was free Friday evening, would I like to have dinner with him? I checked my enthusiasm level and decided I would. But not wanting to appear too eager, I decided to wait until later to reply. After I'd had a chance to run my reservations about him past Logan. Logan was the person I relied on to be brutally honest with me when I needed it. And in this instance, I probably needed it.

It was almost four when there was a knock on my office door. Not Logan's confident rap before he barges in. Not Hudson's polite, rhythmic "knock-knock." But a bold, assertive thwacking that announced someone who thought they were important enough to demand an audience with me on *their* terms, not mine. Instead of yelling, "Come in," I went over and opened the door about halfway in case it was a salesperson or someone peddling their brand of religion.

"You Bryn Baczek?" the man asked. He was wearing casual but expensive looking clothes. Not your average West Coast casual; more international flair. In his fifties was my guess. Tanned face with that leathery "I spend time outdoors" skin.

"Yes. What can I do for you?"

"Can we talk? My name is Shane Reed." He put out a hand through the half-opened door and I automatically responded. That caused me to open the door another few inches. An effective ploy on his part. His hand was rough and his handshake vicelike.

"About what, Mr. Reed?"

"Call me Shane." He smiled with his lips not his eyes.

"Okay, Shane. What do you want to talk about?" I was blocking the entrance, unsure about whether to let him in.

He hesitated, then said, "About your uncle, Wade Payne."

I stepped aside, but I deliberately left the door open. Although it was more symbolic than a good safety measure since there weren't a lot of people around to come to my rescue if I yelled for help.

He took a seat in front of my desk and waited for me to sit down. "I'm sorry for your loss," he said in a tone that told me he didn't really care about my feelings or Uncle Wade's death, but that he knew what he was supposed to say. So did I.

"Thank you," I replied evenly.

"I'm here because I think you may be able to help me."

"And why would I want to do that?" He may have expected a different answer, like "In what way?" because he stretched his neck before responding, as if he needed breathing room.

"Because I can make it worth your while."

I waited, forcing him to continue without feedback on his vague proposal.

"I knew your uncle. He and I went on a couple of trips together."

I continued to wait. There was something about him I didn't like; I had no intention of making his explanation of whatever he was after any easier.

"We were planning a hunt together when he died unexpectedly. I was going to finance it, but he had the information. I'm hoping we can make a deal. You tell me where he was heading in return for a percentage of whatever is found."

"It's not me you should be contacting. My mother is the executor of his estate."

"I thought you might have talked with him about the project."

"I didn't."

"Well, you and your cousins had access to his house and his belongings, perhaps you found something to indicate the location of his intended hunt."

"And how do you know we had access?"

He hesitated, then said, "I talked to his housekeeper, Bianca."

"You mean Bianca Torres?" It irked me that he used her first name only; it felt disrespectful.

"Yes, Ms. Torres." He'd picked up on my irritation but had overcompensated. I decided to let it go.

"And what did she tell you?"

"That someone had searched the house. And that you and your cousin had cleaned everything up." He stretched his neck again. Not a good poker player. I wondered if he had pressured Bianca in some way or offered her money for information. "She said you and some of your other relatives have already removed items."

"Why come all the way to Seattle to see me? You could have called."

"I thought it was a conversation to have in person."

"Have you talked to any of the other relatives?" Had one of them pointed the finger at me to misdirect Reed or to irritate me? Or both?

"Look, I admit his brother and sister think his treasure hunting was a joke. But they both said that *you* believed in your uncle's fantasies. That's why I'm here."

"I don't remember him mentioning you. What *past trips* did the two of you take together?" I got out a yellow pad to write on and waited with pen in hand. "And what proof can you show me that you and he were collaborating on an upcoming hunt?"

"We didn't sign any agreements, if that's what you're asking. It was a gentleman's handshake." Looking indignant and thoroughly ticked off, he stood up and reached into his pocket. I almost dove under my desk but caught myself in time to see him take out his wallet and remove a card. "If you decide you're interested, here's my number."

As he headed to the door, I said, "I didn't remove anything from my uncle's house. But if it's a treasure map you're after, I think you should ask my cousin Kent about it." Take that, Kent, I've lobbed the ball back.

He turned toward me. "You think he found a *map*?" He was almost salivating at the idea.

"I don't even know if a map ever existed. But he and the other cousins were the first ones to search the house." I was tempted to add, *Unless you had a look around the night you pushed Uncle Wade down the stairs.*

"I really did have an appointment to meet with your uncle. I heard through some other hunters that he was onto something. And I wanted to get in on it. You can't blame me for that."

"I don't blame you for anything, Shane. But I'm afraid I can't help you."

The next visitor to come by was Logan. A confident rap and an entrance before I could say "come in." He invited me to dinner with him and his partner Judd. Judd is a good cook, no, better than good, an *excellent* cook, so I leapt at the offer.

"He's making beef Burgoyne. It's a new recipe."

"What's the occasion?"

"Your triumphant return, what else?"

"Seriously."

"He's been working long hours to make a court deadline and is taking a half day off today. When I suggested we have dinner, he decided to make something special. He and Macavity are over there right now cooking up a storm."

I still had a hard time accepting the fact that self-professed cat-hater Judd had an amiable relationship with Macavity. I suspected it was based on a mutual love of salmon, but I was still surprised . . . at both of them. Macavity's what I would describe as an independent and cantankerous loner. I feel honored that he lets me cater to his whims and provide him with food and lodging. Whereas Judd's rational and disciplined demeanor doesn't lend itself to kowtowing to a critter of any sort. Definitely the odd couple.

After a delicious dinner, we settled in with our coffee, satiated and relaxed. It was time to run my plan past Judd and fill in Logan on a few details. Logan was already totally on board for the adventure, and while I trusted his judgement on most things, I was relying on Judd's lawyerly pragmatism to poke holes in the plan. Even though I doubted there was anything he could say to dissuade us from making the trip, we might make some adjustments based on his assessment.

"Tell me more about how you've created this virtual map," Judd said after I highlighted the big picture for him, the Cliffs Notes version.

I described in detail what Ellie and I had found in Wade's house—the light switch cover, mug, placemats, watercolor picture, and the Gollum figure. I showed him the letter I received from Uncle Wade and told him about the one Ellie got. Then I showed him pictures of the replicas that were in the safety deposit box and the snapshot I took of the empty chest in the attic. "We think the artifacts and whatever was in the chest are part of an elaborate hoax. Uncle Wade's attempt to clear the way for Ellie and me to look for the treasure without interference."

"So, there are two major pieces to this—a possible prank and a possible treasure."

"Everyone seems to think he had a good lead. Including the

treasure hunter who came by my office today." I told them about Shane Reed and his claim that he'd made a deal with Uncle Wade to search for the treasure together.

"You think he was lying about both the deal and about working with your uncle in the past?" Judd asked.

"Fairly certain."

"And you think your cousins found a map that Wade intended them to find."

"Yes."

"And you believe the clues he left for you and Ellie are real."

"Yes."

"And you want Logan to go with you to find this treasure."

"Yes."

"And you want to know what I honestly think."

"Yes."

Judd actually laughed. "I think you're all delusional."

you won't believe!

"You won't believe what Bianca told me when I confronted her about talking to that treasure hunter guy. She actually let him look around the house on his own!" I'd called Ellie earlier to tell her about Shane's visit.

"Did she say why she did it?" I asked.

"She admitted he offered her money to let him in, and she felt that since it had already been searched by the family, why not? She also assured me that she surreptitiously kept an eye on him and that she was fairly certain he didn't remove anything."

"Did she elaborate on which family members she thought had already searched the house?"

"Like us, she assumed the male cousins went through everything and made the mess that you and I had to clean up. And that's when our conversation became really interesting. Shane wasn't the first person to approach Bianca or give her money for a peek inside."

"Really?"

"She said that Uncle Wade loved talking about his expeditions and had been pretty excited about the latest one he was planning. Apparently, he'd bent the ear of the guy who has been repairing the front deck, and the other day when she caught him spooking around, he offered her a few bucks not to mention it to anyone. Not good for business, he told her."

"I wonder if he found anything?"

"We could ask him, but I doubt by the time he hazarded a look around that there was anything left to find . . . because there's more."

"Seriously?"

"Apparently when Uncle Wade had breakfast with his male friends, he not only talked treasure hunting to them, he also chatted up the waitress. Her name is Jo something. Before Bianca caught the deck repair guy in the act, Jo and a friend of hers asked for access. She claimed Uncle Wade had some pictures of her that she didn't want getting out, implied they had been having a fling. Bianca said she didn't believe the bit about the pictures for a minute, but again thought, why not?

"The treasure hunter came after the two women and before the deck repair guy, and he apparently paid her the most. She seemed pleased about that. It surprised me that Bianca didn't try to hide what she'd done. I think she was less concerned that I might accuse her of unethical conduct than that I would ask for a cut of the money they gave her."

"She's more enterprising than I thought." I paused. "Should *she* be on our suspect list?"

"I don't see her as a killer. Nor do I get the impression that she believed in the existence of Uncle Wade's treasure map. She did, however, mention how pleased she was to be named in Uncle Wade's will. Although obviously a few bucks in hand to tide her over until she receives the $50,000 distribution was too tempting to resist."

"The one who surprises me the most is the waitress."

"I was curious, so I called Abe about her. He told me she used to chat up all of the regulars. But he thought she seemed particularly interested in Uncle Wade. They teased him about flirting with her, and I have no doubt he tried to impress her by bragging about his treasure hunting activities. And maybe, like the others, she assumed he had a map for his latest project. If so, she was a little slow on the uptake. Not sure whether Bianca told her someone already searched his place before she and her friend did."

"Bianca didn't mention a reporter asking for a look around, did she?"

"No, but that doesn't mean he didn't act on his own and got away unseen."

"What I can't decide is whether asking to search the house *after* he was pushed down the stairs lets all of these potential suspects off the hook for murder. Although, as we've talked about before, if it was an accident and they panicked, they may have run away before making a thorough search."

"On the other hand, approaching Bianca like that might have been an attempt to cover their tracks. Even if they already got what they were after."

"There are too many possibilities, and too many suspects. But I still think it's one or more of the cousins who found the fake map from the chest. If that's what was in the chest. Haven't heard about any 'vacation plans' for them, have you?"

"No, but I'm keeping tabs on what they're up to. And I'm not telling anyone about *our* trip for a while."

I got another call from Ellie Tuesday afternoon. She began by again announcing there was something I would *not* believe. "You won't believe what your cousins have done now."

"*My* cousins. I'm afraid they're *our* cousins. But what did they do?"

"They *all* tried to sell their artifacts." She started laughing. "Together. And are they mad! Of course they are convinced that I kept the 'real' artifacts for myself and substituted the fake ones."

"They actually accused you of that?"

"To my face."

"What did you say?"

"I pointed out that I wouldn't have had time to find reproductions before the funeral, but they weren't buying. They demanded that I come clean. They even got Aunt Regina and Uncle Max to come by for a friendly chat."

"How did that go?"

"Not well. They accused me of being in *cahoots*—their word, not mine—with Uncle Wade to play a cruel trick on their children."

"No mention of Dylan or me, of course."

"Not a whisper."

"I'm sorry you live in the same city. I know that makes it more difficult."

"Well, what I can't decide is whether Dylan wins the pool with his Kent bet or whether we all get our money back because it was a group thing."

Wednesday morning I got still another call from Ellie: "You won't believe what they're demanding now."

"The cousins?"

"The cousins *and* their parents. They want first dibs on Uncle Wade's household contents. It's hard enough just going through everything, but having them paw through it all first, well, that would be a real pain. And another mess to clean up."

"You're not going to let them do it then?"

"I told them they can come through and mark any large items they want, but they can't move anything. And the small stuff is either going to a church or a charity. Period. If I thought they wanted keepsakes, that would be one thing. But it's just another indication of how materialistic they all are."

"I wish I had room for some of his books," I mused. "That's the downside of living on a boat."

"I've asked your mother what she would like, if anything. And she mentioned the books. I'm going to check with Dylan too, to see if there's something he might want."

"I assume no one will notice the few items we took."

"I doubt it. Plastic place mats, a light switch cover, a mug, and a watercolor by Uncle Wade—? By the way, I replaced the light switch cover with one of those standard white ones. And, paranoid that I am, I've put the items we took in my storage locker, splitting them up and adding them to stuff I already had in storage to camouflage them. I did, however, put the globe back together and have it in my living room. I always liked it as a kid and decided to keep it for myself."

"Well, if you're paranoid, so am I. I deleted the pictures of Gollum after writing the numbers in a couple of used books that have a lot of scribbling in them." I had also memorized them, making up a jingle to jog my memory.

***

It was twenty-four hours before the next "You won't believe this" call.

When my cell started playing the partying frogs and I saw Ellie's number, I braced myself. And I was glad I had.

"You won't believe it—my condo was burgled."

"Oh no, you don't think—"

"Yes, that's what I think. I want the police to dust for prints, and if any of *your* cousins are identified, I want them prosecuted."

"Have they ever been in your condo?"

"Not a one. Aunt Regina and Uncle Max have though. So, if they did the deed themselves, I won't have a case."

"What was taken?"

"That's what convinces me that I'm right about it being the cousins. The only thing taken was some money I had stashed in a desk drawer and a couple pieces of jewelry."

"If they wanted to make it look like a robbery, why didn't they take more?"

"Duh, because they weren't smart enough to do it right. They were probably fixated on finding a map. Or the 'real' artifacts. Besides, they may have thought that if they took too many things the police would make more of an effort to catch the thieves."

"Doesn't your building have cameras?"

"Yes, there were two unidentified males who showed up. It could have been Kent and Tuna, but I can't swear to it. They've apparently seen enough crime movies to worry about cameras; they wore hoodies and caps and kept looking down."

"Probably wore gloves too."

"Probably. Darn. What's next?"

On Friday morning I got the fifth "You won't believe this" call from Ellie. Macavity was demanding breakfast, so I put her on speaker while I set out his food. "You won't believe . . ." I cut her off.

"At this point, nothing could surprise me."

"Well, *this* may. Kent's house was broken into and searched. Very little taken. And who do you think he blames? Me, of course. Fortunately, I was out to dinner with a friend, so I have an alibi. But who would have thought I would need an alibi to keep from being a housebreaking suspect?"

"Think they set it up themselves to look innocent of the break-in at your condo? Or maybe it was that treasure hunter."

"I don't know what to think."

When Ellie called again on Friday afternoon, I was almost afraid to answer. "Hello," she said.

"That's it? Hello? No, 'You're not going to believe this?'"

"Well, *you* said it."

"What am I not going to believe *this* time?"

"I'll send you a copy of the article in the paper. It's by that reporter who kept trying to interview Uncle Wade. He makes it sound like our uncle was some kind of obsessed eccentric."

"That's not too far off base."

"But he also ignores his successes and paints him as someone who was destined never to fulfill his dreams."

"That's partly true too, isn't it?"

"I suppose. But there's something about the tone of the article that bothers me. It's like he doesn't want anyone to think Uncle Wade knew what he was talking about at the end."

"Maybe he should go to the top of our suspect list."

Friday evening I received another variation on the "You won't believe this" call. Only this time it was *me* thinking "I can't believe this"! It came to me direct from Kent. He had the nerve to ask why I had told some "pushy treasure hunter" that he had a map to Uncle Wade's last proposed treasure hunt.

"I assumed you retrieved it from the chest in the storage space in the attic," I said pointedly.

"I don't know what you're talking about."

"I don't care one way or the other," I said. "That's why I haven't brought it up. But this Reed guy told me he would be willing to sponsor an exploration. I thought you might be interested." It's so easy to deceive the deceptive. They think they are the only ones who know how to lie.

"Oh. Well, I think he's more interested in getting his hands on the map than sponsoring an expedition," Kent complained.

"That could be," I conceded.

"Did you hear about the break-in at my place?"

"Yes, Ellie mentioned it. Was it a burglary? Or are you thinking it was Reed looking for the map?"

"As I just told you, I don't know anything about a map. But if there was one, Ellie probably took it for herself. She faked those gold figures, you know."

"The replicas, you mean? I think that was Uncle Wade's way of playing one last practical joke."

"Some joke."

Yeah, a very satisfying one.

Saturday evening I met Sophie at our usual restaurant bar for dinner and drinks. We like to eat in the bar because we are never hurried there. Our dinners frequently turn into drawn-out affairs where we leave just enough wine in the bottoms of our glasses to look as though we haven't quite finished yet. Fortunately, the place is never so busy that we prevent others from being seated.

Sophie and I have a bond forged by years of friendship and shared confidences. After a marriage and miscarriage when she was in her twenties, she's divorced and lives alone in a small house in a middle-class neighborhood, is constantly on the lookout for *the* perfect mate, likes good red wines and dark chocolate, and is always watching her calories. In addition, she's not only a loyal and supportive friend, she's someone who doesn't hesitate to call me out if she thinks I'm doing something I shouldn't.

This was the first chance I'd had to tell her about my trip to Vancouver and to share all of the family drama. When I was finished, she summed up her view of what I'd been through with one word: "Unbelievable."

rule of threes

There is evidence to suggest that humans are drawn to the number three. *The three witches give three prophecies to Macbeth. Three blind mice. The Three Stooges. Three times a bridesmaid. The Three Musketeers. Snap, Crackle and Pop. Rock, paper, scissors. Get on your mark, get set, go.* So even though I know that the saying "bad things come in threes" isn't based in science, when I get bad news twice during the week, I worry that something else is about to happen. It's like waiting for the other shoe to drop, although in this instance, that had already happened. Now I was waiting for shoe number three.

Earlier in the week Ellie had let me know that Uncle Wade's cause of death was ruled as inconclusive. In some ways that was good news, but it meant that if he had been murdered, the murderer was home free. So, I put it in the "bad news" category.

Next, she informed me that no fingerprints were recovered from her condo to identify who had broken into her place. There were only three sets of prints: hers, mine and a friend who visited frequently. Another dead end, and "bad news" number two.

She also told me that she had finally been in touch with her step-father about Uncle Wade's death. He was about to leave for Santorini with his new spouse, obviously enjoying their trip, and did not chastise her for not getting in touch with him before the funeral. It was sad that they weren't closer, but the fact that they didn't have a warm family relationship didn't fall in the "bad news" category since it wasn't exactly news.

When no other bad news descended during the week, I was prepared for the third shoe to drop during my date with River. Not that I'm superstitious . . . knock on wood. He wanted to see my boat, so he was coming by the marina at six o'clock. Macavity and I were ready and waiting.

Macavity was probably picking up on my nervous vibes, but I swear he knew that his instincts about people were about to be tested. I'd fed him dinner early. He usually leaves for his evening marina rounds after that, but tonight he stayed put. I've tried to follow him to see where he goes after dinner, but he's too clever, and random, for that. I have to be satisfied that he always returns.

River passed the first test. He called out from the dock to announce his presence. A lot of people step aboard and knock on the railing or cabin roof. But when they see that the hatch is open, it's polite to hail first.

Macavity often leaves when someone new comes by but, in this instance, he stayed, retreating to the corner of the settee, ready to leap off and flee in a streak of orange fur. Or attack, if necessary.

I popped my head up through the open hatch and saw the dark silhouette that was River, the bright sun backdrop forming a halo around him. Although I couldn't see his facial features with the sun in my face, I sensed he was smiling. "Hey, come on down." He stepped aboard and the boat rocked slightly, bouncing against the fenders, the mast swaying, waving to the other boats in the marina.

Next, River passed test number two. He turned around and came down the steps backwards. That way you can hold onto the railings and are less likely to slip and fall.

Then came test number three. He saw Macavity and immediately said, "Hello, there. What's your name?" Macavity didn't answer, but he didn't run either. His nose was in the air, sniffing out the new friend . . . or enemy. River turned to me. "Does he like to be petted?"

"Sometimes," I said vaguely. "His name is Macavity."

"Like the T.S. Eliot poem?"

"A bit too much at times."

River extended his hand for Macavity to sniff, but Macavity kept his distance.

"I'll give him some time, then." He glanced around. "Cozy."

"Is that code for 'small'?"

"I prefer more living space, but I can see why you like it. What's the wood? Mahogany?" He reached up and ran his fingers across one of the laminated beams. "Lovely woodwork."

"Let me show you the rest. That will take thirty seconds."

I stepped aside and motioned him toward the bow. "Bathroom on the left. Closet on the right. Double berth up front." He went up front while I waited. When he came back, I said, "Now you've seen it all."

"I admire you for your minimalism."

"I was living aboard before that term became popular."

"I may not like living in small spaces, but I do like sailing. Maybe you could take me for a sail some time."

"That's a possibility," I said. Macavity and I hadn't made up our minds yet. "Well, shall we go? We can stroll around the marina if you'd like to see my back yard."

"And didn't you say your office is here at the marina too?"

"Yes, but that's off limits. The cleaning service hasn't been around for a while."

I thought I saw him hesitate, as if he was going to say something, but instead he moved on, figuratively and literally. He went up the steps and into the sunshine.

As he stepped off the boat, I texted Logan. We had talked briefly about River earlier in the week, and Logan wanted to meet him before rendering an opinion. We agreed that he would run into us on the dock, allegedly by accident, so I could introduce him to River. First impressions can sometimes be misleading, but in general, I trust Logan's instincts about people. And then he would have an image to go with the name for future conversations.

Macavity followed us outside and disappeared down the dock without comment on my visitor.

"This is a nice set-up," River said, indicating the cement float I think of as my front porch. "What's in the outbuilding?"

"This used to be a fuel dock years ago. That was the office. Now it's used for storage."

River looked around. "It's a surprisingly industrial neighborhood for being so close to downtown."

"Yes, I personally like the feel of the area. Shilshole Bay Marina, a fancier place with locked gates, is right on the Sound with easy access to open water. But I don't mind going through the locks. And this suits me."

He pointed to the name on the bow of my boat. "Where does *Aspara* come from?"

"It's a mythical sea bird in a Utopian novel, *Islandia*, by Austin Tappan Wright."

"Very fitting." He looked at me and smiled. "You're an interesting woman." I immediately wondered if that was a line he used on all of the women he met. Who doesn't want to be considered interesting? Well, I wasn't falling for his bait, at least not yet.

Logan's timing was excellent. We crossed paths at the foot of the stairs. "Logan, hi," I said. He smiled and extended a hand to River as I introduced them. "Logan lives aboard the *Carpe Diem* on the other dock." I pointed in the general direction of his sailboat. "River is from Vancouver; he's a friend of one of my cousins." Short version; no frills; no specifics.

"Another minimalist," River commented. "I admire your ability to live simply."

"I'm not sure there is anything *simple* about living, no matter where you call home," Logan replied. Oh, oh, that sounded a bit tetchy to me.

"What do you do for a living?" River asked, as if he would be the judge of what was simple.

"Professor at the university. And you?"

"Import, export business."

"That covers a lot of ground."

River laughed. "Most people automatically think of the kinds of things you find at Pier One. And they never ask any questions." He nodded approvingly. "I deal primarily with high-end art: painting, sculpture, textiles, rugs, photography, sometimes furnishings—whatever is trending on the international market."

"That must be interesting."

"I enjoy it. Lots of travel involved. I've been living in Europe, although I'm thinking about buying a place in Vancouver." He sneaked a look at me. "Or maybe Seattle—it's also a gateway to the Far East. That's where a lot of my business has shifted to of late."

"You didn't mention looking for real estate in Seattle," I said.

"I want to be somewhere on the West Coast. Since I'm from Vancouver, it seemed like a logical place. But things change."

I put a mental bookmark on that comment.

"We've always liked Vancouver," Logan said.

"We?" River asked, lifting his eyebrows an eighth of an inch.

I knew Logan's "we" meant the two of us. But he quickly added. "My partner and me." I'm not certain why he didn't want to admit we were the kind of friends who took trips together, but I was still glad he'd made Judd the other half of his "we." In case I decided River was date worthy.

The small talk petered out and River and I took our leave.

About halfway through the meal, River brought up the break-in at Kent's, and I mentioned the same thing had happened to Ellie. "Maybe it's just a coincidence," I said lightly.

"That seems like more than a coincidence, if you ask me," he said. "Any ideas what someone might be looking for?"

"A treasure map," I said without hesitation. "I know Kent thinks there's one."

"But *you* don't?"

"Uncle Wade just found out he had cancer and revised his will accordingly. I think he would have mentioned a treasure map if it existed. Why keep it a secret if he wasn't going to be able to follow up on his own?" The argument sounded pretty convincing to me.

"Kent said the artifacts in the safety deposit box were fake. I assume that included your gold coin. What do you make of that?"

"I guess we'll never know whether Uncle Wade thought they were real or not."

"As a life-long treasure seeker, doesn't it seem unlikely that he would be fooled about the authenticity of ancient artifacts? Wouldn't he have had them checked out?"

"Do you have a better theory?" I asked. It seemed to me he was pushing a bit too much, but then, it was an intriguing conundrum.

"Maybe they were a decoy," he said.

"You think he hid the real artifacts away somewhere?"

"It's a possibility."

I forced a grin. "Maybe they're in a box with the map!" He needed to know that I didn't take this conjecture at all seriously.

"From your tone, I assume you won't be digging up his back yard looking for a pirate chest." River made a sound halfway between a snort and a chuckle, a friendly scoff.

"No, I'll leave that for Kent and the other cousins." I wanted to scoff back but was afraid it would come out as more snort than chuckle.

I took a bite of prawn, chewed for a moment, savoring the delicate seasoning, while River gave his steak the attention it deserved.

"There is one thing that bothers me though," I said after a few minutes of chewing and savoring.

River swallowed and took a sip of wine before asking, "And that is?"

"There is some question about whether Uncle Wade fell or . . . was pushed."

River looked shocked or feigned looking shocked. I couldn't tell which. But if he'd been auditioning for a role in which looking shocked was required, he would have landed the part. "Was there an investigation?"

"Yes."

"Autopsy?"

"Yes. Inconclusive results."

"What do *you* think happened?"

"I'm not sure. But all this talk about a treasure map could be a motive for murder." I let the conjecture hang in the air, mingling with other more pleasant aromas.

River sipped some wine. "If he was pushed, then the person who pushed him may have taken the map."

"Assuming there *was* a map. Although I guess all that was needed was for someone to *believe* there was a map. Someone who thought it was worth killing for."

"This must be hard for the family," he said, "not knowing for sure, but suspecting the worst."

"For some. Not everyone was close to Uncle Wade, as I'm sure you know."

"Why should I know?"

"You're Kent's friend." Maybe I should have finished dinner before picking a fight. It was a good meal.

He took another sip of wine before responding. "We need to get one thing straight. I knew Kent years ago. We weren't close then, but we were on the same team. Team members bond. But it was only recently that I got back in touch. And it's become clear that we don't have much in common anymore."

"Except for a curiosity about Uncle Wade's alleged map."

He was studying my face at the same time I was studying his. I don't know what he saw in mine, but I didn't see the face of a murderer across the table. At least I didn't *think* I did.

"Why did you agree to go out with me?" he asked abruptly.

"You're a charming man . . . and I wanted to . . ." I wasn't sure how to finish the sentence. "I wanted to know if you should be on the suspect list. Or if you were looking for the map. Or if you were using me in some way."

"Let me make this clear. I had great respect for your uncle and his treasure seeking. I would have loved to go on an expedition with him. But I have a good job and no interest in leaving it to chase down some elusive treasure." He paused. "And for the record, your cousins aren't very nice people."

I couldn't help myself—I laughed out loud. "You must have picked up that there's no love lost between Ellie and me and the rest of the cousins."

"I guessed but wasn't sure. I could hardly say that I was asking you out in spite of your relatives, could I?" He smiled. "Want to reset over dessert?"

The rest of the evening was fine. Including the brief good-night kiss on the dock. The last thought I had before falling asleep was that the third shoe was yet to drop.

CHAPTER 17

thunk!

The third shoe dropped with a loud *thunk!* on Sunday morning.

Logan called to invite me to breakfast on the *Carpe Diem*. I never turn down one of Judd's breakfasts. This time he was making crepes with raspberries and chocolate. I was salivating in anticipation. Macavity followed me—or his nose—over to the *Carpe Diem*, and I'm pretty sure that he was rewarded with a few tidbits from the chef. Judd was careful not to let me see him spoiling Macavity. But I recognized the self-satisfied look on that usually enigmatic orange face.

After I was fed and starting on my third cup of freshly ground, French pressed, Hawaiian Kona coffee, Logan dropped the bad news. "I probably should have told you I was going to do this," he began. His serious tone made me sit up straight and put down my coffee. "But I had a bad feeling about the guy."

"Which guy?" I didn't need to ask but did anyway.

"River Robinson."

"Oh." I experienced a surge of disappointment looking for a place to lodge itself.

"Oh yes."

"Hit me with it."

121

"Judd, do you want to tell her about what you know first?"

"Sorry, Bryn. But that company he works for, the Cruzzan Group, has been in the news a number of times over the past few years. They seem to have a penchant for being in possession of stolen or smuggled goods. As soon as Logan mentioned that name, I encouraged him to dig deeper."

"I couldn't find any direct links between River and any of the company's past legal problems," Logan said, "but I did come across another name you mentioned." He paused, but not long enough for me to make a guess on my own. "Shane Reed."

"The treasure hunter?"

"Yeah. It isn't clear how much actual hunting he does. But he tracks down valuable pieces of art, ancient and current, and brokers deals. That sort of thing. At least that's what it looks like based on what my friend could find online."

"Your former student hacker friend?"

"Yeah, that's the one. But I didn't ask him to do anything illegal. There's a lot of information out there if you know where to look. And he does."

I settled back on the couch. "I had my antenna up and he still fooled me."

"Don't feel bad," Judd said. "Logan thought he was quite appealing." He shot Logan a teasing smile.

"So did I." Sigh.

"It doesn't necessarily mean he asked you out for the sole purpose of getting information."

"Sure. He likes my red hair and the color of my left eye."

"Did you reveal anything you wished you hadn't?" Judd asked.

"About what we're up to? No. In fact, I went out of my way to make sure he thought I considered the map a joke. And that *if* it does exist, Kent has it."

"Well, someone thinks it exists. And if they haven't found it, you should expect a search. Maybe they'll try the other cousins' homes too. Maybe even your aunt and uncle's."

"I hope that doesn't extend to Mom and Dad's house. Do you think I should warn them?"

"It wouldn't hurt," Judd said. "You wouldn't have to say much; mention that the break-ins of family members suggests that someone is looking for a map, and they might think the executor of the estate has it."

"I'll do it right away."

"Before you go, I have two somewhat related questions," Logan said. "First, did Macavity hiss at River?"

"Macavity doesn't hiss. But he didn't make tracks right away."

"Second question: Did River ask you for another date?"

"No, he said he'd call. That's a laugh, huh?"

"I'm not so sure. But I doubt he has your number on speed dial."

"Groan. You should learn how to soften insults."

"At least you don't have much time invested in him," Judd said.

"And dinner was very tasty," I added.

Later that evening, Ellie called minutes before I was going to call her. We both tried to talk at once. Finally, I said, "You go first."

"No, you go first."

After two rounds of that, she finally told me why she'd called. "Candy came by Uncle Wade's while I was packing up stuff. She said that Pastel remembered seeing a picture she liked in the living room and wanted to know if she could have it. I had to laugh at her saying that Pastel liked it. I remember Candy examining all of the pictures that day when she allegedly came over to help us clean up. I'm fairly certain Pastel doesn't care a whit about the painting but that for some reason Candy thinks it might be worth something. I could have spared her the scrutiny—Uncle Wade didn't buy paintings for their current or future value but because he knew the artist or simply liked the painting. But I went along with the charade. And now I'm glad I did."

"Why?"

"Because she let something slip during our conversation. Guess who is going to be away for 'a few days, maybe a week'?"

"No."

"Yep, Vinny and the three amigos."

"Did you ask where they were going?"

"Of course," she said. "Wasn't that the obvious thing to do? Candy was vague. All she said was that they were going on a camping trip. Just the *boys*. I didn't want to press and sound overly interested."

"It's too bad we don't know if they're going by car, train, or plane. If by car, maybe we could plant a tracker."

"What about tracking their phones?" she asked.

"Not something I know how to do, but I could ask."

"You have someone you can ask?"

"Yes," I said. "The same person who discovered a connection between River's company and the alleged treasure hunter who paid me a visit."

"What?"

"That was why I was going to call you," I said. "The Cruzzan Group isn't apparently always on the up-and-up, especially when it comes to acquiring stolen or smuggled goods. And Shane Reed does freelance work for them."

"Oh, oh. What do you think that means?"

"First, one of them could be the person who pushed Uncle Wade down the stairs. Second, there may be someone with money pulling the strings. And third, River was using me. Sorry about number three. I admit to having an eye on him. But not as a crook.

"And, if he approaches you," I added, "pretend you're interested. Get him to take you to dinner at a nice restaurant and pry any information out of him that you can without giving yourself away."

"That's not an unpleasant assignment."

"I wish there was some way to let him I know about the cousins' trip," I said, "although he and Shane are probably already all over it."

"Really?"

"It depends on how good River is at getting info out of Kent. And assuming he and Shane are working together. Do you know when they're leaving?"

"Mid-week," she said. "Candy told me that she wanted to go with them but has to stay home with Pastel. According to her, Pastel doesn't like to camp. I think she threw that in to make me believe they were really going camping for the sake of camping. She thinks she's clever."

"That's what concerns me—their overconfidence," I said. "I'm certainly not fond of any of them, but if they aren't responsible for Uncle Wade's fall, they could have a murderer on their tail."

"You don't think River is the one who shoved Uncle Wade down the stairs, do you?"

"If you'd asked me that immediately after our date, I would have said *no way*, but now I'm not so sure."

"It could have been that Reed guy," she said.

"Or it could have been someone else. We're looking at River and Shane because they're in our face. But what about that reporter? Or the waitress? Or even the guy working on his deck? They all apparently believed he had a valuable map hidden somewhere."

"For that matter, almost everyone I talked with at the reception knew about his hot lead."

"Well, unless their camping trip involves a boat ride up the Inside Passage, I think we can be assured that the map they found is a phony," I said. "I hate to think how mad Kent and the others are going to be when they figure it out. First the fake replicas and then a fake map."

"You think they'll conclude Uncle Wade didn't know what he was talking about and call it quits?"

"It's hard to say. Maybe they'll start knocking down walls in his house looking for another map or digging up the back yard for buried chests full of gold."

"Well, at least they'll get a camping trip out of it," she said. "I wonder where Uncle Wade's phony map will take them?"

CHAPTER 18

stealing from thieves

I had a normal week doing normal things . . . except for the time Logan, Ellie and I spent planning our trip to look for Uncle Wade's treasure. That wasn't normal. It was both exciting and worrisome. Like standing on a high diving board before launching off into space. You know you will hit water, but you aren't entirely sure what that landing will be like.

Nor was it normal to buy burner phones to communicate with each other. But given how many people seemed interested in the treasure, we had decided not to use email or our regular phones to talk about our plans. It felt a bit silly, like we were criminals planning a heist rather than a sailing trip to Canada. But we did it anyway. There would be a point at which we started telling family members about our sailing vacation, but that bit of subterfuge could wait.

It's one thing to know there are dangerous and unscrupulous people out there—people you might brush shoulders with on the street, sit next to in the theater, even people you might know casually—but it was altogether different when the potential for danger hit closer to home. Still, intrusive though it was, knowing someone was searching the homes of family members wasn't as scary as watching Jack Nicholson in *The Shining*, especially since there was no certainty that Uncle Wade's death was anything other than an accident. Still, the fact that it might have been a deliberate act kept a tickle of fear lingering at the back of my mind, occasionally surfacing as tension in my neck muscles and an increase in my heartrate.

For the most part though, I was able to ignore doubts and misgivings and concentrate on the planning stage of our adventure. Until I got an unexpected call from my mother, that is. She called to let me know about something that had happened to our male cousins, something I'd briefly considered might happen, then put out of my mind.

At first, I was shocked. Then I felt twinges of guilt for not warning them to be careful. Although how do you warn someone to be careful when they lie about what they're up to? If they really had been going on a camping trip, such a warning might have included a suggestion that they take along the seven essentials or watch out for deadly snakes or poisonous spiders. It would have seemed very strange to suggest that they guard themselves against cutthroat treasure seekers.

Shock and guilt at first, followed by self-concern since we were preparing to launch a similar venture. I was just glad we'd decided not to bother trying to track them. If we'd been caught, the police might have considered us suspects. As it was, their story, as related to Mom by Aunt Regina, was a cautionary tale that I intended to take seriously.

According to my aunt, the four cousins had flown to Phoenix, Arizona and rented a camper with the goal of "getting away from civilization" for a while. If we were right about them using the camping trip as an excuse to search for Uncle Wade's hidden treasure using the phony map he'd planted in the chest in the attic storage area, then Uncle Wade had definitely succeeded with *his* plan. Call it a prank or punishment for past character lapses, they'd ended up in a desolate part of the Sonoran Desert where the temperatures frequently soared into the 90s in July, sometimes exceeding 100 degrees Fahrenheit. Although I'd read that camping in the Sonoran Desert was a popular activity, I couldn't imagine my cousins enjoying it. As far as I knew, camping had never been a vacation priority for them. And four men in a cramped camper in the middle of the desert in intense heat didn't sound that great under any circumstances. It had probably not been much fun even before the attack.

According to Aunt Regina's narration of events, they had stopped at a jumping-off place on the edge of nowhere for provisions, a diner meal, and gas. The only people they saw there were the clerk in the grocery and the waitress in the diner. And beyond that pit-stop they encountered nothing but desert . . . for the first thirty miles.

They'd stopped to reconnoiter and have a drink when a car appeared out of nowhere and pulled in front of their cab. Two men wearing ski masks then forced them at gun point out of the camper. They took the cousins' wallets and cell phones and ordered them to lie face down on the ground, hands over their heads. Vinny had apparently been certain they were about to die and begged the robbers to take what they wanted and leave. There may have been a little more to that part of the story, but if so, we weren't going to be privy to it.

My aunt said that Kent resisted lying down and was pushed from behind. When he tried to get up, one of the men kicked him in the ribs and yelled at him to stay down or else. Ignoring the threat, Kent tried to get up a second time, yelling at the three other cousins that they needed to fight back. That's when the man who'd warned him to stay down shot Kent in the leg.

After that, no one tried to fight back.

Before taking off, the two men shot out the camper tires, leaving my four cousins stranded. With no phones, no transportation, and Kent wounded. From Aunt Regina's perspective, no punishment was too harsh for anyone who would do that. My Mom agreed. Even I felt a flicker of sympathy for my cousins.

Given Kent's condition and the lack of any traffic in the area, they'd decided the only sensible thing to do was for someone to head back to the pit-stop to get help. Vinny and Dennis left Tuna to watch over Kent, and the two men started walking. Unfortunately, they didn't take enough water with them and were soon suffering from heat exhaustion. It was four hours before they finally encountered a couple in a Range Rover pulling a small camper. The couple gave them water and a lift back to the pit-stop.

It was almost dark when the police and an ambulance arrived at the camper. By then the robbers were long gone. The cousins weren't able to provide particularly helpful descriptions of either the two men or their car. Neither of the robbers had said much, their voices muffled by the ski masks that also hid their faces. And the fact that they were medium height and weight, probably Caucasian didn't narrow the field much. However, Dennis did notice that the shooter was left-handed. At least he was 85% sure of it. All the cousins could remember about the car was that it was a dirt-streaked, dark sedan. The police recovered the bullet from Kent's leg. That was their only piece of physical evidence.

The good news, according to Aunt Regina's account of what happened, was that Kent's wound was minor, and the only thing the robbers took other than their cell phones and wallets, were two cold beers and a bottle of Old Forester Classic 86 Proof that had been on the table. There was no mention of a map.

Ellie, Logan, and I speculated about whether the cousins had studied the map enough to know where to look for the treasure without it. Even if they were to remember enough details though, they were probably concerned that a second try could either result in another confrontation with their two assailants or finding a huge hole where the X should have been. How disappointing that must have been for them. And how disappointing it was for us not to be able to enlighten them without giving away what we knew about the real treasure. The joke was not only on the cousins but on the thieves stealing from thieves.

In talking about the actual robbery, Ellie, Logan, and I envisioned the same thing: a treasure map spread out on the small camper table, the four unsuspecting men crowded around, sharing a drink while studying the map. Two strangers showing up with guns, the cousins helpless to stop them from taking what they wanted. We found Kent's bravado both admirable and stupid. The same was true for how we felt about Vinny and Dennis trudging off in the heat to get help but not taking sufficient water with them.

We also speculated about what it must have been like for the two robbers to search the desert location indicated on the map and come up empty. Was that the end of it for them, or did they still think there was a map to be found somewhere?

A late summer sailing trip was not unusual for me, and as far as we knew, no one currently suspected us of having Uncle Wade's map. Nevertheless, we were determined to take appropriate precautions, from innocently talking up our vacation plans to divert suspicion and taking along some kind of defensive weapons, just in case.

Our plan was for Logan and me to motor up to Vancouver and go through customs at Coal Harbor. Ellie would meet us there, and the three of us would continue on inside waters, stopping occasionally at tourist spots, until arriving at the first of the three abandoned canneries where we hoped to find a trail that matched the pictures we had from the light switch cover, the mug, and the watercolor. If anyone was following us and searched the boat while we were off on a day trip, they would find charts marked to suggest the places we were planning on spending time, making it look as much as possible like a vacation rather than a treasure hunt.

Our biggest fear was that someone might think we were carrying a map with us and hold us up on some isolated trail. We definitely didn't want to lose our IDs or all of our credit cards. I planned on keeping a credit card and my Enhanced Driver's License tucked in my bra just in case. Logan was going to stow his under the inserts in his tennis shoes. And Ellie said she had a money belt that looked like an ordinary leather belt that was wide enough in back to keep her ID and a little money.

Meanwhile, we were trying to live our lives as usual, going through the motions of getting ready for a touristy sailboat vacation. By this point we'd shared our vacation plans with Mom and Dad, and Ellie had fed the family rumor mill in Vancouver.

About a week before our planned trip, I was surprised by a call from River. He was going to be in Seattle for a few days and was looking forward to getting together. Maybe we could go for a sail?

Logan was opposed to me being out on the water alone with River, and although I didn't like being told what to do or not do, I decided he was right. I told River it was a busy weekend for me and that the only time I had free was a couple of hours on Saturday afternoon. He suggested we go for a walk on Queen Anne, one of the neighborhoods on his real estate list, enjoy the scenery and grab a bite to eat. Since the verdict was still out as to whether River was a good guy or a bad guy, although leaning toward bad guy, I agreed. Maybe I would learn something from him and not the other way round.

If River didn't ask about the sailboat trip, I intended to bring it up. Perhaps mention a few of the places I was looking forward to visiting and how pleased I was that Ellie was joining me. My goal was to sound transparent enough to dispel any lingering doubts he may or may not have about why we were taking a sailboat vacation together.

On Saturday afternoon, I met River at a popular coffee shop on Queen Anne Avenue. There were several tables out front under a couple of spindly trees. It was a bit noisy, but still a pleasant spot. And the coffee and pastries were good.

River had greeted me with a hug and a quick kiss on the cheek. It felt warm and personal, but not overly so. Then, without much conversational foreplay, he asked, "Did you hear about what happened to your cousins?" On the one hand, it was a natural topic of conversation, but it felt like he jumped on it a bit too quickly.

"Yes. The family pipeline is fully functioning in spite of recent disagreements. Maybe you know more, but from what I heard, the whole thing seemed rather strange. It sounded like they were in the middle of nowhere. Who would be looking for targets to rob out in the desert? And why make so much effort and take such huge risks for so little gain?"

"It has crossed my mind that maybe your cousins actually *did* have a map to your uncle's treasure," he said. "Or maybe someone *thought* they did."

"Really? Have you asked Kent about it?"

"I asked how he was doing," he said. "Whether the gunshot was healing. That was about it. If they did have a map, I assumed he would be reluctant to admit someone ripped it off."

"But you actually believe they had a map, and that's why they were there in the desert? And you think the map was stolen by treasure hunters who knew what they were up to? Sorry, but I find the whole map story hard to believe." I felt like I managed to get just the right amount of incredulity in my tone before adding, "Candy said it was a macho camping adventure. Knowing my cousins, that makes more sense to me."

"Well, even if they had a map," he said, "or still have a copy of the map, it's too late now. If my supposition is correct, any treasure buried out there was probably dug up and whisked away shortly after the robbery."

"When you put it like that, I can't say I feel all that sorry for my cousins. If they did find a map, they should have told Ellie. Having someone steal it from them seems like just punishment. Although I'm sorry Kent was shot. And leaving them out there with Kent wounded like that was cold, really cold."

"Heartless," River agreed.

Was his compassion real? Or was he one of the two men who'd attacked my cousins? And, more important, was he in

Seattle because he now knew the map was fake and wanted to see if I knew where the real map was?

"And shooting Kent seemed so unnecessary," I added.

"Well, he can be irritating," River said with a chuckle.

"So, you'd shoot him for being irritating? I admit that I've been tempted at times. It's a good thing I don't go around shooting people, I guess."

"I don't even like hunting," he said. "Never understood the appeal of guns or killing animals."

Really? Was that a gratuitous statement designed to throw me off the scent?

After we finished our coffee, we walked around. Making small talk, I managed to get in my spiel about the upcoming sailboat trip. He responded by saying all the correct things, leaving me no closer to assessing whether his visit was about me or about the map. Then I made the mistake of mentioning the birthday party my brother was throwing for his oldest daughter Catrin the next day. I'm not sure how it happened, but somehow River wangled an invitation as my guest. The instant I agreed, I regretted it. My mother would love River, and the family would think it was significant that I chose to bring him along. It would be a first. How could I possibly explain that this was a dead-end relationship with a possible hidden agenda on his part? And how on earth had I let him trick me into it?

On the other hand, I could use the party as an opportunity to emphasize that the upcoming sailboat trip was one hundred percent vacation, nothing more. My parents and Dylan were still in the dark as to its real purpose, so they would be great witnesses.

I called my parents Sunday morning to let them know I was bringing a friend of Kent's to the party. Fortunately, Dad answered, so I didn't get many questions and was able to explain away his presence by emphasizing he was in Seattle to look for real estate, not to see me. "He's thinking about moving here or buying a house in Vancouver," I said. "He isn't sure which yet. You met him at the funeral. The blond guy who played football with Kent in high school." Another clue planted—everyone in my family knows I'm not a football fan. They consider it a character flaw.

Since it was a birthday party, I upped my clothing game a smidgen by wearing a teal waffle-knit shirt in a southwest design with my usual jeans. River, on the other hand, could have been a model for a Nordstrom ad for men's smart casual dress. His indigo denim shirt looked soft enough to pass the Charmin test, and there was a tiny tag that proclaimed *Mephisto* on the side of his shoes. He probably paid more for this one outfit than I spend on clothes in a year.

Dylan and Angelina were the first to greet us. Dylan looked sporty and well pressed, and Angelina was in her usual frilly attire. River reconnected with Dylan and won Angelina over by crouching down and addressing the twins as if they were real people. I do realize that they *are* human, and I'm very fond of them, although sometimes they seem more like out-of-control miniature alien beings. Next, he greeted Catrin and handed her a box of Fran's chocolates. A rather large box given the price of Fran's confections, but still within the bounds of propriety. "Thank you for letting me crash your party," he said. Catrin responded with a full smile and a glance in my direction that said, "Where have you been hiding him?"

River had apparently talked at some length with Dad at the reception, so in spite of Dad questioning whether "River" was a suitable name for a man, they acted like two old friends who hadn't seen each other for a while. Mother came in to say hello and waved me into the kitchen.

"Let's cut to the chase," she said as soon as we were alone. "No romantic interest? He's a very personable and attractive man."

"Sorry. Pleasant enough, but not my cuppa." Before I could say more Angelina came in to see if Mom needed help. Together we finished up the meal preparations, and Angelina and I put the candles on the cake.

The twins were on good behavior. Emma wore a lace-trimmed green dress with what looked to me like uncomfortable patent-leather shoes. Noah had on a dark polo shirt with tiny sailboats on it and tennis shoes with high curvy soles and Velcro straps. Emma twirled around to show off her dress to me, while Noah proudly pointed to the sailboats. Both of them love being on the *Aspara*, whether it's tied up at the dock or out on the water. They also both love Macavity, but their love for him is not returned. They are too unpredictable and don't show him the proper respect.

Dinner was good, conversation lively, and the birthday girl seemed pleased with her pile of gifts. We all sang slightly off-key and out-of-synch when Mom brought out the cake, and everyone laughed when Emma admonished her not to spit when blowing out the candles.

Afterwards, as we were driving back to the marina where River had left his car, he said, "That was fun. Thank you for letting me tag along. You have a great family."

"I'm fond of them. At least I'm fond of my immediate family."

"I heard you talking with Catrin about your vacation. It really does sound like a fun trip. Wish you had invited me."

"Would you have come?"

"Yes. Maybe another time?"

Instead of responding directly, I decided it was wise to change the subject. "Losing Uncle Wade was hard for both Ellie and me. Did I mention that he left a letter for her? Well, in it he said that one of the great pleasures in his life was boating, so we thought it would be a nice gesture to go somewhere on the *Aspara*. As I mentioned before, we're heading up the Inside Passage, but since Ellie only has two weeks, we don't expect to get too far."

"And you have it all planned out?" It was a natural question, but my antenna was quivering.

"It's going to be a 'go with the flow' kind of trip. It may depend on wind—although I don't expect much on inside waters this time of year. And if we feel like staying some place for a few days, we'll do it. Whatever strikes our fancy." Had I really just used that phrase?

"That sounds like a great way to approach a vacation."

"I always love being out on the boat, especially in the late summer. Logan and I had been planning on a sailing trip after his summer session. He's still going with me as far as Vancouver, probably stay with us for a few days after that. He may stay longer; we're not sure yet. We're going to see how it goes." I hadn't mentioned the part about Logan before, but he didn't seem surprised that we had been planning a trip together. I wasn't sure if that was a good sign or not."

"I would have been happy to make the trip from Seattle to Vancouver with you." He apparently wasn't giving up on the idea of going sailing with me. If I was misjudging him and this visit wasn't all an act, I might be missing out. Although he was a little too smooth for my tastes. Still, Logan and I had concluded it was best to keep him on the "inside of the tent" until we came back from our vacation. As soon as our treasure hunt was over, so was my relationship of convenience with River.

gold!

"I know you said River wasn't your cuppa, but I have to say that he seemed like a nice man."

My mother and I were in the kitchen. I was helping her with last-minute preparations for our Sunday dinner with the family. It followed a little too closely on Catrin's birthday party in my opinion, but we could hardly break with tradition. It might throw the universe out of kilter.

"He may be nice," I said. "But there's no chemistry." I was hoping she wouldn't want to delve too deeply into what I meant by that.

"That's what you said about John," she pointed out.

I'd forgotten. He was an accountant she had invited to one of our Sunday dinners, her version of setting up a blind date. John is a respectable and intelligent man whose personality and interests resemble the three-piece suit he wore on our first and only date. We have become casual friends since then, but he's not someone I want to spend the rest of my life with, not even a weekend. Having coffee occasionally is more than enough.

"Well, it was definitely true in that instance too."

"What about that dashing Irishman who dropped by that

time?" she said. "Don't tell me there wasn't chemistry there. He was hot."

Had my conservative mother just referred to a man as hot? For once we were in agreement. I couldn't help but feel the heat when thinking about the *dashing* Irishman. There had been lots of chemistry with him. Oodles of chemistry. More than enough chemistry to be combustible. Who could resist that dimple in his chin, and his lovely lilting brogue? His sexy smile? But he lived in Ireland, was part of a crime family and, well, he wasn't exactly the boyfriend type. All flash and no steady flame.

"Do you want me to move to Ireland?" I asked, knowing that was a show-stopper for her.

"Of course not. But if you don't watch out, you will end up . . ."

I interrupted her before she could finish her sentence. "No one uses that phrase anymore."

"You don't know what I was going to say."

"Okay, go ahead, finish your sentence . . . you will end up . . .," I prompted.

"Alone in your old age." We both knew she had intended to say *old maid*. Or maybe a spinster. Archaic phrases that cling to the present. I let it pass. It was time to serve dinner.

That evening I stopped by the *Carpe Diem* for a glass of wine. Judd was watching a documentary on Antarctica. It looked interesting, but I needed to vent to Logan about my family's love affair with River and their obsession with my lack of a love life. We sat at the table and I talked while he drank wine and listened. Not a bad division of labor. We take turns complaining about our families, even though we both know how lucky we are to have families who care about us. At times I'm embarrassed by how cliché my issues sound. I could have stolen the script from a sitcom. But when it's your family and they are questioning your life choices, it's hard not to react. I'm fortunate my father is so supportive. Logan has to face disapproval from both of his parents. As an only child, they expected him to fulfill all of their dreams for a perfect family. And it wasn't in the cards.

"Why did he have to come to Catrin's birthday party?" I whined. "I should have been stronger. Said it was family only. Everyone liked him, even the twins, for heaven's sake. And he gave Catrin a huge box of Fran's Chocolates, tied with a champagne-colored bow." I acted like the bow was the final straw, and maybe it was. Emma had appropriated it for a wristband. The final score was 7-1 in River's favor.

"Ummm," Logan offered.

"Maybe in spite of my doubts we'll find out he's an innocent bystander."

"Ummm."

"More likely, we'll discover he was one of the two masked men who attacked my cousins." That roused Logan out of his noncommittal mode.

"If you think that, why did you invite him to the party?"

"I didn't 'invite him.' Well, not exactly. He's an expert manipulator. Still, he doesn't seem like a person who would shoot someone."

"Give it some time. It will sort itself out," Judd said. I hadn't realized he was listening.

My burner phone rang. It was Ellie. There had to be a reason she was calling this late on a Sunday evening on the burner phone. My immediate reaction was that something bad had happened. From the look on Logan's face, he was thinking the same thing. Logan and I started to go outside so we wouldn't bother Judd, but he turned off the documentary he was watching and waved us back. I knew he was concerned about our trip and perhaps didn't want to miss out on anything that might give him fuel to dissuade us from going.

"You're on speaker," I said. "Logan *and* Judd."

"Hi. Well, I hesitate to say 'you won't believe this,' because I've used that line so many times lately."

"Not more bad news." The words slipped out before I could stop them.

"No, this time it's a *good* 'you won't believe.' Remember me telling you about the visit I had from Uncle Wade a couple weeks before his death?"

"Yes."

"I didn't mention this earlier because it didn't seem important, but when he came, he brought me a box of his favorite loose tea."

"And?" What did tea have to do with anything?

"And tonight I was feeling nostalgic and decided to have some of his tea. And you'll never guess what I found at the bottom of the tin."

"A ceramic animal," I said, remembering the years my mother collected Red Rose miniature figurines.

"No, better than that. Drum roll, please."

We all waited while she tapped the phone a few times.

"A gold coin with an Aztec design. It looks like the ones I gave to you and Dylan, Bryn. But I have a feeling that this one is real."

"Why would he put a fake one in the safety deposit box and a real one in your tea?" Logan asked.

"I've been sitting here going over the possibilities. What if he'd already been to the treasure site? That would explain why he was so excited about it. Why he didn't bring more back with him is a bit of a puzzle, unless he did and we haven't found his stash yet. But I'm convinced that he put this coin in the tea to let me know his other clues were real."

"A gold coin in some tea seems like a stretch," Judd said.

"All of his clues are a bit of a stretch," I countered.

"That's my point." Judd frowned.

"For the sake of argument, let's say it's real," I said. "Based on what we know so far, I can think of a couple reasons why he may have left the treasure in the cave. He could have been worried about being followed by one of those other treasure hunters. Or it's possible the trip taxed him too much, and he decided to return when he felt better. That could have been about the time he got his cancer diagnosis."

Logan leaned forward. "If, for whatever reason, he decided to leave the treasure in situ, but couldn't resist pocketing at least one coin, then putting the coin in the tea makes a certain amount of sense. Once he realized he wouldn't be going back on his own, it was one more way in which he was trying to get the two of you engaged."

After we hung up, Judd poured some wine and sat down across the table from us, crossed his arms, and took a deep breath before speaking. "I know you think going after the treasure is a game of sorts. But there are obviously people out there who take the hunt very seriously. Bryn, your uncle was murdered and your cousin was shot. The two of you might want to reconsider this *vacation* you have planned."

"We've taken steps to make it look like a real vacation," I said. "I haven't even enlightened my own family."

"But you don't know who you are setting the stage for. It could be someone who isn't part of the family rumor mill. What if all they find out is that the three of you are on a sailboat headed north? Consider the timing. How is that any different from your four cousins going camping in Arizona?"

"At least we'll know to be on guard," Logan said. "The cousins didn't suspect a thing."

Judd uncrossed his arms and released a torrent of arguments about why we should either give up on or at least postpone our trip. We resisted with the stubbornness of denial and optimism. But some of his points hit home. At the end of the evening, instead of being mellowed by wine and conversation, I made my way back to the *Aspara* feeling extremely on edge.

There was no moon and only a few lights to relieve the

ominous darkness. At least in my urban marina home there were people nearby. Once we started up the Inside Passage, we would be almost as isolated as my cousins had been on their trip to the Sonoran Desert.

CHAPTER 20

Stowaway

Logan and I left for Vancouver early on a Friday morning. Provisioned, packed, and ready for adventure. Hudson was fish-sitting Bubbles V and Friend, reluctantly. Judd had agreed to feed and keep an eye on Macavity, reluctantly. And my mother was letting me out of the upcoming Sunday family dinner, reluctantly.

Ellie was going to meet us after we went through customs in Vancouver on Sunday. She called Aunt Regina and Uncle Max to ask if they wanted us to sprinkle Uncle Wade's ashes on the sound. We were willing to do so, but the call was mainly to reinforce the idea that the trip was a vacation. The investigation was officially closed and his death labeled an accident. He'd been cremated and currently resided in the box purchased for his funeral next to the fireplace in Aunt Regina's living room. Aunt Regina said she wasn't ready to part with her brother's ashes yet, and besides, the whole family should be present for the ceremonial farewell. I wasn't sure where that sentiment was coming from. It all seemed a bit defensive, or overly possessive, but it did let us off the hook while making a point of transparency about our vacation.

Candy must have talked to her mother after the exchange

because she called Ellie for details. Ellie said she'd given her a few highlights before Candy came right out and asked whether we were going to any places that Uncle Wade had visited. Although it wasn't a subtle question, Ellie was glad she asked so she was able to tell Candy that he hadn't talked to her about the Inside Passage and asked if that was something Candy remembered. We knew her answer would be "no" and assumed she would pass along the gist of the conversation to the others. We hoped that would end speculation about the purpose of our trip. But it wasn't over yet.

The next day Dennis called Ellie to ask where we planned on stopping. She was surprised by the call but had a prepared answer: "Wherever the winds take us." When pressed, she told him about her two-week time limit and explained that how far we got and where we stopped depended on weather and whim. Then she told him what she previously told Aunt Regina and Candy about how Bryn and Logan had already scheduled a sailing vacation and were accommodating her by taking her along. The caveat was that they weren't sure yet how long Logan would stay with them.

After that, Ellie received no more calls from family about the trip. But River called me to check in and wish me a fun time. At the end of our conversation, he asked if we'd decided on any specific destinations, and I gave him the same programmed response about winds and whim, hoping that satisfied him once and for all that we were taking a vacation and not going on a treasure hunt.

The trip through the locks was uneventful. Sometimes there are people who don't know what they're doing and you have to worry about being rammed by another boat or slammed against the rough cement walls of the locks. Since the *Aspara* is wood, it's more vulnerable than some of the larger fiberglass boats. I have plenty of fenders, and I have sympathy for minor mistakes, like missing a bollard with your tie-up line and slowly drifting away while the lock attendant screams and bystanders point. But there are also times when the person at the helm is so incompetent or inconsiderate that I have an almost overwhelming desire to retaliate in some way. I've considered printing up sticky-backed warning signs to slap on the hulls of flagrant violators of common sense and etiquette. Like a jokester putting a "kick-me" Post-It on someone's back. But this time everything went smoothly.

We were almost to Everett when we discovered the stowaway.

Logan and I were in the cockpit, enjoying the warm breeze and sunshine when Macavity came strolling around the side of the cabin. For a moment I thought I was seeing things. But when he came over and sat down beside me, all I could think was, "Oh, no—please don't let this be happening."

Logan was staring at Macavity as though he'd seen a ghost. "No," he finally said out loud, shaking his head. "No."

"What is he doing here?" I asked. It was a rhetorical question. What he was doing was sitting there beside me, possibly wondering when we would return to the dock so he could go gallivanting.

"I thought he was with Judd," Logan said.

"Obviously he isn't."

"I was supposed to take him over to the *Carpe Diem*, wasn't I?"

"Yes," I tried not to sound accusatory, but I was upset. Our plans didn't include a cat, and Macavity wouldn't like the accommodations with three people aboard.

"I remember now. I couldn't find him and decided to look for him again just before we left. And in the rush of last-minute chores, I forgot."

"He must have come aboard through his porthole as we were taking off. Otherwise we would have seen him."

"I'm really sorry."

"Not as sorry as Macavity is going to be without his treats and privacy and no daytime strolls or evening jaunts." My thoughts were racing ahead to how this was going to play out. And it wasn't a pretty sight.

Macavity jumped up and went below. I peeked inside and saw him standing next to where his food and water dishes should have been. He stood there for a moment staring at the empty space. Then he looked up at me with a cat's expressionless face but with fire in his eyes.

"I'm going below to give the stowaway some bread and water," I said as I turned and went down the ladder.

"We could stop somewhere and have Judd drive up and get him."

"We could, but that would take too long. Let's just make the best of it, okay?" Macavity butted my leg and made a sound that was part yowl part murble. "Okay, okay, I won't let you starve, but I put your cat food in the locker to make room for people food. So, your palette will have to adjust, at least until we stop somewhere there's a store."

"Maybe we could catch some fish for him," Logan yelled from the cockpit.

"Without a fishing pole or net?" I yelled back. Fish. Tuna fish. "How would you like tuna for brunch?" I asked Macavity. "Maybe for dinner too." I was surprised he had waited so long to ask for food; maybe Judd had given him something to eat earlier.

I gave my pushy cat chunked tuna in a cereal bowl and set another cereal bowl filled with water next to it. He sniffed at the tuna and looked at me as if to ask, "What *is* this?" I patted him on the head, even though I know he doesn't like to be petted while dining, and retreated to the cockpit.

"Will it be possible to keep him inside for two weeks?" Logan asked. His misgivings obviously paralleled mine.

"He can stroll the decks while we're motoring, which will probably be for most of the trip since we're really not the relaxed vacationers that we've portrayed to my family."

"I know other sailors have cats aboard," Logan said hopefully.

"Maybe we can make some sort of leash for him. He won't

like it, but it would get him off the boat occasionally. Otherwise, if we let him run loose, he might not be back on board when we're ready to leave."

"And there really could be some dangerous animals around where we're headed."

I started laughing.

"What's so funny? The thought of Macavity facing down a bear?"

"No, I'm thinking about Ellie sleeping in Macavity's bunk. I wonder what he will do? He's not keen on sharing."

"That makes me glad I have the MRI bunk." We call the quarter berth in the cabin the MRI bunk because it's a tight space between the hull and the engine room that runs under the cockpit. It's like sleeping in a large coffin with an opening at one end.

"Hopefully Macavity won't mind sleeping on the settee for a couple of weeks. Maybe I can let him have a towel to sleep on. I didn't bring any extra pillows or blankets. The real issue will be a litter box. Although I think you can use rice or beans instead of litter until we get to a store."

"That sounds unpleasant," Judd said. "What about beach sand?"

"That could work. If it becomes necessary, we'll see which he prefers."

"The question is where to put it."

"As far away as possible. Maybe at the end of the bumpkin. Make him walk the plank to get to his toilet." We both laughed as we looked at the mahogany spar extending from the stern.

"Well, I'd better call Judd and let him know. He's probably roaming the docks looking for Macavity as we speak."

Fortunately, we had reception and Logan got through to Judd right away. I could tell from listening to Logan's side of the conversation that Judd was not pleased. Either because he'd been looking forward to Macavity's company or it was one more thing about our trip that he didn't think was wise.

"Ah, let me put you on speaker," Logan said.

"What are you going to do about customs?" Judd's voice sounded far away, hollow and tinny. Almost as if he was speaking from a ship's bridge through a voice tube to the engine room.

"I'm pretty sure all I need is proof that he's had his shots. But I'm glad you mentioned it. I need a favor."

"Whatever it is, it's probably easier than feeding your finicky cat every day."

"Could you get Hudson to let you into my office? I keep Macavity's records in my desk, lower drawer on the right. Then text a copy of his shot record to me."

"I can do that."

"Oh, and one other thing."

"What?"

"Please don't look at the mess."

"It's pretty bad," Logan chimed in. "But she really does know where everything is."

We could both envision the disgusted look on Judd's face when he opened the door to my office. He is super tidy, not someone to pile books on the floor or leave a layer of dust on everything. And far too fastidious to tolerate a spider web hanging in a window in order to monitor what the spider catches for its efforts. I thanked him profusely before we disconnected.

Logan made a face. "At least you weren't asking him to get something out of your locker." My locker is piled high with stuff I should throw out but keep for reasons that probably wouldn't pass the smell test. It gets less organized each year I put off going through what's in there. Now and again, I think of something I need and somehow manage to find it amidst the clutter. Proof that intermittent reinforcement really is a strong motivator. Or in this case, a de-motivator.

It was late when we arrived at Sucia, a horseshoe-shaped, uninhabited island in the San Juans, accessible only by water. There was very little wind, the water glassy calm. We anchored in Fossil Bay. There were several boats tied to the dock at the head of the bay and two on buoys near the dock. Once the motor was off and the constant hum ceased, it felt like we had entered another world. Voices floated across the water from the nearby campground and golden light flickered from bonfires. Surrounded by water with rocks and trees along the shore, there was the sense of isolation from the civilized world, in spite of knowing there were other people nearby.

Macavity circled the boat three times before resigning himself to the fact that he wasn't going ashore unless he was willing to swim. Assuming he didn't get desperate enough to test his swimming skills, I didn't feel it was necessary to keep him confined to quarters while at anchor. Even though there wasn't much territory for him to wander. It was a bit like Bubbles V and friend in their goldfish bowl, except Macavity was trapped on board by the surrounding water, not trapped *in* the water by a glass wall. But trapped was trapped, especially for a cat used to his freedom.

Logan and I had pastrami sandwiches and a fruit salad for dinner. Macavity likes grapes but turns his nose up at most other fruit. He had pastrami and grapes for dinner and seemed quite pleased. After dinner we introduced him to a make-shift container made from aluminum foil filled with rice and beans. He glared at us to let us know he wasn't interested, but we hoped when he got desperate to go to the bathroom he would reconsider. Finally, he settled in at one end of the bench seats in the cockpit, closing his eyes instead of appreciating the intense pink sunset streaked with dramatic gray whimsy. I wished I could tell him to "enjoy it while you can."

The sun was peeking over the horizon when we pulled anchor and headed up the Strait of Georgia for Vancouver. It was another calm day on the water. That's not something you can count on, and although the *Aspara* is a good sea boat, it's still a lot more pleasant when the water isn't pushing at you from an uncomfortable direction. Under power, the *Aspara* is best on a bow quarter or in a straight following sea, and not at all good from a stern quarter. When you have a specific destination and limited time, you don't want to go too far off course to adapt for wind and sea conditions. So I was pleased that it was calm.

In the past, I'd chosen out of the way places to go through Canadian Customs to avoid other boat traffic and busy marinas. But we'd decided the easiest way to pick up Ellie was at the same place we went through customs. It didn't turn out to be easy though. False Creek Fisherman's Wharf was packed, and we had a hard time figuring out where to tie up. As soon as we found a spot, we called Customs. Then we called Ellie to let know which dock we were on. Macavity was below throwing a fit because his porthole was secured and the hatch buttoned up. We weren't taking a chance on losing him in Vancouver.

The Custom's official in her dark short-sleeved uniform smiled when she asked permission to come aboard. Going through customs always makes me nervous, even when I'm fairly certain I haven't violated any laws. Once I had a plant that I was forced to give up because you can't bring uncertified soil into Canada. Another time it was potatoes that I had removed from their original bag. It's easy to overlook something or to be unaware of a rule or a rule change. On this occasion we didn't have anything illegal on board, although we knew that might become problematic once Ellie joined us.

Canada allows registered rifles and bear spray, a potent form of pepper spray, for personal protection against wildlife in remote areas. But it prohibits regular pepper spray and brass knuckles. We didn't care about the brass knuckle ban, but we'd decided we wanted three bear pepper sprays, one each. We realized they wouldn't be much good against a gun, but we didn't anticipate running into armed bears. And if we needed to spray a person, it was likely it wouldn't be in a crowded area where we would get caught.

The agent filled out her form, said she would need to see my rifle and the ammunition for it, and asked if we had any pets onboard. I got out my phone and showed her Macavity's shot records. She seemed satisfied, mentioned the processing fee for pet registration, and said that PayPal was fine. The only thing left to do was open the hatch without letting Macavity escape so I could show her the rifle and ammunition for it.

"We need to keep my cat inside," I explained as I prepared to open the hatch. "Logan, stand by."

The agent took a step back.

"He's fine; I mean, he's not aggressive. He just doesn't like being kept inside."

I braced myself for a speeding ball of orange fur to come screaming out of the main salon, so when I cautiously slid back the hatch and nothing happened, I started to worry that he'd found another way out. Maybe he developed a superpower and could pass through walls.

I went below while the agent watched and Logan stood at the ready to stop the orange bullet. When I found Macavity sleeping in the sunshine on what was soon to be Ellie's bunk, I was incredibly relieved. He barely opened his eyes as I removed the rifle and ammunition from the closet.

After checking the rifle, the agent gave us her blessing, and within minutes after she left, Ellie arrived. We left her stuff in the cockpit while we untied. I didn't want to chance Macavity being awake and ready for a prison break.

It was the official start of our expedition, aka vacation. Everything we needed to know about our destinations was in our heads; we'd put nothing on paper. And there was nothing on our cell phones that could give away our real intention. Except for a fold-up shovel that fit in a pack, there was absolutely nothing to suggest we planned on looking for buried treasure.

on vacation

The weather was perfect, and we were in good spirits as we pulled away from the dock. Once under way, I opened the hatch and Macavity streaked up onto the deck with a burst of energy that suggested he was about to catapult himself into orbit. After he circled the deck a few times and assured himself that there was a watery barrier between him and land, he came over to me and actually swatted me with a paw. He kept his claws in though, so I assumed he'd settle for a treat rather than a fight.

"Next stop where there's a grocery," I said. "We'll see what we can find."

"What does he like?" Ellie asked. "I have some jerky—it might not be that good for him, but just this once?" She looked at me for approval. Macavity was also staring at me. There was no way I could deny him something to chew on. Even though as a stowaway he had forfeited most of his rights. Like the right to rations of his choice.

"Will we be sailing a lot?" Ellie asked. She had been on day trips on boats before, but nothing like what we were embarking on. If the *Aspara* could manage more than seven knots, it wouldn't have been such a big ordeal. As it was, we'd charted our course carefully in order to cover enough ground each day to reach our destinations within Ellie's time frame, even though our actual paper charts didn't show our efforts with compass, parallel rule, and dividers. You can't tell everyone you're going with whatever strikes your fancy and then have every leg of your journey visibly mapped out. We might invite the wrong person on board, or someone might sneak a look. We were taking every precaution we could think of to avoid giving away our true purpose for the trip.

"We'll be bucking a lot going north and will probably have to motor most of the time. Maybe some motor sailing occasionally. But it's a long way to any of the most likely spots. We may need to pretend we just love twelve-hour days of motoring."

"I won't mind. I have my Kindle and am looking forward to the scenery."

"You'll also be taking your turn at the helm. You're a working member of the crew, you know."

"Sounds good to me."

"By the way, I have a GPS tracking device that my parents insist I turn on when I'm out alone, and I promised them—and Judd, that I'd use it for this trip. It's a good safety device. What that means though is that anyone could track us if they want to. Even follow from a distance using the tracker."

"But it reinforces the idea that we're on vacation, right?"

"That's what I'm thinking. Although some of our long runs may seem suspicious to someone used to more leisurely boat trips."

"I did tell my Aunt Regina that I'd like to go as far up the Inside Passage as possible in the time we have."

"Let's hope she found that convincing. It's a reasonable goal."

Five and a half hours later we were at our first stop, Secret Cove. We made our way past the buoy that marked the entrance to the harbor and anchored up inside Turnagain Island. Ellie had a book by a woman who kayaked from Anacortes to Juneau, and another on cruising the Inside Passage. But she couldn't find anything about Secret Cove in either of them, and her cell didn't have reception. "Damn, I thought I would educate myself about the history of each place as we went along."

"Live in the moment," Logan said. "We can row over to the dock and stretch our legs."

"Do you think I need to put Macavity below?" I asked as he rubbed up against me. Did he sense we were talking about leaving him behind?

"Do you think a rope tied to his collar is something he would tolerate?" Logan asked.

I thought about it. "We could try. Otherwise, we'll need to keep him locked up every time we get off the boat." I went below to cut a piece of light, 3/16th synthetic rope to the right length, long enough to give him some leeway and short enough to hopefully keep him under control.

Logan and Ellie got the dinghy down while I tied the rope to Macavity's collar. He let me do it, but he glared at me as if he understood—and didn't like—what was about to happen. "I've seen people walking their cats," I told him. But I had to admit I always thought it looked ridiculous.

Logan got in first, then Ellie. I handed Macavity down to Ellie. He didn't panic, but I could feel his body tense and his legs went stiff as I lifted him over the side. Then I got aboard, and we were off.

When we reached the dock, Logan tied up while Ellie and I got Macavity ashore. "If we're going to be doing a lot of this," I told him, "I'm putting you on a diet." Macavity gave me a disdainful look before trying to take off, coming up short when he reached the end of his rope. Literally. He turned back, looked at the rope, and yowled. I thought he was saying, "Get this thing off me," but I wasn't sure.

"You'll get used to it," Ellie said as she bent down to rub his head. Macavity shook her off and started up again, tugging at his leash.

"This is going to be fun," I said.

Logan was laughing. "We could threaten to make him walk the plank if he doesn't behave."

"Nice cat," someone coming toward us down the dock said with a smirk.

"Yes, he is," I said, ignoring the barb.

"Hey." Logan pointed at a large building to our right. "I think that's a restaurant. I can see people eating on that outside deck on the second floor."

"Think they accept cats?"

"Worth a try. We can always take him back to the boat."

We were pleasantly surprised that not only was Macavity allowed in the restaurant's outside seating area, he was welcome. The waiter who showed us to our table called him a "handsome critter," and the person who came to take our order leaned down and tried to pet him. Macavity drew back, avoiding contact. I explained that this was a new experience for him and he was a bit uneasy. Actually, "uneasy" wasn't the word; "furious" was more like it. Especially when he realized he was confined to a small space under the table during our dinner. He was somewhat mollified when we started giving him tastes of the ling cod, clams, and salmon we ordered. He even liked the fingerling potatoes. By the time the trip was over, he was going to be one spoiled, two-ton kitty.

There was another minor crisis at bedtime when Macavity realized he didn't have his bunk to himself. Ellie apologized to him while I picked him up and took him to his new "bed," a bath towel on the settee. He refused to stay put and wandered over to the half berth only to find it occupied. Then he crawled under the table and pouted, a true martyr.

In the morning, I found him snuggled down in his bath towel. Although he was definitely not happy about getting underway before being fed.

Still playing tourists, we headed for Refuge Cove. It wasn't far, a seven-hour motor trip up the length of the Strait of Georgia. There wasn't so much as a whisper of wind, which was in many ways nice. It would have been miserable if we'd had to buck a stiff northwesterly. As it was, we had a relaxed breakfast, took turns at the helm, and enjoyed the sunshine and backdrop of trees and hills stretching into the distance.

When we arrived, we tied to the fuel dock at Refuge Cove and topped off the tanks. Then we moved to another dock so we could see about buying cat food and litter at the small store at the top of the walkway attached to the dock. The store stretched out over the water on pilings, some of which had seen better days. With its weathered planking and huge wood storefront sign that read "Refuge Cove General Store," it looked like vintage Wild West. Inside, it offered customers a potpourri of boater needs, including tackle, T-shirts, books, charts, ice, groceries, and some hardware. Everything except for Macavity's favorite treats and food. Although they did carry "cat litter pellets." The picture on the bag did not look inviting; Macavity might decide he preferred rice and beans.

I bought the pellets, a Rubbermaid dishpan to put them in, and a 14.2-lb bag of Meow Mix Seafood Medley. I would have bought a smaller bag of cat food if they'd had it. The weight didn't make sense—why the extra .2 lbs.? It was too much cat food even at 14 lbs., but at 14.2 lbs. it seemed like way too much. And since I was pretty sure Macavity would rather go hungry than eat dry cat food, I also bought a couple cans of tuna, two of canned chicken and one labeled "beef chunks." The latter was loaded with sodium but at least it wasn't mystery meat. Macavity had once turned down a sliver of fried Spam, letting me know I have pedestrian tastes because I love fried Spam chunks. Anyway, I figured I could mix some protein in with the dry cat food to make it more palatable.

With our bag of cat supplies in hand, we strolled to the Refuge Cove Galley, checked out the local crafts and bought a few postcards. On the way back to the boat we stopped at a dockside deli and bought a pizza. We were roughing it.

Refuge Cove was a busy place, and the best spots for

anchoring were already taken, so we headed across to Squirrel Cove. There were quite a few boats there, too, but the weather forecast was good, so we didn't have to be fussy. We found a spot in the outer harbor and settled in for the evening. Macavity ignored his Meow Mix and went from Logan to Ellie to me begging for pepperoni and sausage from our pizza. The pizza aroma hung overhead like low fog. I understood Macavity's mission, and although I tried to be strong, I failed completely.

While we were eating, several eagles flew overhead, then perched high in the trees that lined the outer harbor, eyes alert for their dinner. "You'd better behave," I told Macavity. "You could be mistaken for a large salmon filet."

That night Macavity headed for his towel on the settee without a fuss. He may be petulant at times, but he knows when to accept defeat.

Monday was a long slog from Squirrel Cove all the way to Alert Bay. We left at first light and arrived before dark, but not by much. We tied to the dock and attached Macavity's leash to the wheel so he could be with us as we sat back and enjoyed the day's end. Since we had eaten earlier to break up the boredom of the long day under power, all we were having was wine. There was nothing for Macavity to beg from us, which he apparently found very disconcerting, glaring at each of us in turn instead of enjoying the quiet that descends once the engine is off. Earlier I'd given him his first meal of dry cat food mixed with canned meat. He'd taken one sniff before retreating under the table. Occasionally I'd glance below from the cockpit and see him come out from under the table and check his food bowl in case something better had appeared. After verifying that nothing had changed, he returned to his under-the-table hideout. Based on this response, maybe instead of gaining weight he might be a lot lighter when we returned home.

We decided not to leave early the next day but to spend the morning in Alert Bay. It's a small First Nations village with a cultural center that Ellie had read about and wanted to visit. Because there were a lot of trails nearby, we talked about whether we should take a short hike to establish a pattern to camouflage our real search for the cave, although as far as we could tell, we weren't being followed by a flock of treasure hunters or bad guys. We were feeling safe.

We left Macavity securely tucked away on the boat and walked to the U'mista Cultural Centre, an impressive wood building with large totems guarding a covered entry. Inside we were pleased to find an exhibit featuring the history of the Potlatch, a celebration in which possessions are given away to enhance prestige. We lingered over the pictures and displays, reading and commenting to each other on their captions. The Potlatch was once banned because it was considered a heathen practice and an impediment to progress. Yet now the cultural practice and its artifacts are usually portrayed as a celebration of the past.

On the way out we stopped at the gift shop and Ellie bought a print by Andy Everson that made me sorry I didn't have a place to hang pictures on my boat. I drooled over a raven plaque that I couldn't quite imagine in my ramshackle office. Logan bought a killer whale mug by a Tsimshian native artist for Judd, while I settled for a raven tea towel. I'm fond of raven designs by native artists, and I appreciate functional art.

The only place open for lunch was a fair distance away on the other side of the marina, so we decided to have a few snacks en route and then have an early dinner in Port Hardy. We had to go into town when we got there anyway because it would most likely be my last chance to find something my picky cat would eat. It was also our last chance to play tourist before we transformed ourselves into treasure hunters.

CHAPTER 22

set free!

It was only four hours to Port Hardy at the northern tip of Vancouver Island, but bucking into a stiff northwest wind was not pleasant. Macavity stayed below, while the three of us hunkered in the cockpit. We couldn't read or relax because we were bouncing in the chop, occasionally lurching side to side, and frequently dodging spray. When we finally got to Port Hardy, we were all relieved to tie to a dock that was only bobbing slightly from wind gusts sneaking into the protected harbor.

Macavity wasn't pleased about being left behind again; it took some gymnastic moves to get out of the boat without letting him escape. "You'll thank me for this if we find some food for you," I told him as I pushed his orange paw back inside before pulling the hatch shut.

"You really believe that?" Logan asked.

"No, he'll be complaining about this trip for months," I said. "No matter what kind of food I come up with."

The walk into town wasn't long; nor was it a nature adventure. It was a mix of industrial and retail with some residential. When we found the grocery, I was pleased to discover they carried both Fancy Feast and Temptations cat food products. With English *and* French descriptions. Macavity might become bilingual on our trip. I purchased two pouches of seafood medley treats but couldn't find his usual Fancy Feast meals. His palate would either adjust to shredded wild salmon and turkey Tuscany or he would be reduced to begging for table food.

Once Macavity's needs were taken care of, we found a small café that served local seafood. Logan and I had ours fried while Ellie asked for grilled. Hers came with a vegetable, ours with French fries which can, I believe, still be classified as a vegetable.

We were relaxed and happy as we headed down the dock toward the *Aspara*'s mast. Masts are as distinctive as faces, and I always feel a sense of well-being knowing my boat is where I left it. However, everything changed the instant I unlocked the hatch and went inside. Macavity wasn't there. He had vanished.

"How is that possible?" Logan said as Ellie checked the boat one more time, even looking in places he couldn't possibly be.

"There was no way he could have gotten out," I said. "The portholes are still latched, the anchor locker is closed, and the hatch was padlocked. He's a clever cat, but he's not Houdini."

Ellie said, "Let's worry about the 'how' later. We have to find him."

"Let's split up," Logan suggested. "I'll search to the end of this dock. Ellie, you check other nearby docks, and Bryn, you start along the shore. We can stay in touch by phone."

I was only a few boats down the dock headed toward shore when a child's voice said, "You're not looking for the orange cat, are you?" She was sitting in the aft cockpit of a large cruiser. A miniature mariner in white and navy blue.

"Yes, have you seen him?" I felt a rush of hope.

"I saw him leave when that man went into your boat. He ran toward shore."

Man? Fighting to remain calm, I asked, "What did the man look like?"

"You know, like a man."

"Dark hair? Blond? Tall? Short?"

She pursed her lips so hard I was afraid her face would crack. Then she smiled and said, "I don't know. Just an old man."

I thanked her and headed for land. Someone had broken into my boat and had been careful enough to put the lock back. As if I wouldn't notice my cat was gone. We should have known better than to assume we were safe just because we hadn't seen anyone following us. Now I wasn't sure what to do. How do you find a cat who is anxious to be on his own after being cooped up for days? Was he out getting some exercise? Searching for something to eat? Or looking for trouble?

Even in a strange place, I assumed he would be able to find his way back, so if he got hungry enough, maybe he would return for his dinner. I only wished he knew he had more than dry cat food waiting for him.

Eventually Logan and Ellie caught up with me and we divvied up the territory again. I didn't mention "the old man" yet; there would be time later to discuss what that meant for our trip. Macavity was our first priority. Would he stay near the water? Follow the road? Explore buildings? There were just too many possibilities. I headed away from town along the shore while Logan and Ellie took separate routes toward town.

The day was starting to fade when I got a call from Logan. For a moment, I thought he was going to say "I found him." Instead, he said, "It will be dark soon. I think we should go back." I didn't want to give up, but I knew he was right.

I was the first one back. As I approached the *Aspara* I realized that in my panic over discovering Macavity was gone, I had left the hatch open. Great. What if some other unwelcome visitors had come and helped themselves to whatever they liked?

When I stepped aboard and glanced below, I felt a surge of happiness. There, sitting next to his empty food bowl was my runaway stowaway. "Macavity!" I quickly went down the stairs and picked him up. He wanted food, not hugs, but this was *my* reward for finding him. Well, technically I didn't find him, but it all came down to the same thing.

I closed the hatch and called Logan. He and Ellie had met up and were almost to the dock. There was barely time to give Macavity some shredded salmon and glance around to see if anything obvious was missing before they stepped aboard.

Macavity quickly gulped down his dinner, obviously pleased with the new fare, at least by comparison with his last meal. Ellie, Logan, and I gathered together on the settee watching Macavity finish his dining experience by washing his face before deciding to take an after-dinner nap on Logan's pillow.

Logan started to protest, but Ellie stopped him. "He's back; that's the important thing."

We continued to watch as Macavity made himself comfortable, smiling sappy smiles, like we were viewing a Disney film.

Suddenly I remember that I needed to tell them about the man the little girl had mentioned seeing. "Let's take a stroll," I said, holding a finger up to my lips. "I feel a need to stretch my legs some more." Although I hadn't thought it completely through, it seemed possible that whoever had broken in had been looking for a map, and after not finding one, perhaps they'd planted a bug or tracker on board. Although they'd obviously already been successful locating us.

Once away from the boat I told them about the man who had allowed Macavity to escape.

"We knew it was a possibility," Ellie said. "But he couldn't have found anything since there was nothing to find."

"Think he was tracking us with your GPS?" Logan asked.

"I thought we were in the clear. Wishful thinking."

"I assume from the way you shushed us that you assume the boat may be bugged. Why?" Ellie asked.

"Because that's what I'd do."

"If they put a bug somewhere, I think it would have to be inside the cabin," Logan said. "Too much weather and salt spray outside."

"Isn't there a distance issue?" Ellie asked.

'Yeah, I think so. I'm not sure how close they have to be to listen in. Just in case, we need to avoid mentioning anything about abandoned canneries or looking for treasure when we're inside."

"Are you going to turn off the GPS?" Ellie asked.

"That might send the wrong message, don't you think? Besides, it's too late for that."

"So, we let them follow us—assuming someone is," Logan said. "Avoid loose lips when in port, and keep an eye out."

"I hope they got a good look at our charts and noticed that there are no marks on it except where we've been on this trip so far. With a few notations about possible tourist attractions up the line."

"Should we search the boat for bugs when we get back?" Ellie asked.

"Let's wait until we're under way tomorrow. Tonight, let's chat a little about shopping in Port Hardy and call it a night. Act like the tourists we are."

We returned to the *Aspara* and went into performance mode. To me, we all sounded a bit strange, but if there was someone listening, they wouldn't know we weren't usually such stilted conversationalists. It was a good thing we were turning in early.

Tomorrow was going to be a long day of motoring. Maybe some motor sailing if the winds were right. We were aiming for either Namu or Bella Bella, depending on the weather. Leaving Port Hardy and heading across Queen Charlotte Sound in a small boat, even a seaworthy boat like the *Aspara*, can be harrowing. The waves may look small from a distance, but when you're rolling over them, rising to the top on a cresting wave before dropping into the trough where all you see is water, it can do things to your mind as well as to your stomach.

The sky was barely starting to lighten when we left, blue-gray and cool. We checked around the cockpit for listening devices but didn't find anything. Not that we were entirely sure what we were looking for. Then Logan and Ellie went below and continued the search, making stilted conversation again, avoiding anything that might give away our concerns or what we were intending to do next.

Macavity didn't like it when they interrupted his early morning nap to search *his* bunk. He'd made a beeline for it the instant Ellie got up. When she picked him up to move him to my side of the conjoined bunks, he howled in protest. For a cat who loved routine, life was not being kind.

It was daylight when we got to open water. As soon as we started fighting the waves, Ellie got seasick. She was sick all the way across the Sound, staying below in *her* bunk, holding a plastic bag full of processed breakfast. Logan was fine as long as he stayed at the helm. And I was fine as long as I didn't go below. Macavity was stretched out on the floor under the table, probably wondering why he hadn't stayed in Port Hardy.

Five hours later, we made it to calmer water behind Cape Calvert. The rest of the way was pleasant. Ellie came topside and managed to eat a slice of dry bread and drink some tea. Macavity came up to let me know he hadn't had breakfast yet, and I was able to go below to get him something to eat. We were making good time and decided to try for Bella Bella. If someone *was* following us, I hoped that they had been seasick all the way across the Sound.

The scenery up the channel was lovely, but after a while, all the tree-lined banks tended to look the same. And the steady drone of the engine was unrelenting. We resorted to snack food and taking turns at the helm to while away the hours, occasionally checking the radar to see if anyone was following close enough to be detected. No one was. We were convinced they were tracking us using my GPS. Or a device they may have planted in case I turned ours off. We took turns looking for a tracking device below, starting in the bow. But there were just too many hiding places. And again, we didn't know what we were looking for. The only thing we knew for sure was that they hadn't planted anything on Macavity, since they'd let him escape.

We were relieved to finally reach Bella Bella, a Heiltsuk village on Campbell Island. Arriving late, we were pleased—and amazed —to find a space at the dock. We didn't have to raft up and climb over other people's boats to get ashore. We all wanted to get off the boat and feel the ground beneath our feet. I decided to put Macavity on his leash and let him join us so he could be a land-lubber for a few minutes and so no intruder would let him out again.

We walked down the ferry dock and onto a road. Macavity seemed pleased to be outside, even while on a leash. I took a picture of a sign that said: *Welcome to Heiltsuk Territory Bella Bella*. It had native art on both ends and looked like it had been there a long time. The store we came to was closed, and there were no people around. It was starting to get dark, so we returned to the *Aspara*. We were all exhausted by the long day, even though we spent it sitting.

The next morning we considered walking around Bella Bella, maybe do a short hike to establish a pattern for potential observers to note, but again decided to keep moving. We had already skipped Namu and its abandoned cannery, and although Klem-tu's abandoned cannery was the least likely on our list of possibili-ties, stopping there would reinforce the idea that we liked exploring small villages and, at the same time, give us a chance to look around.

Six hours later we were approaching our destination, a village of the Kitasoo tribe of Tsimshians located in the Great Bear Rain-forest. We were pretty sure we would find a trail to hike there, and that would hopefully camouflage the hikes we had planned for our next two stops. Although I wasn't particularly excited about wandering into an area with the word bear in its name, especially armed with only one rifle, some bear bells, and three cannisters of bear spray. In the past, I always avoided possible encounters with wildlife, especially bears. I wasn't confident that I could stop a bear with a lucky rifle shot—and given my expertise with a rifle, it would *have* to be a lucky shot. Nor did having bear spray put me at ease. You weren't supposed to spray until you were at about the 25-foot mark, almost close enough to do a dental exam.

Most tourists stop at Klemtu to see their traditional Big House, but we were going to take a short hike and leave the next morning for Butedale. Another time I'd like to see the Big House. Pictures of it are very impressive.

We ate on the way to Klemtu so we wouldn't have to carry any food with us, just water, weapons, air whistles, light sources, a GPS, and our trusty folding shovel. As it turned out, there was plenty of room on the dock. We tied up, made sure Macavity was confined to quarters by tying him to the table stanchion, and headed off for our hike. We did manage to find a trail of sorts leading into the forest, but it didn't match the proximity to the abandoned cannery nor the terrain Uncle Wade had depicted. We followed it anyway for show. Logan had his handheld GPS with him in case we ran into trouble, but our main goal was to stay out of trouble. And to look like we were enjoying ourselves. It was a good thing there were no cameras in the woods.

I can't express how relieved I was when we arrived safely back at Klemtu. The first thing I did was release Macavity from bondage. Unlike me, he is quite capable of expressing his feelings when he's upset. He backed off with a loud, elongated yowl before retreating to the forward bunk, ignoring all of our entreaties, even the piece of jerky Ellie held out for him as compensation for being left alone and tied up for hours. He eventually came back to the main salon for dinner, but he still refused to have anything to do with us.

We prepared dinner on the boat, chatting casually about this and that, and went to bed early. Even though we hadn't mentioned it in case there were ears listening in, tomorrow was going to be a big day.

CHAPTER 23

a cave in the forest

Ellie only had three weeks of vacation a year and, given that she'd taken a week off when Uncle Wade died, we'd set two weeks as the outside limit to look for the treasure. Although we'd told everyone we were making it up as we went along and that Logan might not stay with us for the entire trip, that was not the plan. We were going to try to find the cave before Ellie's two weeks were up, and at the two-week mark, we would put her on a plane for home. Logan and I would finish out the return trip on our own. With the help of Macavity, of course.

We got up early and made it to Butedale before noon. Butedale was technically uninhabited, although we'd read that there were a few homesteaders nearby. Based on topography maps, it was one of our best leads. It had the prerequisite abandoned cannery, a hill behind the cannery leading to a lake, and hopefully a cave just beyond the lake to the northeast. We wouldn't know for sure until we hiked up there and had a look around.

The dock was empty when we arrived; there would probably be more boats later. Our packs were ready to go, so we quickly secured the boat, and I was about to lock up, when Macavity slipped out of the mostly closed hatch by compressing his body in

169

an unnatural way. He leapt onto the dock before I could stop him and turned into a bolt of orange lightning headed for land. "No!" I yelled. "Not again!"

"Sorry, I noticed his rope was coming loose. I should have done something about it." Ellie looked stricken.

"Don't worry. We'll find him," Logan said.

I locked the hatch, like closing the barn door after the horse has bolted, although in this case it was a crazy willful cat who had bolted, hightailed it, skedaddled, fled, taken off . . . with nary a glance back. T.S. Eliot had nailed it: he was "a fiend in feline shape."

At the top of the ramp, Ellie went left and I went right while Logan headed uphill. There was a scattering of old buildings lining the shore, beyond them nothing but trees, an impenetrable looking mass of evergreens. First, I searched for Macavity along the shore, then I headed up the hill to what appeared to be the main cannery building. It was pretty dilapidated. Some of the exterior wall boards were missing or canted outwards, and a short flight of stairs had partially collapsed. I was starting to get really worried. What if Macavity fell through rotted floorboards and was trapped? Or, what if he was attacked by a wild animal? He was a scrapper, but he was still a city cat.

When I caught a glimpse of something orange disappear around the corner of the building, I was fairly certain it was a wayward cat and not a quick red fox. I picked up my pace. I also registered movement near the edge of the clearing to my right but didn't stop to get a better look.

As I rounded the end of the building, there he was, sitting there, looking at me as if to say, "What took you so long?" When he didn't resist letting me pick him up, I wondered if there were smells in the area that made him hesitant to wander further on his own. Maybe he was making a point about being in charge of his own destiny. Or maybe he was becoming lazy and had run far enough. "You silly cat," I said, rubbing his ears. "Please don't keep doing this."

When I got back to the end of the building, I remembered the movement near the tree line, paused and peeked around the corner in time to see a man heading toward the beach, staying in the shadow of the trees. There was something furtive about his actions, although he couldn't have been following us if he was already here. It was more likely that he was a homesteader, a squatter, or a hunter.

I caught sight of Ellie in the distance and waved at her. Moments later, Logan came out from a ramshackle building, saw me carrying my orange bundle and started back down the hill.

It didn't take long to secure Macavity and start out all over again. I did note that there was another boat tied at the end of the dock, although I didn't see anyone around. It was about a 35-foot cruiser. The name on the stern was the *Jolly Roger*. I tried to remember if I'd seen it in Port Hardy and didn't think I had.

"Did you see who was on that cruiser when it came in?" I asked Ellie and Logan as we headed toward the abandoned cannery. They both shook their heads "no." Like me, they had been so focused on finding Macavity that they hadn't noticed. I told them about the man I had seen, and we started speculating.

"Someone could be on our tail. But ahead of us? We never referred to Butedale, did we?"

"It's possible they were clever enough to anticipate where we were headed. There aren't that many places of interest to stop around here."

"Maybe they *were* ahead of us and turned back once they saw where we were stopping."

There were lots of possibilities but no real answers. "I say we take some extra precautions but stay with our plan," Logan said.

"Extra precautions?" I asked. "What are you suggesting?"

"When we get near where we think the cave might be, I'll split with the rifle and stay out of sight on the trail."

"What will you do if someone shows up? Shoot them?"

Ignoring my sarcasm, he said, "First, I'll put some distance between me and whoever I see, then use the air whistle to warn you. Two short blasts. Ellie can be your lookout at the cave, Bryn. Assuming you find one. If she hears the whistle and you don't, she can let you know."

"I'm not sure I can go into a cave." Ellie's voice was tight, and her breathing suddenly became shallow.

"You won't have to," I said. "Just yell."

"What if there *is* a cave, but they spot Logan and take a different route and show up with a gun while you're inside?" Ellie's panic-driven description of the worst-case scenario was definitely disturbing.

"Look, given the number of steps or distances listed on the Gollum rock, the cave must be pretty good-sized. If someone gets past Logan, you need to give two whistle blasts to let him and me know, Ellie. With luck, I can hide until Logan gets there with the rifle. If not, I'll have bear spray and a shovel to protect myself."

I didn't feel as brave as I was trying to sound for Ellie's sake, but I was fairly optimistic about our chances of avoiding a confrontation. If I were following us, I would wait until *after* we found the treasure before attacking. My guess was that the same thought had occurred to Logan, but it wasn't something that Ellie needed to hear if she hadn't ready considered the possibility.

Logan said, "If it's any comfort, I won't hesitate to shoot."

"You won't hesitate to shoot, but can you hit what you're aiming at?" Ellie asked, only half kidding.

"I suggest you hit the deck if I start shooting," he said lightly. "If there are stalagmites, Bryn, hide behind one . . . if you're still in the cave when I start shooting, that is."

"You're trying to make it sound less dangerous than it may be," Ellie said.

"I understand why you're having second thoughts," I said. "But if we don't do this, we'll never know if Uncle Wade's dream was real."

Ellie took a couple of deep breaths, slowly exhaling. "Sorry. You two have been so supportive. We're here; let's do it."

A little adrenaline rush can be helpful, but too much can

make you jumpy and cloud decision making. Like Ellie, I was worried about the possibility of someone tailing us, but I really wanted to see if there was a cave beyond the lake. And if there was, I couldn't imagine simply walking away without following the directions I had memorized leading to the X.

We found what appeared to be a fairly well-traveled trail behind the main cannery building. It ran alongside a stream that came from above. The path was narrow, with spaced out splotches of vegetation. I was in the lead. We hadn't gone far when I noticed a print in the dirt. "Oh, oh," I said, squatting down to study the print. "Five toes, about six inches long, narrow trail." I looked at Ellie and Logan. "You know what that means."

"I already noticed a couple of prints back a way," Logan said. "But we'd be more likely to encounter a bear in the early morning or later in the day."

"Bears?" Ellie's voice cracked. "Now we have to worry about bears? Bryn, do you have your bear spray handy?"

"I think they pick off the last one in line," I said, keeping my tone light. "You're in the best spot . . . until they snatch Logan."

"Killer bears and killer treasure seekers," Logan said. "We've got it all."

I would have felt reassured by Logan's kidding if I hadn't known that's how he handles situations when he's nervous. "Where are those bear bells?" I asked. "They need to hear us coming." I had no faith that the bells would ward off bears, but it was the only preventive tool we had. And if someone *was* following us, they already knew where we were.

Ellie searched in her pack until she found the bells. She and I hung one each on our packs before continuing, like a couple of Salvation Army volunteers, but hoping to *deter* rather than *entice* attention. Logan declined; he wanted to stay silent once he let us go on ahead.

After about a half hour we came to an embankment above the lake. To the right was a stretch of open trail that eventually disappeared into the trees. According to the picture from the bathroom, the cave wasn't far from the lake, but unless the trail led right up to it, it might be hard to find.

Logan decided to hang out near where the trail re-entered the trees. With the lake to his right and a large clearing, it was a good vantage point. Ellie and I continued on, a growing sense of anticipation and anxiety churning in my stomach.

The surroundings looked like what Uncle Wade had painted. There was even a giant Douglas fir at a sharp turn in the trail. I noted the bear marks on the tree but didn't call them out to Ellie. Did bears hang out in caves during the day?

When the trail veered to the left, we could see a small hill ahead. If the picture was accurate, the cave should be directly in front of us near the base of the hill. I'm not much of a bushwhacker, but the underbrush wasn't dense, and as we got close, it wasn't hard to spot a gaping black hole about twenty feet up the rocky hillside.

Eureka!

We decided it was best if Ellie remained out of sight in a clump of trees at the bottom. Although it seemed unlikely to me that someone would know where we were at this point, there was still plenty of reason for caution. Ellie's forehead was beaded with sweat. "Look at the trees and the trail, not at the cave," I advised. She nodded weakly and took up a position next to a large red cedar with her back to the cave entrance, a whistle in her right hand, bear spray in the left.

When I reached the opening, I got a headlamp out of my pack, took a deep breath, and held it a few seconds to soothe my nerves, silently repeated the directions I'd memorized and moved from sunlight into the dark recesses of the cave. It was instantly about ten degrees cooler. I paused to let my eyes adjust to the dim interior.

I knew from our research that Vancouver Island had the largest concentration of caves in North America, and I had studied images of the most popular ones, but I was still unprepared for the cave's high ceiling and impressive limestone formations. As I looked around to get my bearings, I noted that the uneven floor was littered with rocks of all shapes and sizes, but no stalagmites. And thankfully, as far as I could tell, I wasn't disturbing a den of sleeping animals.

Counting my steps, I headed in. That seemed like the most logical reading of the numbers on the Gollum figure. And since I'm tall, I assumed that my step length would be at least close to my uncle's. As I navigated the uneven surface, I began to wish I'd brought a pick-axe rather than a shovel. What if I reached "the spot" and the ground was too hard to dig with a camp shovel?

At the point where I was supposed to turn left, there was a huge pile of rubble straight ahead. Then beyond it, I was able to turn right as directed. It was all looking good. The final steps took me to a location near the cave wall about mid-way back. When I reached the metaphoric X, it looked as though someone had already been digging there. A patch of untrammeled dirt stood out in the middle of an otherwise rocky surface. Was this where Uncle Wade had dug up the coin he left in the container of tea? My hands were shaking as I removed the shovel from my pack. This was the moment of truth.

Twenty minutes later I returned to the entrance, climbed down the rocks, and found Ellie right where I left her. I held a finger to my lips and motioned for her to follow me. She obediently fell into step behind me as I headed back toward the trail on a circuitous route through the brush. Once on the trail, we'd gone about a hundred yards when Ellie came up close behind me and asked in a low voice, "Well?" It seemed to me that she'd shown tremendous restraint. I'm not sure I could have waited that long even if admonished to remain silent.

"There's something there," I whispered.

"What does that mean?"

I stopped, turned to her, and kept my voice low. "The ground was so hard I was barely able to dig. I needed a better shovel. I did, however, find a gold coin and a ring about eight inches down. The area had been dug up before but tamped down pretty good. Then I started thinking it might be wise to leave them there and come back another time. But we can talk about that later. We need to get going."

"But you think this is the spot?" she asked my back.

I gave her a thumb's up.

Since it was downhill, it didn't take us long before we reached Logan. He hadn't seen anyone, and I quickly filled him in on what I had found and the unilateral decision I'd made. He agreed, said he'd had similar thoughts while watching the trail. It was going to be hard not knowing what I might have found if I'd been able to dig a little deeper, but at least we had succeeded in finding the spot.

"Ellie, when we get back you can contact the guy you know at the Museum of Anthropology and give him the coin you found in the tea as proof. I wish I could at least have taken a picture of the ring, but I didn't want it on my phone. It looked a lot like the one from the safety deposit box though."

"You're right. If someone is following us, they could attack and grab our packs or search the boat again."

"I thought about that before, but it really hit home when I realized we definitely have the right place."

"Leaving whatever we found there should probably have been our plan all along."

We continued on, half expecting to be ambushed before making it back to Butedale. But we weren't. The *Jolly Roger* was still at the dock when we returned, with no one visible. There was also a large sailboat tied up across from the cruiser, and we saw a couple with two children roaming the shore. It would be interesting to see which boat they returned to. We left our packs on the cabin roof while Ellie and I went below for drinks and Logan walked down to the end of the dock to check out the other boats. A natural thing to do. We decided that if someone was watching, we didn't want them to think we had something valuable in our packs.

We gathered in the cockpit with sodas and a very unhappy cat on a leash. Then we walked up the dock with Macavity, as if giving him a little exercise and emphasizing how little regard we had for what was in our packs. We didn't bother taking them below until after dinner in the cockpit, a thrown together meal because we were too tired to do better. While we were eating, the family returned, pausing briefly to say hello before following their children back to the sailboat.

Around midnight I got up to go to the bathroom and looked out of the porthole at the end of the dock where the cruiser was moored. In the light of the half-moon, I saw someone rowing a dinghy toward the *Jolly Roger*. Then a man climbed aboard and two men hauled the dinghy up and hung it off to the side on a pair of davits. I couldn't see facial features and nothing stood out for me other than that it was a strange time to be out rowing a dinghy back from shore.

The next morning we left before the cruiser did, and although I thought I saw a face at a window as we motored past, I couldn't swear to it. If they were somehow tracking us, I wondered if they would show up at the Hot Springs, our next stop.

CHAPTER 24

hot springs

It was only three hours from Butedale to the Hot Springs at Bishop Bay in the Monkey Beach Conservancy. The Hot Springs can only be reached by boat or float plane. We thought of the area as being remote and were surprised at the number of boats anchored in the bay when we arrived. Although we were hoping to enjoy a soak, we also considered this isolated location another diversion for anyone tracking us.

"Looks like there may be some competition for enjoying a bath," Logan said.

"I don't think you're supposed to use it for bathing," Ellie commented.

"I read you can use soap and shampoo in the outer pool. Then you are clean for the inside pool."

"Kind of like a Japanese bath house or sauna."

"Except I bet people using those are much cleaner to begin with—they aren't coming from days spent on small boats with limited bathing facilities."

"I doubt Judd would go for it," Logan observed.

"Well, *we* are going to," I said. "I read that the flow is over eight gallons per minute with water temperatures over 100 degrees Fahrenheit. Sounds good to me."

We decided to take the dinghy ashore rather than raft up at the dock. I left a bowl of treats out for Macavity and hoped he didn't have to entertain visitors or decide to take a swim. But today was one time I definitely couldn't take him with us. After our trip to the hot springs, we were planning on disappearing into the woods for a while. As far as we knew, there were no official trails in the conservancy, but a lot of people did wilderness camping in the area, so we anticipated we would find a trail without too much trouble. We left the rifle on the *Aspara* because we didn't want to deal with it while we were in the bathhouse, but we were equipped with bear bells and spray.

Once ashore it was a short walk on a well-maintained boardwalk to the bathhouse. The pool was smaller than we anticipated, so we were pleased to find its current inhabitants getting ready to leave. Once they were on their way, the three of us crowded into the changing room and stripped down to our bathing suits. Ellie and I headed straight for the indoor pool, while Logan took a bar of soap and made for the outdoor pool.

"Join us after you get clean," Ellie called after him.

There was a single pipe shooting hot water into a space that was about half the size of a backyard swimming pool and barely three feet deep. A collection of boat floats and flags dangled from the ceiling, and people had carved their initials in the wood posts supporting the roof. Other than that, all you had to look at was the gorgeous view and the steam coming off the water. After over a week of long days and tension, it was blissful.

When Logan joined us, the three of us clung to the edge of the pool while taking in the view and luxuriating in the warmth of the water. We lingered longer than we should have. Our leave-taking was encouraged by several other people showing up to indulge themselves. We left reluctantly but refreshed.

We'd decided in advance that heading in the opposite direction from the hot springs on the boardwalk past the camping platforms made the most sense for our incursion into the woods. Campers seemed more likely than bathers to go for a hike in the wilderness. When we reached the ramp leading to the dock, we paused to check out the boats in the harbor. The *Aspara* was barely moving at anchor, and we thought we could see an orange blob on the cabin roof. "He's sunning himself," Ellie said.

"Or getting sunstroke," I said.

Logan was scanning the bay. "I see a couple of cruisers anchored out, but I don't think the *Jolly Roger* is here."

"Well, we need to play this out just in case. The *Jolly Roger* may not even be the right boat."

The boardwalk led us to some wood camping platforms that were piled high with gear. There were people sitting on folding chairs alongside one of the tents. We waved as we went by, beyond the boardwalk, hoping to find a trail to justify a hike into the woods. When Logan spotted what could have been an animal trail angling off up the hill, we didn't hesitate. After all, we only needed to be gone long enough to indicate that we considered a short hike in the wilderness a typical vacation activity for us.

After about twenty minutes the trail petered out at a small clearing next to a stream. There was a fallen log that looked inviting. We accepted the invitation and sat down to enjoy the food we brought with us to pass the time.

When we heard noise in the brush off to one side, we all stopped eating. "Maybe we shouldn't have brought food with us," Ellie said. "Animals have a keen sense of smell."

Logan picked up his pack and rang his bear bell.

"If that's a bear out there, I hope he doesn't think that's a call to dinner," I said.

"If it's a predator, we put down our food and back off," Logan said.

"And hope we don't end up as the main course."

A bird flew up out of the bushes, and everything was suddenly still.

"I don't care if it was only a bird. Next time it might be a bear," Ellie said. "I don't want to add another phobia to my repertoire."

"We've probably been gone long enough anyway."

"We don't even know if anyone cares."

"Quiet," Logan whispered, holding up his hand for us to stop talking.

We heard people coming in our direction. I reached for my bear spray, as did Logan. Ellie looked like she was about to make a run for it. Then we heard laughter, and I felt my muscles relax. "Sounds like hikers," I said as two people popped into the clearing. They stopped when they saw us. And smiled.

"Hi. We were wondering if there were any more camping spots in this direction."

"Right here might be good," I said. The ground was level, there was running water, and a place to sit. "Unless you're worried about bears."

"Nah, I'm told if you don't surprise them on a trail, they won't bother you." He held out his hand. "I'm Blue by the way, and this is Reena."

Logan shook his hand and gave them our first names before adding, "I've heard about bears dragging campers out of their tents at night."

Blue hesitated. "You're kidding, right?"

"No, I'm saying it pays to be careful. Well, we need to be going." Logan picked up his pack, and Ellie and I picked up ours.

"Have fun," Ellie said as we headed back the way we had come.

Once we were out of earshot, I said, "That was rude."

"I agree," Logan said. "But that guy's macho behavior puts both of them at risk. It's like people taking selfies at the edge of a cliff to get a shot of themselves in a dramatic location. Why take the risk? Better to play it safe."

"Like *us* playing it safe," I said.

"Ouch," Ellie snickered.

"Okay, point taken. I need to chill."

"And I would like one more chance at heating up," Ellie said.

"Let's see if we can get in the bathhouse again before the evening rush."

We managed about a fifteen-minute soak before a crowd lined up on the boardwalk, waiting their turn. There were no time limits posted, but it didn't feel right to stay when this was our second time.

We rowed along the shore a way just for fun—and to check out the other boats—before returning to the *Aspara*. As we climbed aboard, Macavity came to greet us. He rubbed against Logan and Ellie, ignoring me. "Okay, Macavity, I get it," I said. "You're still mad at me. But you brought it on yourself."

The sun was shining overhead. There wasn't so much as a ripple on the water. And best of all, we'd accomplished our mission. The only bad thing was not being able to talk about what was really on our minds for fear of being overheard. We read for a while, Ellie and I stretched out in the cockpit, Logan on the bow, his back against the cabin. In that moment, it felt like we were three friends on vacation together. Later, Logan fixed dinner and we ate outside, Macavity joining us after devouring his own dinner, still hoping for more. Everyone gave him a little something. Together we watched the sun go down.

Tomorrow was a long slog to Bella Bella, and the next day to the last abandoned cannery on our tour. Even though we had already crossed the Namu cannery off our virtual list.

CHAPTER 25

blindsided

For the second time we arrived in Bella Bella after everything was closed. It was barely still light. We had already eaten dinner and decided to take a very short walk to stretch our legs before calling it a night. Macavity wasn't thrilled about going with us, but once on the dock, he seemed to enjoy himself.

We were looking forward to reaching Port Hardy the day after tomorrow. Ellie was hoping to catch a plane to Vancouver from there. She was anxious to get home and get the ball rolling with UBC. Logan and I could decide the details of our return trip after that. But we, too, were starting to look forward to getting back. We hadn't seen the *Jolly Roger* since leaving Butedale, but we were still avoiding talk about the treasure when in the cabin or when other boats were around.

When we left the following morning, we looked for the cruiser but didn't see it. It could have been anchored out of sight nearby, or we could even be looking out for the wrong boat, so we didn't assume we were entirely in the clear. There didn't seem to be any option other than trying to act natural and continue our trip. After all, whoever had broken in didn't know that we knew about it.

Barring any sudden weather changes or mechanical problems, we anticipated we would make it to Namu in time for a little exploring. And since we were clearly heading south, we thought it possible that any followers might take advantage of our absence to search the *Aspara*. I hated the thought of someone on my boat without my permission, but the sooner they assured themselves that we didn't have any treasure on board, the better. Assuming they were still on our tail.

We'd had good travel karma for the entire trip, and it was still with us for the leg to Namu. Ellie was excited about stopping there. She'd read about its unique history and location. An archaeological site that spanned 10,000 years, the rise and fall of the fish cannery, which included Japanese and Chinese labor, and its isolation created by being surrounded on three sides by a dense coastal rainforest. We regretted not being able to spend more time sightseeing, but that afternoon we took in as much as we could in the amount of time we had, all of our exploration on foot. Macavity got tired and Logan carried him for a while. At the end of the day, we were all exhausted. I was concerned about what we might find when we got back to the *Aspara*, but everything looked exactly like we'd left it. If someone had searched the *Aspara* in our absence, they'd been remarkably professional.

The next morning we motor-sailed down the channel and put up a full sail in a mild westerly on Queen Charlotte Sound. The *Aspara* was like a butterfly that had been set free, riding the waves with grace and ease. Ellie was pleased to find that she wasn't seasick for the crossing, and we all enjoyed the trip to Port Hardy. Well, I can't speak for Macavity. He stayed below on the forward bunk that used to be his alone.

When we arrived at Port Hardy, we felt lucky to find a spot on one of the floats at the busy marina. Within minutes we were headed to town for dinner. It was a nuisance taking Macavity with us, but I wasn't comfortable leaving him behind. We found a small, busy restaurant and had just ordered when I had an idea.

An idea for doing something that was probably unnecessary, even ill-advised, but once it took hold, I couldn't shake it.

"If I go back to the marina, will you have my food boxed up?" I asked.

"Aren't you feeling well?" Ellie sounded concerned.

Logan looked suspiciously at me before asking, "You want to see if the *Jolly Roger* has come in, don't you?"

"So now you're a mind-reader. Hey, they stayed out of sight while we were in small bays and places with only a single dock, but here, in a larger marina, they might feel they can blend in without being noticed. And if they think they have the docks to themselves for a bit, they might let down their guard."

"I can do that if you want," Logan said, starting to push his chair back.

"No, you stay here. I can use the walk, and I ate enough peanuts earlier to stave off any hunger pangs." I stood up before he could argue. "Keep an eye on Macavity, and don't give him too much people food." The waiter hadn't questioned us bringing Macavity in and didn't blink an eye when I asked about a back door. Maybe he just assumed anyone from the US was a bit odd.

It probably wasn't necessary, but just in case someone had followed us to the restaurant, I took several side streets and cut through a parking lot and across a field to get back. Once at the marina, I started my search on the far side from where the *Aspara* was moored and was immediately rewarded by spotting the *Jolly Roger* on a float about halfway out on the main dock. I did a mental happy dance as I strolled down the dock, casually looking around, hoping to catch signs of life on the cruiser. But the only person I saw was a man on a fishing boat moored on the main dock at the foot of the float I was scoping out. He was working on a gurdy when I went by and didn't look up.

When I reached the end of the dock, I turned back. I had no plan in mind, but as I reached the float where the *Jolly Roger* was moored, I made an impulsive decision. I walked over to the boat and climbed aboard. Once in the cockpit, I didn't think anyone could see me from the main dock, but I knocked on the door both for show and in case someone was there. If someone *was* below, I wasn't sure what I would say if they answered. When no one did, I tested to see if the door was locked. The handle turned and the door opened an inch. I almost took off at that point. Someone could be sleeping below. Or in the shower. Or not want company.

But I'd come so far—too far to turn back. I opened the door a little further and called out, "Anyone aboard?"

When no one responded, I glanced around to make sure there was no one observing me, then stepped inside. On the table was a Canadian map. There were tiny x's at all of the stops we'd made. I took out my cell and snapped a picture. There was a plastic glass with a little water still in it next to the map. I found a paper towel, used it to pick up the glass, dumped out the water, wrapped the glass in the paper towel and tucked it in my pack. Next, I calmed myself by inhaling deeply and counting to four before exhaling.

Then I headed for the forward bunk area, half expecting to see someone asleep there. But there wasn't anyone. I rummaged around and had almost given up, when I came across a box of ammo. I removed one bullet and put it in my pack. Maybe it would match the one taken from Kent's leg. It wasn't much, but it was a start.

I knew I should probably get going, but I hated to leave without learning something that would help us identify the men who were most likely tailing us. The boat appeared to be equipped with only bare-bone essentials, nothing personal visible in the main cabinet. Probably a rental then. I went through drawers and cabinets but couldn't find any documents to indicate who owned or who was leasing the boat. With the name and boat registration number on the hull, we could probably track that information though. I would copy it down when I left.

I felt rather than heard someone step aboard. My heartbeat went into overdrive. Stupid, stupid, stupid. I got out my bear pepper spray, hoped they didn't charge inside with their gun at ready, and waited. When no one came in right away, I became fairly certain they either didn't know I was there or they were waiting for me to make the first move. I crept toward the entrance, praying that whoever was out there wouldn't realize that the boat's slight movement was caused by a person moving around inside rather than waves entering the harbor.

When I finally saw the door opening, I felt as visible as a black spider on a white wall. I let the man get a couple of steps inside before pepper spraying him. At the same time, I reached out, grabbed his arm, and jerked him further into the room. He screamed, lost his balance, and tumbled at my feet. I leapt over him, climbed out onto the float, and ran. When I reached the end of the float, I made another quick decision. Instead of continuing down the dock, I jumped onto the fishing boat and went in through the open door.

The white-haired man holding a mug of coffee looked surprised but didn't miss a beat. "Do I know you?"

"No, but I need to hide. Someone will be coming after me from the cruiser down the way. Please don't say I'm here."

He motioned me to an open hatch, and I went below, hoping I wasn't making a big mistake as he closed the hatch lid. I could hear someone yelling outside but couldn't make out what they were saying. I felt the boat bounce and guessed the fisherman was going out back to see what was up . . . or to rat me out. I would find out soon enough.

It wasn't long before the hatch opened and he said, "It's safe to come out now, although I wouldn't leave just yet."

"Thank you." My adrenaline high was fading. And my eyes smarted from being so close to pepper spray.

"He went charging down the dock. Not very happy. Said something about being pepper sprayed." He looked me in the eye. "Well?"

"I sprayed him," I admitted and quickly added, "He has a

gun." At least I was fairly certain he had a gun. "Sorry to involve you. But I didn't know what else to do."

"Want some coffee?" he asked as if I was a guest.

"What I want is to contact the police." I got out my phone and realized I didn't know the emergency number in Canada. "Do you know the number?" I asked. "I'm not Canadian."

"I guessed that," he said with a grin. "The Coast Guard has a dock not too far away. I can take you there if you want. Easy enough to crank up the engine and untie."

"You're willing to do that?"

"Never heard of a burglar who asked to be taken to the police. You must have a reason."

Minutes later we were on our way. I called Logan to let him know. The Coast Guard dock was within walking distance of the restaurant. He said that he and Ellie would meet me there. I cautioned them to watch their backs and to be quick but not to look like they were running away. The fisherman smiled as I issued the warning.

I put my phone back in my pack and held out my hand. "I'm Bryn Baczek by the way."

"Louis. My friends call me Lou." His thick-fingered hand was rough, his grip strong.

"Well, Lou, I don't know how to thank you for doing this." Then it hit me; he might be able to give a description of whoever was on the cruiser. "Any chance you can tell me how many men were aboard the cruiser and what they looked like?"

"You don't know who is after you?"

"Actually no. We're pretty sure they've been following us. And we think we know why, but we haven't seen anyone. I was hoping to find a name or names. That's why I was, ah, *on* the *Jolly Roger*."

"On or in? No, don't answer that."

"The bad news is that I didn't find anything and almost got caught for nothing."

"Well, I don't have any names, but I did see two men. Both

were pretty average—average height and weight, brownish hair, casual dress, boating caps. No visible scars or tattoos." He paused. "Not too helpful, huh?"

"Sorry, did I look disappointed?"

"There is one thing—I heard one of them call the other *Shane.*"

on the lam

Logan and Ellie beat me to the Coast Guard station. When I went inside, I found a Guardsman kneeling down, rubbing Macavity behind his ears. Macavity was purring. "Love your cat," the Guardsman said. He had on a uniform consisting of a light-blue shirt, dark pants and a nametag that said "Tremblay."

"What happened?" Ellie asked. She and Logan both looked concerned.

"Ah . . ." I wasn't sure how much I should reveal in front of Officer Tremblay, so I opted for vague. "I was trying to find out who was on the boat that's been following us and was, ah, caught. A fisherman helped me get away and brought me here on his boat."

Logan gave me a hug. "I was worried," he admitted.

"The fisherman overheard a name—Shane."

"Isn't that the name of the guy who paid you a visit in Seattle?" Ellie asked.

"Yes. Shane Reed."

"What are we going to do?" Ellie and Logan looked at me and then glanced at Tremblay who was still seemingly focused on Macavity but no doubt listening carefully to our conversation.

"Well, I'm hoping Officer Tremblay will help us get in touch with the Vancouver police."

Tremblay stood up. "Certainly. Do we need to contact the RCMP?" he asked.

"Well, my guess is that the two men who've been following us have illegal handguns with them, but I can't prove it. We can't even prove they've been following us. But I think they may be involved in a Vancouver police investigation. I need to pass on what I've learned to someone who can check it out."

Tremblay let me make the call from a landline in a back room. He left me alone and shut the door, so I felt more comfortable being honest with the Vancouver officer I talked to about what I'd done to get the information and evidence I had. I fudged a bit by not admitting that I didn't know one of the men was Shane Reed until after I'd taken the picture of the chart and removed a glass and a bullet from the boat. Although I didn't think they would get too excited about following up on the break-ins, I also mentioned that we suspected Shane might be involved in the attack on my cousin in Arizona. That was my reason for taking the bullet. We agreed that Ellie would drop off the evidence when she returned to Vancouver. Meanwhile, they wanted us to stay put until they had a chance to coordinate with the RCMP.

Officer Tremblay gave us coffee and we settled into the lobby to await word from the RCMP. I was a bit concerned about the *Aspara*, although Lou had promised to keep an eye on it once he was back at the marina. Macavity climbed onto my lap, and after some experimentation, found a comfortable position and immediately fell asleep. He might not be happy with me, but my lap was better than the floor for a place to nap.

I texted the picture of the chart to Ellie and turned over the cup and the bullet. It wasn't much, but with the police spotlight on him, it might be enough to get Shane off our backs. And as soon as the treasure was secured, we could share that piece of information with the police.

While we waited, Ellie made a reservation to fly back to

Vancouver. There was no morning flight, so she wouldn't be able to leave until 3:00. "I'm sorry the two of you have to do the long return trip on your own," she said.

"It should be a lot more pleasant after today. I'm sorry you won't be enjoying it with us."

"Me too," Logan added.

"Maybe we can do this again under less nerve-racking circumstances," Ellie said.

Then Logan put into words the nagging concerns at the back of my mind: "If we don't tell the police about the treasure and the phony map, do you think they will take this being followed stuff seriously? And if we only share it once the treasure has been recovered, will they be upset?"

"You mean like upset enough to press charges for withholding evidence?"

"Evidence of what?" Ellie countered.

"This *is* complicated," I agreed. "We don't want news of the treasure to be leaked to the press in case that encourages someone else to come after it. And even if we accept the risk of telling the police about everything that's happened, we can't prove that Shane committed any crimes. We couldn't even prove Uncle Wade's death wasn't an accident. There are too many unknowns and too many suspects."

"I agree," Logan said. "Only the people at UBC need to know about the treasure at this point."

Maybe it was having Macavity's warm soft body in my lap that was slowly bringing me back to my pre-treasure hunting mentality. As my body relaxed, my brain did too. I felt okay with not having all the answers. And I was confident that someone— not necessarily me—would eventually figure it all out.

When two RCMP showed up, I had to wake Macavity and put him on the floor. Not surprisingly, he was unhappy and had to be pulled along as we were ushered into the back room. The atmosphere wasn't unfriendly, but I could tell by their demeanor that it was going to be a serious conversation.

The RCMP wasted no time in getting to the heart of the matter. "We understand that this man, Shane Reed, may be wanted in the U.S. for questioning about an assault, but we have nothing to hold him on. The Vancouver office wants to see the evidence you have, but they have no reason to detain him either, unless requested to do so by the Arizona police. They would, however, like to talk with him. So far, we haven't been able to locate him or the other man who was seen with him on the boat."

"You've checked the *Jolly Roger* at the marina?"

One of the officers looked visibly affronted by the question, but the other maintained a neutral expression. "No one is at the boat. We have someone waiting there in case they show up. We believe the boat was rented in Vancouver. The Vancouver office is following up on that." The officer looked at me. "Do you want to press charges? I understand he attacked you."

"Well, not exactly. I don't know what he would have done if he'd caught up with me, but since he didn't, I'm not sure what you would charge him with." In truth, he probably had a better case for charging me with something than I had for making a complaint against him.

"There is one thing we would like you to do," Logan said. "We're pretty sure they were following us. Would it be possible for you to check our boat for listening devices and a tracker?"

"You're *pretty sure* they were following you." He sounded a bit incredulous.

"Yes, they're treasure hunters, and we believe they think we have a map to a hidden treasure. It's a long story."

The two men exchanged amused glances.

"We don't have a map," Ellie added. "But our uncle was a treasure hunter, and he hinted that *he* had a map. When he died, his home was broken into and searched. My condo and another cousin's house were broken into. And earlier on our trip, Bryn's boat was broken into and searched. We believe these two men were responsible for all of these break-ins."

"Did you report the break-ins?"

"All except the most recent one. But there was an eyewitness who saw a man go inside my boat while we were gone. Nothing was taken, but they let my cat out."

"They have every place we've stopped marked on their chart," Ellie said before I could stop her.

"Where did you see this chart?" the officer asked, looking at each of us in turn before the needle stopped at me.

"I admit that I went on board their boat without permission. But the door was open, and I called out to see if there was anyone there. The chart was right there on the table."

"Is that why he chased you?"

"Probably," I reluctantly admitted.

"So, if we find them, it's possible they might want to press charges against *you* for trespassing."

"Humph," Logan said.

Logan might say "humph," but I feared the mention of pepper spraying someone who discovered you on their boat might have serious consequences. Still, I wasn't about to confess unless I had to. I felt certain that the two men had more to be guilty about than I did.

The two RCMPs stepped into the hall for a brief discussion. While we waited, we didn't talk. There was nothing to say until we heard what they were going to do. When they returned, the one who seemed to be in charge said: "Unless you have something else to tell us, I don't see any reason to detain you further."

In some ways, that was good news. "Will you let us know if you find them?" I asked. "And we really would like to find out if my boat is bugged or being tracked. Is that something you can do? Or can you suggest someone we can hire to do it for us?"

The officer who seemed to be in charge hesitated, then shrugged. "Sure, we can do that. First thing tomorrow morning?"

"There's one more thing," Logan said. "Ah, we'd really appreciate a lift back to the marina. We have a tired cat . . ." His voice trailed off as the officers both scowled. Then the officer in charge shrugged again. "Sure, let's go." On the way there he asked us how we were enjoying our trip, as if nothing unusual had happened. Logan mentioned our Bishop Bay stop and soaking in the hot springs. Ellie said she hoped to someday return to Namu. And I added that the wind had made for a lovely sail across the Sound. Then he dropped us off at the marina with a friendly wave.

Lou's boat was tied up ahead of the *Aspara*. He stepped out on the dock when he saw us. "Everything okay?" he called out. Logan took Macavity and returned to the *Aspara* while Ellie and I went over to talk to Lou.

"I see the RCMP brought you back."

"You do have a sharp eye. And yes, everything is okay." I introduced Ellie. "They haven't caught up with the two men yet—you haven't seen them, have you?"

"No, but there's an officer waiting over there in case they do show."

"Like I said, you have a sharp eye."

Ellie yawned, and I barely managed to stop myself from joining her.

"Looks like you two are ready for a rest," Lou said. "I'm leaving early tomorrow. If I don't see you before I take off, have a safe trip home."

"Thank you," I said. "I can't tell you how much I appreciate you saving me."

"It makes a good story," he said with a smile. "So long, Bryn Baczek." He pronounced it correctly. "And you too, Ellie."

bugged & tracked

Since Ellie's flight wasn't until 3:00 pm, that meant we needed to hang around Port Hardy until afternoon. Logan made pancakes, and we enjoyed a leisurely breakfast, lingering over coffee, not talking about anything important. Then we switched to reading mode. We didn't want to leave the boat, but we didn't want to talk about what I'd done, what we'd discovered, and what we were going to do next—until we knew it was safe to do so without being overheard.

When a Mountie showed up carrying a black canvas bag, we welcomed him like royalty. We didn't bow or anything, but all three of us stepped onto the dock, thanked him for coming, and explained what we wanted him to look for.

"I hear someone thinks you have a treasure map on board."

"Don't we wish," Ellie said. "Our uncle liked to tell stories, and I was named in his will. That's how all this started."

"You know about Oak Island, don't you?" he said. "People really want to believe in that sort of thing."

"We all need our dreams," Logan said. For a moment, we were silent, apparently each of us pondering our own dreams.

"Well, I'd better get on it," the Mountie said as he climbed aboard and unpacked his bag. "Lovely boat, by the way."

"Lots of hiding places inside," Logan commented. "We've looked but didn't find anything."

"Well, I'll be able to tell you shortly if you missed something." He did the outside first, with a thoroughness I found impressive. We watched from the dock as he started at the bow, crisscrossed the cabin, went around and into the cockpit, and circled the deck. "Nothing," he said. "But there's more likely to be something inside than out."

He was right. He found two trackers and a listening device inside. One of the trackers was in the engine room in a location where we felt we should have spotted it when we were doing our own amateur search. The other was under my bunk in a cubby that was awkward to access. I was amazed anyone managed to mount one up and under inside the space. "Pretty sophisticated," the Mountie said. "With this battery this little beauty can last for up to two months on standby. It sleeps when the boat isn't in motion and gives regular updates every few minutes when it is. Impressive."

"Wouldn't it be on all the time? The boat is never what you would call 'still.'"

"There is a parameter setting that takes that into account. Like I said, sophisticated."

The tiny listening device was in one of the food compartments. Again, it was tucked up under an opening. If we'd run our hands along the upper edge, we would have found it. "Also fairly sophisticated," the Mountie said. "Not cheap. You have enemies that think you are worth listening to." He chuckled as if he'd made a joke. "There's probably a noise depressor function, but I think it wouldn't have picked up much unless you were in this main area with the motor off. And the person had to be nearby."

"What if they were several floats over on another boat?"

"That could work."

"But we're clean now?"

"Absolutely." He looked at the devices. "You might be able to trace where these came from, but it won't be easy. I've disabled the trackers, but the bug was no longer functioning."

"We're going to turn them over to the police in the States. They're working on an assault case that involved tracking a van. It will be interesting to see if the devices are similar."

"Any idea when they planted these?"

"Yeah, the last time we were in Port Hardy, about a week ago. They let my cat loose but locked up when they left."

"I can't say for sure how long it was operational, but I doubt they heard much when you were under way."

"They didn't actually have much to hear. I regret we didn't know for sure that someone was listening; we could have made it more interesting for them."

We thanked the Mountie for helping us out and called Tremblay to tell him about the devices and thank him again for his help. He informed us that they still hadn't caught up with the two men from the *Jolly Roger*. They had literally jumped ship.

Ellie left in a taxi for the airport early afternoon. Before we headed out, we made one last call to the Coast Guard and the RCMP to see if they'd located Shane and his companion. The *Jolly Roger* was still tied up at the dock, and we hadn't seen anyone coming or going from it. The RCMP told us they managed to track down the boat rental place in Vancouver, but the person who signed the papers wasn't Shane Reed. They were working on finding both men.

Before leaving, I called my mother to let her know our GPS tracker would be off for now. I mumbled something about a malfunction, vowing to myself that I would explain everything to my family as soon as Ellie had the treasure situation squared away. Well, almost everything. I might leave out the part about sneaking aboard someone's boat and using bear spray to escape.

It felt good to be tracker free and to escape from Port Hardy. It was late, so we only went as far as Alert Bay. We stayed on the boat that evening, tied to the dock. At first Macavity protested being on a leash by tugging and yowling in frustration, but he finally settled down, unhappy but resigned. Every time a new boat entered the harbor, we got out the binoculars and had a look. There was no sign of the *Jolly Roger,* nor of the two men who had been on it.

"We're probably okay, but I'm still worried," I admitted after scanning the harbor for the umpteenth time.

"Me too. And Macavity isn't having fun. I say we give up on a leisurely trip and make a beeline for home."

It took us five more days to get back to Shilshole. We didn't linger anywhere and made good time, spending our evenings at anchor. It was tempting to row ashore for meals, but we were still gun-shy. It was easier to stay with Macavity and get creative with the remaining groceries on hand. We made an exception at Friday Harbor. We tied to the dock, and I stayed with Macavity while Logan went ashore for takeout before we anchored up in the south bay for the evening.

In some ways the trip was idyllic—the days were gorgeous and the weather remained settled. We had modest northwest breezes in the late afternoon to give us a little following sea and a push by sail. The sunsets were dramatic. And spending time with Logan is always good. We read, chatted about life, and enjoyed the time capsule that is travel by boat.

When we could get cell reception, we checked in with Ellie, Judd, and my parents. Each time we talked with Ellie, we expected her to say that the police had caught up with Shane or his buddy, but no such luck. Judd was glad we were safe and almost home. And my mother talked about what was happening with the family and, as usual, didn't seem particularly interested in what we were doing. That made it easier to hold some things back.

Monday, we made the trip from Friday Harbor to Shilshole in record time only to miss getting into the large lock by a couple of boats. The small lock didn't seem to be operating, so we knew we had to wait a full cycle for the lock to fill, open its doors to discharge its current load, let more boats in, lower the water level, and then discharge that load before we could get in. We tied to a timber on a wood barrier the other side of the railroad drawbridge and waited. Two other sailboats ended up rafting to us. Sailboats with tall masts can't make it under the drawbridge when it's down, so they often crowd into the small area to avoid getting caught on the wrong side. Even boats that can travel under the bridge often hang around close to the entrance, like airline passengers jockeying to be first to board.

When we finally completed the transition from salt to fresh water without incident, the tension in my muscles vanished; I could almost feel the level of cortisol dropping like the change in body temperature when a fever breaks. Logan was smiling, and Macavity was pacing in anticipation of finally being a free cat. Although how he knew we were close to home, I'm not sure.

The instant the *Aspara* came alongside the familiar spot on the cement pier, Macavity raced off. As soon as I had the lines secured, Logan departed. One minute we were huddled together in the cockpit, and the next I was all alone. It felt good.

By Tuesday mid-morning it was as if I'd never been away, except for the pile of dirty clothes waiting to be washed that I'd stashed in the corner of my office until I could manage a trip to the laundromat. Bubbles V and Friend were back in their bookshelf home, swimming around and around and around. There was still a pile of books on my office floor, a spider web hanging in one corner from the ceiling, and a thin layer of dust on everything.

I was busy sorting through the pile of emails that had accumulated while I was gone when there was a firm yet respectful knock on the door. Not knowing whether Shane was lurking out there somewhere, I'd kept my bear pepper spray handy. Cannister in hand, I went over to the door and asked, "Who is it?" That may have sounded rude to whoever was out there, but it felt like the safe thing to do.

"Ben Peterson."

"Oh, sorry." I opened the door to a detective I'd worked with before. He has a pencil thin mustache, a perfectly manicured line of facial hair that is a turn-off for me. Still, the rest of him looks darn good.

"Hi, have a few minutes?" He glanced at the pepper spray as I put it on a bookcase shelf. Then his eyes traveled to the goldfish bowl.

"*Two* goldfish," he commented as he took a seat in the chair across from my messy desk.

"Bubbles V and Friend."

"I don't know who to wish luck to, you or them." He laughed, a glint of white teeth under the line of darkness.

I smiled, but I had an uneasy feeling about this unexpected visit. "You here on official business?"

"Yes and no."

"Which means?"

"I have a friend in the Vancouver police. We coordinate on some cross-border crimes from time to time. He said your name came up in connection with an assault on a Canadian citizen that took place in the U.S."

"That would be my cousin, Kent. Although there were three other cousins with him at the time, Kent was the only one shot."

"And you reported having a problem with another boater in Port Hardy."

"Wow, the Canadians have a good communication network."

"My Mountie friend wanted to know if you were a reliable witness."

"And you told him . . .?"

"That you can't keep a goldfish alive for more than a few months at a time but, other than that, you're okay."

He was being supportive whereas I was being deceptive. I wasn't sure it would make a difference to any of the ongoing investigations, but I felt I owed Ben a version a bit closer to the truth. "Ah, I did leave out a thing or two when talking to officials about the Port Hardy incident," I confessed.

Ben raised one eyebrow, leaving the other at rest. When we were about seven, Sophie and I had practiced doing that for hours. We thought it was cool. But Sophie always squinted when she raised one brow, and I looked like an owl about to hoot. Ben was good though, just the right display of questioning and disdain to let the person he was interrogating know he meant business.

"After Kent was attacked and Ellie's condo was searched, we were concerned about being followed while we were in Canada. Someone seemed to think one of the cousins ended up with a treasure map. Ellie purchased bear spray, and all three of us carried it in our packs. She bought it legally," I added quickly. "For our wilderness hikes in bear country. But I not only went aboard a boat without permission, I pepper-sprayed one of the men renting it in order to get away when he caught me."

"You didn't tell the RCMP about any of this." It wasn't a question.

"Why would I incriminate myself?"

"You also took a picture of a map and 'removed' a cup and a bullet."

"I admitted that to the RCMP, and Ellie turned it all over to their Vancouver office. Furthermore, the RCMP found two trackers and a bug on the *Aspara*."

"Nice to know you're not unjustifiably paranoid." Was that a hint of a smile I detected? The dark line had quivered slightly.

"Do you know if anyone claimed the *Jolly Roger* yet?"

"No, the two men are still in the wind. But . . . maybe that's all you need to know." Now I was certain he was teasing me, so I responded in kind.

"I wouldn't want you to share official police business with a mere civilian. Even the victim of a crime."

He laughed. "Okay, you were right. The prints on the cup belong to one Shane Reed, a man of dubious reputation, but someone who has never received more than a fine for some sleight of hand with stolen artifacts and unreported antiquities."

"Did the bullet come from a gun like the one used on Kent?"

"Yes, apparently it did. But without the actual gun used in the shooting, that doesn't prove anything."

"There's more," I said.

"You going to share?"

"Unofficially?"

He thought about it.

"It's nothing illegal," I assured him.

"Then spill it."

I told him about Uncle Wade's death and how Ellie and I had put together the clues he had left for us and that was the reason for our *vacation* to Canada. "Ellie has lined up a team from UBC to retrieve the treasure. As soon as they do, we'll make an announcement and inform the RCMP. Then we can quit looking over our shoulders."

"You found buried treasure?" Both of his eyebrows shot upward.

"Yes, we think Uncle Wade had already been there once and was prevented from going back to recover it for some reason."

"And you have people from the University of British Columbia involved?"

"Yes, if they find what we think they'll find, the artifacts will most likely end up in a museum."

"I'm impressed."

"It would have been our uncle's biggest haul. At least that's what we think. I only dug up enough stuff to know I was in the right place. An Aztec coin and a gold ring."

"I'm sincerely impressed. You actually found buried treasure. A lot of people spend a lifetime trying to do that."

"Well, it's my first and last treasure hunt. My next boating vacation hopefully won't involve bears or tracking devices or unhinged treasure seekers."

"I'm curious, did your cousins who were attacked also have a map?"

"Yes, a fake map they stole from Uncle Wade's house. Although we're pretty sure it was a set-up, our uncle intended them—or Shane, or some other treasure hunter—to find the phony map. It was his way of pranking from the grave."

"Amazing."

"After the team from UBC retrieves the artifacts, Ellie is going to ask that they credit Uncle Wade with the discovery of their location. He would have liked that."

Ben studied me a moment before saying, "You are a clever and gutsy woman."

"Since you didn't add foolhardy, I'll take that as a compliment."

For a moment I thought he was going to ask me out, but the moment passed, and he stood up to leave. "Make sure I'm on speed dial in case Shane Reed shows up on your doorstep, okay?"

"You're definitely on speed dial," I said, bestowing what I hoped was a playful grin. From his abrupt departure, however, my grin may have looked like I was experiencing gas pain.

Tuesday mid-afternoon I had another visitor. This time it was Hudson. When I opened the door, he was standing there with a large box in his hands.

"I didn't order anything," I said.

"It's a present. Can I come in? I need to set this down; it's heavy."

I stepped aside and watched as he tried to figure out where he could put the box. I would have made space on my desk, but when I glimpsed the product photo on the side of the box, I wasn't sure it was a present I wanted to accept.

"I'll just put it on the floor," Hudson said.

"Please tell me it isn't . . ."

"Let me explain."

"It *is*!"

He glanced at the box and realized the picture was a dead give-away. "I can explain. It was my wife's idea."

I sat down and waited for him to continue. He was a good man and a great landlord. I needed to hear him out before rejecting his gift.

"When goldfish were first kept as pets, they lived mostly in ponds. Eventually they were kept indoors in bowls, and many people still do that. But it isn't good for the fish. They might survive for a short time—like the four before Bubbles V—but fish breathe oxygen and release carbon dioxide. In nature, currents and photosynthesis by aquatic plants replenish the oxygen."

I held up my hand. "You sound like a science textbook."

"I'm just trying to explain that your past fish needed more oxygen and less waste in their water to survive. In addition, fish need space to swim and places to hide."

"Anything else?"

"Since we have chlorine in our water, you need to treat the water you put in the aquarium to dissolve the chlorine. You also need a filter, a heater, and plants. I've included the filter and heater. And . . ." Hudson hesitated, looking uncomfortable.

"And?"

"You need to clean the aquarium regularly to remove waste and algae build-up." He delivered the message quickly as if he thought I would try to stop him. Instead, I asked, "Why are you doing this to me?"

"So your goldfish don't keep dying."

"It won't be long before Emma will be able to cope with the death of a pet goldfish. It's part of growing up."

Ignoring my comment, he said, "There's one more thing."

"What's that?"

"You shouldn't dump dead goldfish in the lake. Their bodies transmit bacteria and disease."

With that, Hudson stood. Mission accomplished. "If you

want help setting this up, let me know." He started to leave, then turned back, Columbo style. "Since you have two fish, the aquarium should probably be larger. But you can't get a bigger one in your bookshelf. I measured."

I summoned up the better me and said, "This is a very thoughtful gift. Please thank your wife for me." He looked so pleased with my comment that I knew I was trapped. Bubbles V and Friend would soon have a new home. And I would somehow become a responsible goldfish owner.

But the first chance I got, Emma was going to receive a gift. Then it would be up to Dylan and Angelina to clean the aquarium on a regular basis.

CHAPTER 28

double trouble

The expedition to retrieve the artifacts was scheduled for Saturday. It had taken little more than a week to organize, record time. The Mounties had been notified so they could provide protection. But until they had the artifacts in hand, nothing would be released to the public. Logan and I regretted we wouldn't be there for the dig, but we were pleased Ellie was going to lead the group to the cave, stopping short at the entrance, of course. She was staying with a friend until then, bear spray at her side.

I was starting to feel like it was over. The treasure would be recovered and relocated. When the officials caught up with Shane and his buddy, they might be able to link Shane or both men to the incident in the Sonoran Desert. Maybe they would reopen the investigation into Uncle Wade's death. The Sunday family dinner was scheduled for next month. Macavity would return to his usual independent and demanding self. And I could direct my energies into the consulting projects I had lined up.

So, imagine my surprise Friday evening when Shane came from behind the building across from the *Aspara* with a gun in his hand.

"Just act natural," he said. "We need to talk."

There's nothing natural about being held at gunpoint. I stumbled getting aboard the *Aspara* and had to steady my hand to get the key in the lock. If only Macavity was a Doberman who attacked on command instead of a cat that would undoubtedly leave as soon as he caught sight of a stranger coming aboard.

Sure enough, there was a flicker of orange as he disappeared into the forward bunk area as Shane slowly made his way down the stairs facing forward, without taking his eyes off me.

"Take it slow and easy," he commanded, pointing with his gun for me to sit down behind the table, while he remained standing. "And keep your hands where I can see them." I sat, leaving my hands resting on the table. "You know why I'm here," he said.

"You're too late."

"What does that mean?"

"UBC has the artifacts," I bluffed.

"If they did, I would have heard about it."

"They are going to hold a press conference to make the announcement. Tomorrow or maybe not until Sunday. They want it to coincide with some other news."

"I didn't see you bring anything back." He was no longer pointing his gun at me, but he still had it in his hand. His *left* hand, like the guy who shot Kent.

"After we got rid of your tracking devices, we went back and picked it up."

"No you didn't." He sounded confident. Had he followed us from Port Hardy? Hired someone else to follow us? Or had he simply calculated how long it took us to get back to Seattle?

"Okay, so I admit that we wanted to go back and dig them up, but because of you we gave directions to the Mounties to complete the job instead. They got the artifacts and are turning everything over to UBC."

"If that's the truth, why didn't you just tell me that right off?"

He was good. "Because I'm still ticked. If it hadn't been for you, Ellie and I would have been given credit for finding them. This way, we're an afterthought."

"Is that why you went after the treasure? For glory? I would have thought greed played a role."

"I have all I need to be happy." As long as he didn't shoot me.

"Hand me your cell phone. And do it real slow."

I reached in my pocket, wishing my cell phone was a Bond gadget, a deadly weapon, rather than a simple phone.

"Put it on the table."

I obeyed.

"Now call your cousin. I want to see if you're telling me the truth. Ask her if she has the artifacts in a safe place, okay? And put her on speaker." He waved his gun at me. "Now."

Everything was on the line; one slip-up and he would know the treasure was still in Canada. And he would also assume that I could tell him its location. Once he had that information, what would happen to me?

I dialed Ellie's number and was truly sorry that I got her instead of voicemail. "Elspeth, I said brightly with a slight lisp. "Just wanted to make sure that the artifacts are in a safe place."

Ellie only hesitated a few seconds. "Sorry, I'm distracted. The cat just brought in a rat as a present for me." She held the phone away and we could hear her say, "Scram Ginger. And take that with you." Then she was back. "Now where were we?"

Since she didn't have a cat, I was confident she was ready to go along with whatever cues I gave her. "I'm concerned about the artifacts. You've stowed them some place safe, right?"

"Of course. Don't worry."

"Well, I admit I *am* a bit worried. It's hard to find some place that's really safe. Think of how thoroughly they searched Uncle Wade's. Assure me that you've thought this through."

"Well, actually they're with the appraiser I've found. He's going to get back to me within a day or two on how much they are worth."

Shane mouthed "The name. Ask her the name of the appraiser."

"Ah, what's the appraiser's name?" We had been doing so

well, but I was afraid this was the point at which Shane figured out we were lying.

Ellie was silent for what seemed like forever. Then she said. "I know you're there, Shane. I've already alerted the police and the marina's landlord. So, if you know what's good for you, you will either exit quickly or start thinking about how you are going to spend your years in jail."

"Damn you," Shane shouted at me. "And damn you," he screamed into my cell phone. He waved the gun at me one last time, then turned and hurried up the steps. I moved out from the settee but didn't go after him. He had a gun and I didn't.

I could hear Ellie asking what was happening, but I was distracted by a loud voice from outside demanding: "Stop where you are, drop the gun, and step off the boat."

"What are *you* doing here?" Shane said. Then I heard him drop the gun and felt him step ashore.

"Bryn, Bryn, what's happening?" Ellie shouted from my cell as the voice from outside yelled a message to me: "Bryn, stay below. Don't try to follow us."

I suddenly recognized the voice—it was River! It sounded like he and Shane were leaving together. But how had he made Shane drop his gun? Did *he* have a gun? And why?

"Bryn, please answer," Ellie pleaded.

"It's okay, Ellie. Shane is gone."

"Are you okay?'

"I'm fine. Did you really call the police and Hudson?"

"There wasn't time."

"Hang up—I'm calling them now. I'll get back to you." I quickly dialed Ben. When he answered I spoke as fast and as clearly as I could, and he immediately said to hold. At that point, I dared to poke my head up to make sure Shane and River were gone. The gun was where Shane had dropped it, but there was no one on the pier near the *Aspara*. I got out, went around the back of the building, and peered down the dock. They were halfway up the stairs already, Shane in the lead. I watched, hoping to see what kind of a car they got into, but River must have parked in front of the building instead of in the parking area because they took a right and disappeared from sight.

Ben came back on the phone. "Do you have a description of the two men? And of their car?"

"I couldn't see the car they left in, but I can not only describe the two men, I can give you their names. And I have Shane Reed's gun. His friend made him drop it before they took off."

After I told Ben everything I could, I called Ellie back, thanked her for being so quick-witted and promised to get back to her as soon as I learned anything. Then I called Logan and asked if he could come over and keep me company until the police arrived. He didn't bother asking for details but said he would come immediately.

I left the gun on the deck and sat in the cockpit, trying to piece together what had happened. When Logan arrived, I motioned for him to join me and said not to touch the gun. "Shane dropped it after threatening me with it."

"If it's one thing I've learned from watching TV, it's not to pick up a weapon when you come across a crime scene." He stopped and stared at the gun. "Is *this* a crime scene?"

"It almost was." I quickly explained about Shane holding me at gunpoint and making me call Ellie. How Ellie had tricked him into believing the police were on their way. Then River showing up and ordering Shane to drop his gun. And the two men leaving together.

"Do you think River and Shane came here together?" Logan asked.

"If they came separately, then Shane's car should still be here."

"Do you think they were working together but had a falling out? Why else would River show up, order Shane to drop his gun, and then leave with him? Unless forcing Shane to go with him was an act for you. And if it was, why?"

"Maybe they haven't been working together," I speculated. "Maybe they were keeping track of each other so if one of them got hold of the treasure map or the artifacts, the other could steal them."

"If that's the case, was River also on our trail in Canada? And, more importantly, was he with Shane when they attacked your cousins? Or was that the other guy who was with Shane in Canada?"

"Even if we can't figure out Who's on Third, let's hope this gun will answer at least one of the questions we have—did Shane shoot Kent?"

a river runs through it

Saturday was a long day. I kept trying to focus on business-related tasks, but my mind flitted from one thought to the next. When was Ben going to call? Were the police making any progress on linking Shane to the attack on Kent? What was the relationship between Shane and River? Where had they gone after they left? And most important, what was happening at Butedale with the UBC team? I'd had a troublesome thought, which once considered, I couldn't shake: what if Uncle Wade had seeded the spot with a few relics, maybe even fakes, and there wasn't any real treasure there? What if it was another piece of his elaborate prank?

I finally gave up trying to concentrate on work and turned to something I thought would be less mentally challenging: watching a video titled "Ten Easy Steps for Setting up Your Aquarium." I should have known that anything with *ten* steps wasn't all that easy.

The video winked the title and immediately panned to a woman standing behind a long table covered with an array of products. She quickly ran through these essentials, pointing at a bag or picking up a box and waving it at viewers as if she was doing a late-night infomercial. Many of the products had unfamiliar names, to me at least. Things like "substrate" and "safes-tart." It was hard to digest what she was saying before she held up still another indispensable product.

Once she completed her rapid-fire product display, she jumped into a fast-paced discussion of filters and heaters, cultivation practices, tank decorations and why you needed to regularly test the water. By the time she got to the part about how to fill the tank—not as easy as simply dumping in water—my brain was swirling around and around like Bubbles V and Friend swimming in their bowl. In addition to being confused, I didn't have most of the stuff I needed to complete the job anyway.

I almost gave up. Instead, I decided to at least get a start by removing the aquarium from the box and showing it to its new tenants. I set it down gently on a pile of papers in the middle of my desk and scooped up the directions from the bottom of the box. That earned me a paper cut, but at least the directions only had *seven* steps listed. Seven steps with three to five bullets per step, that is. The bottom line was that I needed to do what the woman in the video had talked about: buy soil substrate, gravel, plants, fertilizer, extra heat cartridges, water purifier tablets, and a water test kit before I could even think about step two.

In the meantime, I needed to determine the best location for the aquarium. According to the directions, it had to be some place flat with a stable surface that did not get any direct sunlight and that was near an electrical outlet but not so near that I would splash water on it. The first two requirements eliminated my bookshelves in their current state. Unless I wanted to share a desk with my fish, I needed to beef up and level my shelving. I had some wood and tools in my locker that would do the job, but it would take some effort to get at them.

That was the point at which I considered tossing both fish in the lake. Maybe they'd grow into giants and terrorize swimmers. They might enjoy that. In the end, I got a grip, fed Bubbles V and Friend in their existing bowl, and promised them a new home soon. Meanwhile, I put the aquarium back in its box and set it on the floor in front of the bookshelves. Maybe I would trip over it and break the glass.

Feeling unsettled, irritated and at loose ends—a bad combination—I decided to calm myself by going for a walk. Excite my endorphins and readjust my attitude. I started along the lakeshore road with its industrial businesses and occasional stretches of sidewalk and made my way to Gasworks Park on the north shore of Lake Union. Once there, I found a grassy spot in front of the knoll I usually climb to take in the view.

There was a sailboat race in progress, small boats gliding across the water, occasionally changing directions with sails going slack before snapping back into place. There were several boats with colorful spinnakers that didn't quite have enough wind to billow out properly. Having had similar problems on the water when the winds refused to cooperate, I felt sorry for the sailors as they kept manipulating their sails to get as much windage as possible. I admired their persistence but questioned their judgement.

I was enjoying the show and starting to mellow, but that was no excuse for letting someone sneak up on me. "Don't panic," River said as he sat down beside me. "I can explain."

I looked straight ahead and warned: "With all of these people around, I can scream and attract a lot of attention."

River actually laughed. "You *could*. But I hope you won't. Hear me out, please."

"This better be good."

"I think I can answer most of the questions you must have. Although you may not like some of what I have to tell you." He suddenly sounded somber. "Let me start at the beginning . . . I *do* work for the Cruzzan Group, doing what I've described. That's how I know Shane Reed. He acquires art and artifacts for us from time to time. He's in what is commonly referred to as 'acquisitions.'"

I couldn't help but interrupt. "*Acquisitions?* Do you mean he *acquires* stolen art and antiquities for your company? Is he a criminal or merely a dishonest entrepreneur?"

"I can understand your skepticism. We didn't realize initially that he wasn't always on the up-and-up, or we wouldn't have continued doing business with him. When my boss finally got suspicious, he wasn't sure what to do. By then we had sold a lot of the inventory we'd purchased from him. We wanted to be sure of our facts before turning him over to the authorities. Labeling him a criminal has serious financial and reputational consequences for us.

"That's where I came in. With the help of a detective, I've been tracking Shane's movements."

"Why you?"

"Because I know the business, and we wanted to keep the investigation discreet."

That made sense to a point. "Go on."

"Things became complicated when I tailed him to your uncle's house the evening he died. I saw Shane pick the front door lock and go inside. I wanted to know what he was up to, so I looked in a side window and saw him bending over a body at the foot of the stairs. The next thing I knew, he was out of the house and making tracks. He didn't even bother shutting the door."

"You're suggesting that he wasn't the one to push Uncle Wade down the stairs because he didn't have enough time to do it?"

"He definitely didn't have enough time. I was at the window within a minute of him entering the house. I'm pretty sure he intended to search for the map, but when he discovered your uncle's body, he fled instead."

"What did you do then?"

"I went inside and checked to see if Wade was alive. He wasn't. Sorry."

"Then you just left?"

"I didn't see how I would explain my presence there without telling the police why I was following Shane, and I wasn't ready to do that. If Wade had been breathing, I would have called 911. And if his death had been ruled a homicide I would have gone to the police."

"How do I know you're telling me the truth?"

"Because I turned Shane in last night. You can check with your police friend."

My police friend? "If you intended to turn him in, why didn't you simply call the police when he stepped off the *Aspara*? Why play vigilante cop?"

"Because I had a few questions for him first. He was rattled by being caught like that and was actually quite talkative. I implied that I might let him go if he gave me the information I wanted about the goods he had sold us. Knowing where he'd obtained the artwork we bought from him gives us a chance to negotiate reparations and hopefully mitigate damage to our reputation. If we wait for this case to work its way through the criminal justice system, it could take years. And become very complex, very costly, and very public."

"If you were following Shane, does that mean you followed him following us to Canada?" That sounded convoluted, so I added, "You know what I mean."

"No, you fooled me; I actually believed that you were going on vacation. But I did know that Shane and his friend rented a boat. Unfortunately, I decided it was both unnecessary and too difficult to follow them without being seen. I should have put two and two together, but I didn't. At least not right away. I'm sorry for being so stupid. Really sorry. I thought they would give up when they figured out that you were on vacation. By the time I realized how wrong I was, it was too late. Again, I can't tell you how sorry I am. But even then, I didn't think you were in danger."

"But when he got back, you started following him again."

"Yes."

"And you followed him to my boat."

"Yes, I underestimated him, not for the first time."

"Well, once you realized where he was headed, why didn't you do something sooner? Like before he got a chance to take me hostage? Or while we were on the *Aspara*? Why wait until he was leaving?"

"I didn't know about what had happened in Canada at that point. And I didn't know he was carrying. By the time I had it figured out, my options were limited. There was no way I could take him by surprise after he got on your boat. It seemed safer to wait for him to leave."

"He could have shot me."

"Which actually seemed more likely if I'd come aboard. In fact, then he might have shot both of us."

"You could have yelled for him to come out."

"Then he could have used you as a shield."

I had to admit his version seemed plausible, but it didn't make me feel any better about how things had played out. "What about in Arizona? Did you follow him there?"

"Only as far as the last pit stop. I couldn't tail him after that. There was no way to stay out of sight."

"But you must have had some idea of what he was up to."

"I was pretty sure he was a thief and that he might be after the map your cousins had taken from your uncle's, but I didn't think he would shoot anyone."

"And after you found out he shot Kent, why didn't you come forward then?" In my opinion, he had made a ton of bad choices.

"I didn't actually *see* it happen. What was I supposed to tell the police—I was previously following this guy who I suspect *may have been* responsible for attacking Kent? And how would I have explained why I was following the two men following your cousins, when your cousins never admitted why they were in the desert in the first place?"

"You could at least have placed him in the vicinity. Didn't you feel an obligation to report that to the police?"

"I'm not proud of how I handled everything," he admitted. "But I had the big picture in mind."

"The big picture being to do what was best for your company."

"And to not get mired down in unprovable accusations."

"Let's say I believe what you've told me . . . and Ellie is right about Uncle Wade's death not being an accident . . . what's your best guess about what happened that night?"

"You won't like what I think."

"Try me."

"I think Kent's responsible, either directly or indirectly."

"What does that mean?"

"Kent isn't the type to do something on his own. He needs someone along to build up his ego."

"Like Tuna or Vinny."

"Most likely Tuna, in my opinion."

"So, you think the two of them are responsible for Uncle Wade's *accident*?"

"I don't have any evidence, but you asked what I thought. I can picture them breaking in and getting caught. If so, it could still have been an accident."

"Then why didn't they call an ambulance? They could have made the call anonymously."

"Perhaps for reasons similar to mine."

I studied his pleasant face and his dark brown eyes. I wanted to believe him.

"There's one question I have for you," he said. "Something I'm curious about. Where did you and Ellie find the real map?"

It was a question a lot of people were probably going to ask. We hadn't decided yet how much we were going to make public. It was a complicated story; not one that could easily be explained. And one that felt personal, part of Uncle Wade's legacy to Ellie. "I may tell you someday," I said, "But I'm not ready to share anything with you just yet."

"Fair enough." He seemed disappointed but not surprised. "I do hope you will find it in your heart to forgive me for deceiving you."

"I assume your story about moving to Vancouver or Seattle was a ruse."

"I have been thinking it would be nice to own some real estate closer to my roots."

"But you came because of Shane, not to look for a place to live."

"Yes, but . . ."

I'd heard enough. Even if everything he said was true, I wasn't sure how I felt about him. "You can leave now," I said abruptly.

For a moment he didn't say anything. Then he stood up. "As I said, I hope that someday you can forgive me."

I stared straight ahead and didn't respond.

Then he walked away.

CHAPTER 30

severing family ties

Ellie called me from Butedale. "I'm calling from outside the cave," she said. "On a satellite phone I borrowed from one of the UBC team members." She was so animated that I immediately knew she had good news.

"It's so exciting. They had no trouble finding the spot, and they're making great progress. Although they have to take it slow so they don't damage any of the artifacts. They were apparently dumped in a hole, not in any kind of container. Whoever left them there must have been in a hurry. At least that's what one of the UBC people told me. So far, they've brought out half a dozen coins, the ring you saw when you were here, several warrior figures, a snake brooch with what looks like emerald eyes, and a mask. The mask is sensational even covered with dirt."

"All Aztec gold artifacts?"

"That's the way it looks so far."

"That *is* exciting. I confess that I was worried the site might not yield much. I'm so glad it's looking good."

"I was worried too. I kept wondering if Uncle Wade had been able to dig deep enough to know what was there or was simply taking a wild guess."

221

"Well, if it was a guess, I'm glad he guessed correctly. I just wish he could have been here to see this."

"Me too. But at least he will get some recognition. They've agreed to publicly credit him with the discovery when they announce the find as well as when they display the artifacts."

"It sounds as though the team is really happy."

"They are thrilled. Ecstatic. Euphoric even."

"Are you at all tempted to go inside to see the actual spot where the artifacts were buried, maybe watch a few of them being removed?"

"Very funny. I tried exposure therapy, and it worked for me to an extent with tunnels, not so much with caves. What helped the most was Uncle Wade emphasizing that a phobia doesn't define who you are. He kept telling me that finding ways to cope with a phobia makes you mentally strong, even if you don't completely conquer your fear. He said that someone with coulrophobia doesn't need to crowd into a clown car to show they are okay with clowns. Nor does someone with arachibutyrophobia need to eat a whole jar of peanut butter to prove they can do it without breaking down completely."

"Arachi . . . what?"

"Arachibutyrophobia, fear of having peanut butter stick to the roof of your mouth."

"Just thinking about that almost makes me phobic. But I'm impressed with how the names of phobias roll off your tongue."

"I was in a support group for a while. You'd be surprised what phobias came up. That said, I'm happy enough seeing items as they bring them out of the cave. Although I recognize that it is ironic that something I fear is a source of so much pleasure."

After the call ended, I made myself a cup of tea and sat on the settee, wishing I was with Ellie at the dig. Macavity wandered over and laid down beside me, resting his head on my thigh. Maybe he, too, was reflecting on recent events.

The idea of chains of thieves chasing down hidden treasures

was intriguing, and at the same time, mind boggling. The end of the thriving Aztec empire had been quick and brutal, a combination of smallpox, attacks by Spanish warriors seeking gold, and Cortez forging an alliance with their native rivals to complete his conquest. It was hard to imagine the treacherous and circuitous journey Uncle Wade's Aztec treasure had traveled from the early 1500s to now.

The Spaniards were evidently interested in riches and not the Aztec culture, thus most of the gold artifacts they acquired had been melted down for ease of transport. But some survived, ending up in private collections, museums or in the hands of people who knew how to turn a profit in the black market. That explained how this particular treasure may have gone from place to place, but not how our uncle had come across a map that led him to their location so many years later.

When my thoughts turned to River, as they inevitably did, my reflections bounced in another direction. I went over the lies and deceptions—on both sides—and considered our final conversation in the park. Then my thoughts took still another turn, and I made a decision. As soon as the treasure was secure and Ellie was back in Vancouver, I was going to organize a cousins' confab.

Ellie picked me up at the airport. She had called the cousins and managed to arrange a meeting for Saturday morning, a week after UBC started digging up the treasure. They had finished on Wednesday and planned on making an official announcement about the discovery soon.

So far as we could tell, the press was still in the dark. There hadn't been a whisper in social media about the artifacts and not even a passing mention that we could find in any local newspapers. My hope was that nothing would get out before I had a chance to talk with my immediate family. Meanwhile, there was a window of opportunity to leverage what we knew and the cousins didn't.

To get the cousins to agree to a meeting, Ellie hinted that she had information about the location of the treasure. Actually, she could have told them *exactly* where it was—at UBC in a securely locked basement room. But that wasn't the point. From our perspective, we were thinking of the get-together as halfway between an intervention and a Perry Mason showdown. Although we didn't expect a tearful confession, we were going to use what little we did know to see if we could trip someone into a misstep. Maybe they would reveal a contradiction or a tiny lie that we could use to pry out the truth. At the very least, we were hoping to learn something that would compel the police to reopen the investigation into Uncle Wade's death.

Everyone agreed to meet at Candy's. Candy and Vic had a fire pit in their back yard and enough chairs to accommodate all of us. Initially she'd been worried about what to serve, but we'd assured her the meeting wouldn't last long. Vic was a bit put off that he wasn't included. He argued that he was not only family, but directly affected by any decisions the blood cousins made. It helped that Dennis's wife wasn't included either and, since children were not invited, someone had to stay with Pastel. After a puff of macho bluster, he finally agreed to remain inside with his daughter.

The seven of us sat in a circle around the unlit fire pit: Kent, Dennis, Tuna, Candy, Vinny, Ellie, and me. I explained that Dylan was sorry he'd been unable to come and gave no explanation as to why. Not that anyone cared. To be honest, I hadn't invited him. I told myself I was trying to spare him from what was bound to be an uncomfortable confrontation. But it was more than that. I didn't want him to try and talk me out of it. Ellie and I were on the same page, partly because of what we had gone through together. Dylan might not only disagree but be tempted to tell Mom and Dad, and I was fairly certain my mother wouldn't approve.

"So, what's this all about?" Kent said, taking the lead.

"Uncle Wade," Ellie said.

"How he died," I added. In the brief moment of silence that followed, I saw Tuna wiggle his feet and shift positions in his chair and noticed Kent giving him the stink eye. Everyone else just sat there staring at me, waiting for what I was going to say next. After a dramatic pause, I took the plunge. "So, Kent and Tuna, why don't you tell all of us what happened that night."

There was a collective gasp around the circled cousins. Except for Kent and Tuna who were momentarily frozen by the accusation.

Kent recovered first and said, "I have no idea what you mean. Tuna, do you?"

Tuna shook his head, his face several shades paler than it had been moments before.

In poker, a stone-cold bluff is the art of getting another player to reveal their hand when you have little chance of winning otherwise. In this instance, all I had was a poker face and a loosely fact-based lie to back up my bluff. "You obviously weren't aware that there was someone watching the house the night Uncle Wade died, waiting for Shane Reed, a dodgy treasure hunter, to show up. As it happened, you two were there first. Looking for the map, I imagine."

Candy, Dennis, and Vinny had turned to stare at Kent, wary, but unwilling to speak up. They obviously all knew where the map had been found, but were they aware that Kent and Tuna searched for it the night Uncle Wade died?

"Reed arrived not long after you left. The witness saw him go in and immediately approached the house and peeked in a window to see what he was up to. He saw Reed walk over to the foot of the stairs, find Uncle Wade lying there, and quickly depart. So . . . the only question is whether you pushed Uncle Wade down the stairs and staged it to look like an accident, or whether he tripped and fell on his own. Murder or accident—which was it?"

"I thought . . .," Dennis began, but Kent held up his hand for him to stay silent.

"I repeat, I don't know what you're talking about." This time he didn't ask Tuna for backup. He probably thought, like we did, that Tuna was the weak link.

Ellie stepped in. "We're certain that all of you helped search for the map and were present when it was found in the chest in the attic. And Candy, in spite of what you said to me, you knew that the map was stolen a second time from them . . ." she waved her hand to indicate the male cousins ". . . when they were on their *alleged* camping trip." She paused and lowered her voice. "What I don't know for sure is whether all of you were aware of that first time Tuna and Kent searched for the map. If you were, then you are all accessories to murder."

Candy, Vinny, and Dennis were exchanging shamefaced looks. Before they could speak up, Kent leapt in. "We all searched the place *after* Uncle Wade's death, not the night he died. You can't think Tuna and I would hurt Uncle Wade."

"Tuna? Is that true?" I asked. "Which is it? Are you a willing accessory to murder or do you have a personal reason for lying?"

Tuna's face turned the color of a bad rosé wine.

"Don't answer that, Tuna," Kent said. "She's trying to trick you."

"No, I'm trying to clarify the circumstances under which Uncle Wade died." I looked around the group. "None of you believe it was an accident. At least not one caused by Uncle Wade going upstairs in the middle of the night and slipping on a rug that had never been there before."

"But it *was* an accident," Tuna whined. "It *was* an accident."

"Shut up!" Kent screamed at him. "We're leaving." He got up and motioned for Tuna to come with him, but Tuna scrunched down in his chair, apparently broken by the accusation and perhaps by remorse.

Kent stomped out alone, yelling over his shoulder, "You can't prove anything."

Candy went over to Tuna, knelt beside his chair, and put her arm around his shoulder. "It's going to be okay," she assured him.

"No, it isn't," Ellie said. "That's why Bryn and I thought we should all be together to talk about this. Tuna, why don't you tell us what happened. We know you didn't mean to kill anyone."

Tuna made a few snorting noises as tears formed, droplets clinging to his lower eyelids before dribbling slowly down his face. "We didn't push him," he said, barely loud enough for us to hear. "We didn't push him."

"Then what happened?" I prompted.

Tuna sat up straight, pulled his shirttail out of his pants and dabbed at his face. "He caught us looking for the map." He spoke slowly, as if reliving the moment in his mind. "He knew right away what we were there for. He said we needed to get out and never come back. The next thing I knew, Uncle Wade was falling down the stairs." He looked around at the others. "It all happened so fast."

"Tuna!" Candy backed away from him. "Why didn't you tell us?"

"Kent made me promise—"

"If it was an accident," Dennis said, "you should have reported it. Right away."

"And admit why we were there in the middle of the night? After he fell, there was nothing we could do for him."

Silence descended while the cousins were either struggling with the moral dilemma they faced or were trying to come up with ways to justify their own actions and avoid any negative consequences.

Ellie and I waited, hoping someone else would take the lead from that point forward. When no one stepped up, Ellie said, "Tuna, you need to go to the police."

He shook his head vehemently. "I can't do that; Kent would never forgive me."

I hesitated for a moment before saying, "You aren't being completely honest with us, Tuna. I have absolutely no doubt that

Kent shoved him. Maybe it was in the heat of the moment, maybe he felt threatened. If that's the way it happened, it was still an accident." As I pressured Tuna to confess, I had no qualms about lying to him about the law. Given those circumstances, what happened would most likely be considered culpable homicide in Canada, not an accident. But I wanted Tuna to believe it wouldn't be considered murder if it was a spontaneous act so he would keep talking and truth would out. I remember reading that Aristotle believed truth always prevailed, but that sometimes it required help from persuasive discourse. It was up to me to find the right argument to persuade Tuna to tell the truth.

Tuna's pale, tear-streaked face and defeated demeanor were pathetic. Caught like a fish on a hook, still hoping to wiggle off, but the more he protested, the more likely it was that he could not escape his destiny. "He didn't mean to. Honest, he didn't mean to. We just wanted the map."

Ellie went over and stood in front of Tuna, glaring at him like a judge looking down at a defendant. "Tuna, do you want me to take you to the police or should I call them and have them come here to arrest you?"

"Ellie, what are you doing?" Candy protested loudly. "You heard him—it was an accident. Why do we have to involve the police?"

Dennis and Vinny seemed to be in shock, their eyes moving back and forth between Ellie and Tuna as if the answer lay somewhere in between. But in my mind, there was only one answer: Tuna needed to turn himself in. And tell the truth, even if it meant betraying the cousin he had blindly followed all his life.

I stood up. "The police have to become involved because Uncle Wade is dead, and his death wasn't an accident."

Candy made a few more attempts to dissuade us from calling the police, but when it was clear we weren't going to give in, she and Vinny agreed to take Tuna to the station. Ellie told them she was going to contact the Mounties and let them know they were on the way. Dennis said he would see if he could find Kent and tell him what was happening.

Vic had obviously been eavesdropping enough to realize what was going on. Just as everyone was about to leave, he burst into the room and made a show of telling Ellie and me that we were personas non grata in the future. He also informed us that he would personally see to it that Aunt Regina and Uncle Max were told about our treachery.

the aquarium

There was no feeling of elation when Ellie and I departed, more like an emptiness, a realization that something that could never be repaired had been broken. But there was also closure, for us and for Uncle Wade's memory.

On the way to her place, we stopped at a restaurant to debrief. Ellie ordered two glasses of wine while I called Ben and then Logan to let them know what we learned during the family meeting. Then I had to drink almost the entire glass of Chardonnay before calling Mom to warn her that she might want to avoid answering calls from any of the Vancouver relatives until I had a chance to explain in detail what had happened.

"What have you done?" she asked.

"Hey, have a little faith—it's not about what *I've* done but about what the other cousins have done. I'm staying with Ellie tonight and would like to do a conference call later with you, Dad, Dylan, Angelina and Catrin, if she's available. Can you set that up for around 8:30?"

"You really think it can't wait until you come home?"

"I really do. Sorry." I did think the sooner the better for the conversation we had to have, and I wanted Ellie there as back-up. Talking on the phone was also part copout—I wouldn't have to see their faces, and it would be harder for them to gang up on me. Furthermore, I could hang up any time I wanted. That is, I could try to end the call any time I wanted. There was no way I would hang up on my family.

Ellie and I ordered some food and another glass of wine. We needed fortification for what lay ahead.

Mom wasn't pleased to learn how we tricked Tuna into a confession, but her love for Uncle Wade won over her dislike of the tactics we used. Dylan sounded put out that we hadn't included him, but he allowed as how a cover-up was out of the question; Kent had to be held accountable. Angelina surprised me by not only agreeing with what we'd done but thanking Ellie and me for having the courage to stand up for what was right. Catrin didn't know the players as well as we did and quickly moved on from the fact that they were guilty to asking about the treasure. Mom erupted again when she realized that the purpose of our trip up the Inside Passage had not been for sightseeing.

Ellie tried to take the heat for the deception about the trip, but it was clear I would be hearing more about my role in it from Mom. I've learned that you're never too old to be scolded for what your mother considers bad behavior.

In order to end the call, I had to promise to provide details about everything at our Sunday dinner. No one was completely happy about having to wait to hear more, but they finally acquiesced. I had no doubt that our next Sunday dinner would turn into an interrogation. I'd be lucky if they didn't shine a reading lamp in my face during our meal.

UBC made their announcement the next day, but only a few local stations picked it up. There were more exciting things to be discussed than a team of archeologists finding a few Aztec artifacts in a cave on a remote island in British Columbia. It didn't matter that they were centuries old, made of gold, and their discovery was completely unexpected. After all, there were celebrities getting divorces and cute cat videos and people complaining about politicians spending too much money while food prices were on the rise. My irritation at the lack of recognition for Uncle Wade's success was softened by feeling relieved about the current news in general. There are days when I'm afraid to read the headlines about what's happening around the world. Even though it's a cliché, sometimes no news *is* good news.

Unfortunately, Kent and Tuna *did* make the news. Several local television stations mentioned that two former residents of Seattle had been arrested in Vancouver, one charged with manslaughter and the other with obstruction of justice. Fortunately, the reports were light on facts and either didn't know or didn't care that the two men had relatives in the Seattle area. There was also a paragraph about their arrest on page three of the *Seattle Times,* but it didn't add much to what had already been on television. Be grateful for small blessings I told myself—another cliché that is sometimes good advice.

Their arrests made much bigger headlines in the Vancouver media. The Canadian press mentioned the Seattle connection and seemed to claim Uncle Wade as their own while disowning Kent and Tuna. Both were identified as suspects in a murder investigation.

Although I welcomed the closure the two arrests brought, it added another layer of gloom over the mourning for Uncle Wade.

The story that appeared in the *Vancouver Sun* by Todd Walker the following Saturday was more detailed than most obituaries. Perhaps in part because it was the last story Walker would be writing about Uncle Wade. He skipped over our uncle's sketchy past and focused on his final triumph, his post-life denouement. It was a flattering and inspirational story. That's how I want to remember my Uncle Wade.

Walker quoted the UBC announcement and provided some new context, including an explanation of Uncle Wade's role in tracking down the treasure. The artifacts were known to have been in a small museum in Portugal at the end of World War II. The documentation of their acquisition was questionable, most likely those in charge had taken advantage of art made available by the looting that took place during and at the end of the war.

Then in the 80s, the collection was stolen from the museum. One of the suspects was a Canadian art dealer. He was found dead in a cabin near Edmonton, Alberta. It was alleged that an accomplice, a Prince Rupert salmon fisherman, may have been responsible for his death. But the authorities never caught up with him, even though it was rumored he had fled to his sister's home in BC.

Walker's speculation was that Uncle Wade had tracked down the sister's family in the Prince Rupert area and that they still had some of his possessions, including the map leading to the cave at Butedale. Perhaps they didn't realize the map's significance. Or maybe they were unaware of its existence—it could have been hidden in a book binding or sewn into a jacket. All that was known for sure was that the accomplice contracted a mysterious illness and died shortly after returning to BC.

Walker concluded with: *We will never know the details of Wade Payne's final treasure hunt, but we honor his persistence in pursuing his dream.*

Our next Sunday family dinner started off as if we were all bad actors reading a stilted script. Thank heavens for Noah and Emma and their enthusiasm over the gift I'd brought for them—an aquarium. "Have your daddy set it up, and I'll bring over Bubbles and a friend of his for you."

Angelina and Dylan scowled at me. It had been a hard week, and I was filled to the brim with guilt already; their scowls didn't faze me.

"Noah," I said, "Since Emma named Bubbles, you can name his friend." Noah was elated, Emma a bit jealous. But together they immediately started coming up with possible names: Goldie, Nemo, Splashy, Cheeto.

"Bear," Emma said and they both giggled.

I jumped in and suggested Sushi; they gave me blank looks. "Tankerbell?"

They groaned and turned back to their own rapidly growing list.

Catrin took me aside and whispered, "Which generation of Bubbles is the one you'll be bringing over?"

"Just keep your fingers crossed that I can keep them alive until your father figures out how to set up the tank."

In some ways I was sad to see Bubbles V and Friend leave, but it was better than trying to shore up my bookshelves and worrying about a leak all the time. Hudson would understand. He might even be relieved. Although Logan was already threatening to buy me a hamster.

The conversation slowly improved during the course of the meal, lulled by good food and everyone getting caught up in the story I had to tell. Dylan was obviously hurt not to be included in all of the intrigue and said several times that he wished he'd been there at Butedale for the hike up to the cave. Angelina rolled her eyes and patted his hand to remind him he was a married man with children. Emma and Noah wanted to know if the treasure was in a chest and whether there were diamonds as well as gold coins in it. Mother asked about how Ellie handled being so close to a cave. And, although I downplayed the danger that stalked us, I could sense Dad reading between the lines.

Macavity, the stowaway, provided comic relief. I showed them pictures I'd taken of him walking on his leash and one I was particularly fond of in which he was staring at the water while we were at anchor. Everyone agreed he was trying to decide whether to make a break for it and swim to shore.

Over dessert, Mother forgot for a short time that she was mad at me and asked about the trip up the Inside Passage. That gave me an opportunity to shift the conversation away from the treasure hunt part of the trip and to our role as tourists. I told them about the abandoned canneries and small native villages, the long stretches of wilderness, and the Hot Springs in Bishop Bay. There is something magical about sailing to remote locations, and just talking about it had a calming effect on everyone. By the end of the meal, things were starting to feel normal. Then Catrin asked about River.

"At one point I thought he was one of the two men who attacked our four cousins in Arizona," I admitted. "He wasn't pleased about that. But he lied to me about why he was here, so I guess we're even."

"Does that mean you'll see him again?" Catrin asked.

"I honestly don't know. There may be too much baggage to deal with."

"Don't worry," Dylan said. "I'm sure Mom will find another blind date for you."

not me!

The following week was tough. I experienced a letdown, a mammoth drop from the adrenaline high of the trip, and I began wallowing in mixed feelings about my role in getting Kent and Tuna arrested. I even felt nostalgic about the empty space on my bookshelf where Bubbles V and Friend had circled round and round and round . . . and round. Emma and Noah had insisted I drop them off even before their new home was ready. Dylan called several times with questions about how to set it up—as if I knew —and to complain to me about how much trouble maintenance was going to be. I purchased some plants for it along with the appropriate fertilizer, a packet of water purifier tablets, and a water test kit. It was the least I could do.

The following Saturday, Logan suggested a dinner to cheer me up. Logan, Judd, Sophie, and I met at an Ethiopian restaurant that had a table tucked in an alcove in the corner of a large dining area. There was the illusion of privacy even though you could see the other diners and they could see you. We shared an assortment of spicy appetizers and were waiting for our entrees when Sophie finally brought up what she knew was troubling me.

"You've got to quit feeling like you are responsible for what your cousins did," Sophie said, very matter-or-fact. Like it was that simple. When two people have known each other as long as Sophie and I have, it's hard to pretend you're not feeling something when you are. She knows I've always suffered from excessive guilt over things I think I should be able to control.

"That's easy to intellectualize, but it's hard to get my gut to agree," I said.

Sophie, always the loyal friend, jumped in with her verdict. "The bottom line is that Kent is a despicable human being who should pay for what he did, and you shouldn't feel bad about being the one to call it out."

When I didn't immediately respond, Judd asked, "Does this guilt trip stuff run in your family? Well, obviously not in *all* members of the family."

Logan changed the subject. "Speaking of family, how's Ellie holding up? It can't be easy living so near the viper pit."

"She's doing okay. She may come down some weekend for one of the family dinners. I want her to know that we're here for her."

"So," Sophie persisted. "Can you let this go?"

"Our family was already fragile. Now . . . I don't know if it will ever be whole again. Aunt Regina and Uncle Max have made it clear they want nothing more to do with Mom and the rest of us. Even though Mom and Dad had nothing to do with anything that happened. Ellie is also on the 'no contact' list. They never interreacted much before, but they are still family. And Mom feels bad . . . and seems to blame me, at least in part."

"What I don't understand," Sophie said, "is why the other cousins aren't angry with Kent. After all, he was the cause of their uncle's death. They all heard Tuna admit what happened."

"Tuna has backed off from his original version of events," I said. "He claims we pressured him into admitting something that wasn't true."

"Not surprising," Judd said. "I'm assuming Kent and, ah, Tuna, have lawyered up. And if I had to bet, I'm not sure the testimony from your other cousins will back up the original story either.”

“You think they will lie under oath?” Sophie asked.

“It’s been known to happen,” Judd replied. He turned to me. “They will waffle. Or they’ll claim you and Ellie are lying or that you misunderstood, one or the other. Maybe even both. You need to prepare yourself for that.”

“You think Kent will get off?” I asked.

“It wouldn’t surprise me.”

“Well,” Logan injected, “at least Shane Reed and his colleague will get their comeuppance for attacking the four cousins.”

“You’d think your cousins would be grateful for that,” Sophie said.

Judd laughed. “They stole a phony map and lost out on a buried treasure. Who do you think they’re going to thank for *that*?”

“Not me! I said. “Definitely not me.”

Acknowledgments

The trip up the inside passage is based on the many trips my husband and I made from Seattle to Alaska and back when commercial fishing. I've tried to be accurate in my descriptions, although things change, memories fade, and sometimes a writer needs to be creative to make the storyline work. I apologize for any inaccuracies.

I thoroughly enjoyed the research I did on phobias, caves in British Columbia and treasures thought to still be "out there" somewhere. May we conquer our phobias and may our dreams of discovering lost treasures never die.

Finally, I am grateful to my readers who have given me an excuse to continue living vicariously through my protagonist's very exciting life. I only wish that Macavity was a real cat, although there are advantages to having a virtual pet.

About the Author

Award-winning author Charlotte Stuart PhD writes mysteries that fall into a number of different sub genres: cozy mysteries, character-driven mysteries featuring a female PI, a laugh-out-loud comedic series, as well as more traditional mysteries. She's also coauthored a legal thriller with Don Stuart. In general, she favors twisty plots with a dollop of adventure. Before she started writing full time, she left a tenured faculty position to go commercial salmon fishing in Alaska, spent a year sailing "around the world" in the Washington and Canadian San Juans, became a partner in a management consulting group and later a VP of HR and training. After living on boats for over a decade, boating and forays into wilderness areas often find their way into her stories.

Not Me! Speluncaphobia, Secrets and Hidden Treasure (A Macavity & Me Mystery #3) has won several awards including: Reader Views Silver, Global Book Award Bronze, Book Fest Honorable Mention, and an Eric Hoffer Award finalist.

Charlotte lives on Vashon Island in the Pacific Northwest and is the past president of the Puget Sound Sisters in Crime and a member of the Mystery Writers of America and the International Thriller Writers.

Other books by Charlotte Stuart include:

The Discount Detective Mysteries

The John Smith Mysteries

Bogged Down (A Vashon Island Mystery)

Raven's Grave

Midnight for Justice, a legal thriller by Charlotte Stuart and Don Stuart

You can visit her website at www.charlottestuart.com, or contact her on social media:

facebook.com/charlotte.stuart.mysterywriter

instagram.com/cstuartauthor

bookbub.com/authors/charlotte-stuart

goodreads.com/goodreadscomclstuart

www.ingramcontent.com/pod-product-compliance
Lightning Source LLC
Chambersburg PA
CBHW020423110726
47899CB00006B/2102